Wicked Payback

Daisy Dexter Dobbs

ELLORA'S CAVE
ROMANTICA PUBLISHING

An Ellora's Cave Romantica Publication

www.ellorascave.com

Wicked Payback

ISBN 9781419960826
ALL RIGHTS RESERVED.
Wicked Payback Copyright © 2006 Daisy Dexter Dobbs
Edited by Briana St. James.
Cover art by Lissa Waitley.

This book printed in the U.S.A. by Jasmine-Jade Enterprises, LLC.

Electronic book publication May 2006
Trade paperback publication September 2010

WICKED PAYBACK

છ૭

Trademarks Acknowledgement

∾

The author acknowledges the trademarked status and trademark owners of the following wordmarks mentioned in this work of fiction:

Oscar: Academy of Motion Picture Arts and Sciences Corporation

Dumpster: Dempster Systems Inc.

Prologue

ဢ

Uttering a tiny gasp of wonder, Meredith gazed at the shimmering lights of the city skyline. "Oh, Jack...have you ever seen anything quite so magnificent?"

"Never."

At the husky sound of her new husband's voice, she turned to find Jack's gaze locked directly on her instead of the breathtaking expanse of Chicago's lakefront. One glimpse of the hunger in his eyes brought a rush of warmth to her cheeks.

"I meant the view from up here on the fortieth floor, silly." She gestured at the massive floor-to-ceiling window and smiled.

"Oh...that," Jack said, as if the million-dollar view was nothing more than a shopping mall parking lot. "Yeah, that's nice too." Winking, he flashed a cavalier grin.

Overflowing with love and brimming with the exhilaration, hopes and dreams of a new bride, Meredith hugged herself as she turned back to the window. "It's like we're on top of the world together, Jack. Just the two of us."

"This is what it'll be like for us all the time in a few years, baby, you'll see." Jack wrapped his arms around her from behind and nuzzled her neck. "Once we get on our feet financially, the sky's the limit. All I need to do is to build a solid reputation as a motivational speaker and once those speaking engagements start rolling in we'll be staying in hotels like this every weekend if you like."

"I hope for your sake that it does happen," Meredith said, leaning back and brushing her cheek with his. "Because I know how happy it will make you. But I don't really care all that much about being rich. I'd be just as happy if we stayed at home in our cozy little apartment and just lived happily ever after." She breathed a contented sigh.

Jack smoothed his hands up and down her arms, capturing the fingers of one hand and bringing them to his mouth to kiss them. "You deserve so much more than that, Meredith. I just wish to hell I could have afforded to take you somewhere really special for our honeymoon. Someplace exciting, romantic and exotic like Paris or Barcelona or maybe London. And for at least a week, instead of downtown Chicago for just one night."

"But, Jack, don't you understand? This *is* special." Turning to face him, Meredith cupped Jack's face in her hands and smiled warmly. "As long as we're together, my adorable bridegroom, it doesn't matter to me if it's forty floors up in a fancy hotel here on Michigan Avenue, or some rinky-dink little motel along the highway or in a tent on the Sahara desert. All I care about is being with the man I love. My *husband*," she added with a bright smile.

With two broken engagements behind them due to Jack's dallying with a couple of coeds, there was a time when Meredith doubted she and Jack would ever make it to the altar. It wasn't Jack's fault. Not really. He had a roving eye and exuded the kind of magnetic charm that attracted women like dieters to fresh-baked bread. He couldn't help it if women were always throwing themselves at him. And he felt terrible that he'd succumbed to temptation on those two different occasions and hurt Meredith. But that was in the past. Jack had assured her that it would never happen again and she believed him—because she knew he loved her. Meredith was certain of that. And as long as they loved each other they could surmount all odds. Together. So, no, she didn't care about things that only money could buy. All she cared about was Jack and being with him forever.

"You're an angel," Jack said, kissing her. "And I don't deserve you. You're too good for me."

"Hmm…well, it's a little late for that admission, don't you think?" Meredith laughed. "I honestly never expected to be staying anyplace as fancy as this honeymoon suite for our wedding night." She gazed around the large, elaborate two-level suite and sighed. "Marble, silk, satin and gold and it's even got a second level. Amazing." She shook her head as she studied the ornately carved doors to the bedroom upstairs. "Like something out of a fairy tale. What a wonderful, thoughtful wedding gift. We'll definitely have to invite the professor over for a thank-you dinner."

Jack nodded. "Professor Henkel said every person in the drama department contributed a little something. Guess it pays to be a professor's assistant, huh?" Arching an eyebrow, he blew a puff of air across his fingernails and polished them against his lapel.

"Well, I'm sure being his assistant didn't hurt." Meredith fingered his bow tie and shirt studs, thinking that Jack looked a whole hell of a lot like James Bond in his tux. "But I'd say it probably has a lot more to do with the fact that Professor Henkel and the rest of the university's drama department thinks you're destined to become the greatest orator since Winston Churchill." She beamed a proud grin. "And I happen to agree with their assumption."

"Well, if that's true," Jack tipped Meredith's chin up with his finger and brushed his lips across hers, "it's all because of the sacrifice you've made, Meredith — working those two jobs to put me through school. I'll never forget that. Ever. And I promise that one day I'll make it all up to you."

"Oh, Jack, don't talk that way." Meredith tsked. "You don't owe me anything." She smiled and hugged him tight. "Except your love. If the situation were reversed, you'd be doing the same for me. That's what people do when they love each other."

"I appreciate your selfless attitude, sweetheart," Jack returned her affectionate squeeze, "but, like it or not, once I've made it to the big time, you'll be living like a queen. Go ahead, just close your eyes for a moment and picture us twenty years from now when—"

"Twenty years?" Meredith's closed eyes popped open. "Jesus, Jack, I'll be forty. That's ancient—almost half a century. I can't picture myself that far ahead."

"Okay...if forty sounds too old and decrepit let's make it twenty-nine then. Better?" Meredith smiled and nodded. "So," Jack continued, "envision us just nine short years from now... We're nibbling Beluga caviar on toast points and washing it down with vintage champagne during one of our average weekend getaways at our villa on the French Riviera. We're discussing our wedding night and how broke we were and we're laughing because we can hardly believe it."

"Will I get to have a crew of hunky cabana boys at our villa?" Meredith asked with an all-too-innocent smile. "You know," she shrugged, "in case I need to have someone peel a grape for me or something."

Jack arched an eyebrow, shooting her a warning glare. "I'm all the man you'll ever need, sweetheart." He yanked her close, grinding himself against her and sliding into a devilish laugh.

"Well, gee, I don't know." Meredith tried to look concerned. "After all, Jack, in nine years you'll be..." she counted on her fingers, "thirty-two. That's practically over the hill." She batted her eyelashes at him.

"Don't worry, smarty pants." He gave her a playful swat on the butt. "My virility, or lack thereof, is one problem you'll never have to worry about. I guarantee it. So you can just forget about cabana boys, got that?" Meredith grinned and nodded in response. "Stick with me, sweetheart, and you'll be traveling all over the world, first class all the way. I'll have you swimming in lobster, caviar, the finest European chocolates, diamonds, furs and French champagne."

"Mmm, sounds like a deliciously soggy mess." Meredith laughed. "Actually, I'll be perfectly happy with a yearly vacation, free-flowing bubbly and an unlimited lifetime supply of chocolate. And you, of course." After licking her lips, she squeezed him tight and laughed.

"Speaking of chocolates and bubbly," Jack said, gesturing toward the table, "you'll note that we have an ample supply of both for the evening."

Meredith sauntered over to the gilt-edged table and popped a chocolate truffle into her mouth, closing her eyes and moaning her pleasure at the sweet creaminess and silky texture. "Scrumptious. Delicious. Divine. Are these from the drama department too?" she asked, placing another fancy chocolate candy on her tongue and sinking into the rapturous bliss of chocolate heaven yet again.

"Nope. That was all my idea. I figured I couldn't go wrong keeping you inebriated on champagne and drunk on chocolates. I love it when you get that look on your face, Meredith. It's the same one you get when you're in the midst of an orgasm."

"Mmmm..." she paused while finishing her third chocolate confection, this one filled with hazelnut nougat, "I'm not surprised," she finished. "Seeing as how sexual pleasure comes in at a very close second to chocolate bliss." She winked.

"Ooh, baby." Jack reveled in a hoarse laugh as he tugged Meredith hard against his arousal. "I've been itching to get my hands on your juicy body all day. Ever since I saw you walk down that aisle looking like Cinderella, Mrs. McKenna." He curved his fingers over her wedding-gowned ass, nearly scorching her through the satiny fabric with his heat.

"And when I saw you standing at the altar looking so incredibly handsome and impossibly sexy in your tux," Meredith purred, "I felt my thighs quiver, longing to have you between them." She looped her arm through Jack's, indulging in a tuneful, satisfied sigh. "Oh, Jack, it was a beautiful wedding, wasn't it? Perfect."

"All except for the part where your maid of honor started wailing after you said *I do*." Chuckling, Jack rolled his eyes and shook his head. "That was a little much, don't you think?"

"Yeah...Karyn did get a little carried away with the moment, didn't she?" Meredith mused, cringing slightly at the memory of her best friend unexpectedly breaking into happy sobs. "Still," she shrugged, "it was the happiest day of my life."

"Me too," Jack whispered against her ear. "But the best part of the day—or should I say *night*—is yet to come." He kissed the mound of pale flesh spilling over the décolletage of Meredith's soft ivory-colored gown.

"Mmmm," Meredith purred against the tiny pleated folds of Jack's dress shirt. "Who could ask for anything more than one sexy, private, delectable, perfect wedding night together at the top of the world?"

"Driving each other wild," Jack added, "as we tantalize each other between the sheets."

Her lip curling into a wicked smile, Meredith arched a brow. "We're going to have a ball...doing all that balling." She put her fingers to her lips and giggled. "Hmmm, I must admit that was rather clever."

Jack sighed in mock dismay. "Ah...it appears that this once naïve and innocent little virgin has become a wanton woman." He skimmed his hands from her breasts to her thighs and back again. "A wickedly, wonderfully, lusty little vixen."

"It's true." Meredith hiked one shoulder in a shrug and laughed. "What can I say? But it's your fault. You corrupted me, Jack McKenna. Turned me into a veritable sex addict who's in a near-constant state of arousal. You have only yourself to blame, my darling, far-too-sexy husband." She punctuated her statement by dropping her hands to his groin and firmly cupping his erection.

Jack sucked in a deep breath. "I'm going to do my damnedest to keep you just one heartbeat away from expiring due to excess orgasm the entire night, babe."

"What a way to go." Meredith gave a saucy laugh. Jack's pledge sent a delicious jolt of heat straight to her pussy. Ever since she'd surrendered her virginity to him when they first became engaged, after contending with his endless reasoning, cajoling and tempting, Meredith felt like an entirely new woman. Why ever had she insisted on protecting that damned cherry for so long? Because she was a born and bred goody-two-shoes of course. Thank God she finally gave in and let Jack save her from herself and her puritan principles.

Oh, God, how she loved the man. From his handsome face, thick espresso-brown hair and hazel eyes to his beautifully sculpted muscles, to his wit, limitless skills and talents, Jack McKenna was the ultimate man of Meredith's dreams. The man who'd brought boundless love, laughter and magical hopes and dreams into her life. The man she would spend the rest of her life with, doing her best to make him as happy as he'd made her.

And tonight, her wedding night, the somewhat nervous Meredith was eager to put her newly acquired carnal knowledge to good use, tempting, tantalizing and satisfying her new husband.

"How about that champagne now," Meredith said, deciding she could use an extra bit of courage.

Jack made a sweeping bow. "Your wish is my command, my love." Deftly opening the bottle of bubbly so that there was just a slight pop and no runover, Jack poured them each a glass and then held his flute aloft in a toast.

"To my sweet, beautiful, sexy, good-hearted bride. May you always love me as much as you do this night."

"And to the man who's vowed to keep me swimming in chocolate for eternity—and who will never renege on that promise if he wants my love to remain constant." Beaming a smile, Meredith clinked her glass against Jack's and they drank, intertwining their arms continental style.

After enjoying a second glass of champagne, Meredith gifted Jack with a chaste kiss on the tip of his nose and a suggestive little wink. Then she took a few steps back from the table, a bit jittery and swallowing hard as she prepared to give him his wedding night gift of a sexy, *mostly* uninhibited bride. Turning her back to him, Meredith tugged at the zipper of her wedding gown as she slowly ascended the stairs. With a little shimmy, the gown slid down over one shoulder. One more sensual shake had it slipping off the other shoulder, dropping to her waist. And then with an energetic swirl of her hips and lively thrust of her pelvis, the entire bodice of the gown fell to her knees. Meredith glanced over her shoulder at Jack with a teasing smile and then stepped fully out of the gown, leaving it to drape casually across the stairs. She turned to face him and licked her lips slowly as she modeled her sexy wedding night ensemble.

He stared at her without saying a word, which made her a bit uneasy. She hoped she didn't look ridiculous, especially considering the fact that she was far from being model-thin and never thought she'd have the guts to wear a blatantly sexy outfit like this. It was so distant from her goody-two-shoes sense of morality that just wearing it made her feel wicked, sinful. But if her mirror, and Karyn, hadn't lied earlier, then she was reasonably certain she looked good. Damned alluring even.

Meredith remembered shopping for the silky peaches-and-cream garments a few weeks before with Karyn—the less inhibited of the pair. They'd had a ball searching through a variety of sexy getups and erupting in bawdy giggles as they practiced come-hither looks and suggestive poses. They finally agreed on a strapless ivory-colored waist cincher that stopped just below Meredith's breasts and laced up the front with peach satin ribbon. The bra, a lacy confection with nipple cut-outs in shades of ivory and soft peach, showed off her large breasts to their best advantage. The rest of her fantasy garb consisted of an ivory-lace garter belt with peach satin garters attached to sheer ivory stockings and a pair of peach-colored crotchless silk panties trimmed with ivory satin and lace.

Karyn assured her that Jack's eyes would pop, and now, much to Meredith's relief, it looked as if she may have been right.

After staring at his bride slack jawed and silent for a long moment, Jack finally seemed to regain his senses. He let out a throaty wolf whistle while devouring Meredith with a ravenous gaze. "Holy shit," the future great orator uttered, and Meredith had to bite the inside of her cheek to keep from laughing.

She almost thought she could hear Jack swallow the lump in his throat from across the room. With a slow smile she removed the pins from her hair as she climbed the next few steps and shook out her long auburn curls, fingering them to fluff out over her shoulders. The fiery tendrils stopped just above the bare tips of her breasts.

"You mean that was hiding under your wedding dress all day?" Jack marveled.

"Uh-huh. And every time the fabric of my gown scraped my bare nipples," Meredith's voice quavered a bit as she turned to him, "I thought of your fingers pinching them." Her gaze never leaving Jack's, Meredith tugged at her nipples, rolling them hard between her fingers and allowing a little moan of pleasure to escape her lips. She'd never spoken that way before or touched herself in front of him. She just hoped to hell she was doing everything right.

"Oh my God." Jack threw his head back and groaned. "You're a vision. A goddess, Meredith." He followed her trail up the stairs. "My very own personal sex goddess." He kicked off his shoes and tore at the rest of his clothing, leaving the pieces haphazardly strewn in his path.

"Oh goodness," Meredith cooed in mock surprise. She was really starting to enjoy this new wanton side of herself. "My panties are damp and I'm all hot and wet between my legs." Posing at the top of the stairs, her legs spread about a foot apart, she slipped her fingers between her legs, stroking herself back and forth slowly, and then held up her glistening fingers. "See?"

"Shit." Jack let out a low guttural groan. "Jesus, Meredith, you're driving me fucking crazy." Struggling to shuck his dress pants quickly, he tripped while hopping out of one pant leg and stumbled on the stairs. "Christ, my cock's so hard it could hammer nails."

"Well, why don't you come on up here and hammer that great big hard cock of yours into your new bride's tight, hot, wet little pussy, hmmm?" On that teasing note, Meredith backed into the bedroom, satisfied that she'd performed quite well indeed — for a diehard goody-two-shoes sort of girl, that is.

"You wicked, wanton woman, you," Jack said, bounding up the staircase. "Just wait till I get my hands on you."

"And your tongue," Meredith called from the bedroom. "Don't forget your tongue."

Breathless, Jack crossed the bedroom's threshold. Clad only in a pair of black silk boxers, his jutting erection tented the fabric, stretching it to the limit.

"Ooh." Meredith eyed the way his cock ached to escape its confines. "Is that for me?" Propped against the pillows on the bed, she spread her legs and crooked a finger, loving the way Jack's eyes bugged as his gaze flew to her crotchless panties and the moisture glistening at her pussy and inner thighs.

"Oh yeah." Jack swallowed hard. "All for you, baby," he said huskily as he crossed the room to the bed. "And if I don't plunge into you soon, I swear to God I'm going to burst." Bending over her with a gleam of anticipation in his eye, Jack smoothed his hands up over her silky stockings from her ankles to the garters.

"Oh, we can't have that now, can we?" Determined to draw out the deliciously scintillating anticipation, Meredith held up her hand before Jack could jump into the bed. "But not yet." She almost laughed when his face fell. "I want you to just stand there still for a moment so I can thoroughly inspect that amazing gravity-defying cock of yours." Meredith slipped off the bed and stood before him, wrapping her hands around the bridegroom's impressive arousal and purring. "Mmmm." She stroked the length of his cock through the whisper-thin silk.

"*Meredith,*" Jack uttered hoarsely, glancing down as her rigid nipples grazed his chest. Grasping them between his fingers and twisting, he drew a moan from her throat. "You're so goddamned hot, Meredith. Every fiber of my body is on the verge of detonation. I don't think I'm ever going to be able to breathe again."

With a mirror-practiced come-hither smile, Meredith slipped off Jack's shorts, breaking into a full grin as she eyed his erection springing to full attention. Curling her fingers around the broad base of his cock, she whispered against his ear, "I want you to fuck me, Mr. McKenna. Hard. And fast. Until I'm senseless." And then she swooped her tongue across his sculpted pecs and ground herself against him.

"M-Meredith … you're killing me."

"Not a bad way to die, hmmm?" she asked teasingly.

Not wasting another minute, Jack lifted Meredith and tossed her on the bed, with himself following right behind her. "I'll have you know you're not the only one with wedding night surprises, Mrs. McKenna." A low, wicked chuckle rumbled in Jack's throat. "How about engaging in a round of MAGCC? That is," he arched a brow, "if you think you're woman enough to take it, of course."

Slanting him an eager, inquisitive expression, Meredith popped up on her knees, straddling Jack. "I've never heard of that. What's a MAGCC?" She quickly held up her hand in stop sign fashion. "And whatever it is, Mr. McKenna, I can assure you that I'm more than up to the challenge." She laughed.

Jack captured her nipples with his fingers, tugging hard and stopping her laughter in its tracks. Meredith threw her head back and moaned as the pleasurable action launched shivering waves to her pussy. He continued to twist and pinch as she helplessly mewed and purred.

"The initials stand for Michigan Avenue G-Clit-Cock," Jack clarified. "I like to call it *magic* for short."

"Sounds intriguing. And just what sort of magic have you con-*cock*-ted?" Meredith couldn't help giggling.

"It's my own personal invention," Jack explained proudly, still playing with her breasts. "In honor of our honeymoon night at this grand hotel on Michigan Avenue. If it works the way I hope, it'll drive you so incredibly mad with passion you'll beg for mercy. Are you ready to test it out, my sweet?"

"Oh God, yes. Do it!"

Maintaining an unyielding hold, Jack intensified the exquisite firm pressure against her nipples, teasing them mercilessly as Meredith leaned back. The union of pain and pleasure drove her almost to the edge as he drew her forward by clamping firmly on the rigid buds and tugging.

"Okay, that's it, Jack. I need to feel you inside of me *now!*" Without further ado, Meredith impaled herself firmly on his rock-hard cock. An unabashed cry of joy escaped her lips as she rode him, enjoying the delicious sensation of fullness.

"Hold it!" Jack said through clenched teeth as he stilled Meredith's swiveling hips. "Jeez, Meredith. You're going to be the death of me yet." He laughed. "We have to switch positions. This will work best if I'm on top." With that, he cupped her ass firmly and, still buried inside her, they rolled so that Meredith lay flat against the mattress.

He pulled himself out slightly and then plunged into her swift and hard.

"Mmmm. Great start," she panted.

"Tell me when you feel something, um...different." Jack tilted her hips up slightly, guiding the tip of his cock back and forth and to the left and right. With a grunt he screwed himself in even deeper, burying his long thick cock to the absolute hilt. Meredith gasped. "Well? Feel anything yet?" he asked.

"You mean aside from the usual sensation of blinding pleasure?" She gave a throaty laugh. "Other than that, I don't know what you—" She stopped and her eyes widened. Wheezing a monumental gasp, Meredith said, "Oh! Yes. There!" She began to writhe and moan. "Oh dear God, Jack, what is that?"

"That, Mrs. McKenna, is your G-spot. I read about it in one of my buddy's medical books at the university."

Meredith gulped. "The...the G part of the MAGCC, I assume?"

"Precisely, my dear." Jack grinned. "My magical cock, obviously being the last part of the name."

"Oh Jack...it's...it feels... I don't know how to explain it," Meredith murmured, feeling almost drunk with inexplicable pleasure. "The sensation is overwhelming, like nothing I've ever felt before. Oh God," she swallowed hard, "I never want this to end."

"According to everything I read," Jack said, "if we do this right, you'll be able to achieve an internal orgasm, stemming from the muscles of your uterus contracting. It's supposed to be more powerful than a clitoral orgasm. But my dastardly plan is to give you both types of orgasm—simultaneously."

"The pleasure might kill me," Meredith panted madly as Jack continued his deft stimulation of her G-spot, "but I'm willing to make the sacrifice. Ooooooh! Mmmmm. Damn, that's just incredible. You were right about the cabana boys.

They definitely won't be necessary." She managed a slight chuckle.

"Damn right." Jack winked. "Right now your job, my lovely bride, is to just relax and enjoy." He lifted her hand to his lips and kissed her fingers. "And you need to let me know if you feel yourself on the brink of orgasm inside, at the G-spot area. Damn…it's hard, but I'm going to do my best not to come too soon."

"Okay," Meredith barely got out as every one of her nerve endings melted in ecstasy. "Feels…so…good…" Her eyelids fluttered closed.

"I wish we could stay like this forever, Meredith." Jack kept moving in slow, cautious circles, driving her past the point of all reason. "You have no idea how much I love being inside of you like this."

"Yes, just like this. Exactly like—" Meredith's eyes flew open and she gasped. "Jack! N-now!"

Continuing his internal massage of her G-spot, Jack reached down and began fingering Meredith's clit.

"Wait! No! Jack…stop. It's too much." Meredith's head thrashed against the pillow as the intensely erotic waves practically did her in. "Seriously. I'm not kidding. I can't take it."

"You can take it, sweetheart," he assured with a hoarse chuckle. "Just go with it, baby. Give in to the passion, the pleasure. Let the *magic* overtake you. I want to watch you come, both inside and out."

"Yes…okay…" Meredith's hands flew up to Jack's abdomen, where she dug her fingers in and pressed, clinging for dear life. A moment later her scream reverberated around the room as her hips bucked violently off the mattress. Undulating torrents of pleasure washed through her entire being. The dual orgasm rocked her to her very soul, pulsating and contracting inside and out.

As her muscles clamped hard around him, pulsating strongly against Jack's cock, he roared out a howling growl and she felt his hot cum spurting into her depths. It was a devastatingly magnificent and mutually magical first climax as husband and wife.

Crumpled into a musky, sweaty heap, their arms wrapped around each other as they lay panting in the afterglow of a most amazing sexual journey.

"And that, my precious, beautiful wife," Jack said through short fast breaths, "was Jack McKenna's patented Michigan Avenue G-Clit-Cock."

Meredith gazed into Jack's eyes and began to cry.

He looked at her in surprise. "Oh, honey, what is it? What's the matter?" He stroked her cheek gently. "I didn't hurt you, did I?"

Shaking her head back and forth, Meredith turned to Jack, taking his face in her hands. "No, sweetheart. I'm crying because I'm so happy. So blissfully, miraculously, unbelievably happy." She brushed a kiss across her husband's lips.

"Whew!" Jack chuckled. "You had me worried for a minute. I thought maybe my MAGCC did you in after all."

"Are you kidding? It almost did!" Wiping the tears from her eyes, Meredith laughed. "I'm just so happy to be your wife. I feel just like a princess who's been carried away by the handsome prince on his white charger." She trailed a path of kisses from his jaw to his chest. "Oh, Jack, let's never lose the magic—or the MAGCC." She winked. "Let's promise to always be this happy."

"I love you, Meredith. With all my heart and soul." Jack kissed the top of her head. "Neither hell nor heaven could persuade me from your arms." He enveloped her in his embrace and kissed her soundly. "I promise you that our life together is going to be beautiful, wonderful, perfect."

Stretching with a contented sigh, Meredith cooed, "Especially if you continue to invent exotic methods of cataclysmic orgasm like that." She gave a wicked smile and hiked an eyebrow.

"Hmmm." Jack played at being in deep contemplation. "When we're carefree and filthy rich we'll have to travel all over the world and, one by one, I'll concoct a new method of orgasm or sexual position in honor of each place we visit. How does that sound?" He flashed a bright, little boy smile.

"Mmm-hmm." Meredith nodded. "Sounds good to me. How about the Torrid Toronto Tumble...or the Irish Shamrock Screw...or the Horny Houston Handful...or the—"

"Or," Jack interrupted, "how about the Parisian Stuffed Pussy." He licked his lips and jiggled his eyebrows. "Or the Lip-licking Londoner...or the Barcelona Buck and Howl."

Jack and Meredith looked at each other for a long moment and burst out laughing.

"You know," Jack scooped her against him as she snuggled close, "all kidding aside, maybe we succeeded in making a baby tonight." He kissed the tip of her nose. "Wouldn't that be fantastic?"

"Oh goodness." Meredith laughed. "A baby conceived using the Michigan Avenue G-Clit-Cock method!"

"Maybe I should patent the technique. We could make a fortune." Jack smiled devilishly. "I can see it all now." He skimmed his hand across an imaginary panorama. "Seminars, books, T-shirts, mugs and, of course, *Michigan Avenue G-Clit-Cock--The Movie.*"

"Uh-uh," Meredith said, laughing. "No way. I'm keeping your brilliant discovery all for myself." She kissed Jack's chin. "I'm much too selfish to share this one."

They untangled themselves from each other and sat up against the bank of pillows at the headboard. Jack brought his arms up, folding his hands behind his head as he leaned back with a contented sigh.

"I'm a supremely happy man, Meredith," he boasted through a broad smile. "Married to the woman of my dreams. And it's only going to keep getting better from here. You, me, a houseful of kids and a big sloppy dog."

"And don't forget the unlimited lifetime supply of chocolate you promised me," Meredith teased as she gently coaxed her husband's cock back to attention. "And the pricey French bubbly," she added with a resolute nod. "The deal's off without those."

"I'm a man of my word," Jack said, quickly slipping his fingers into her unsuspecting cunt and laughing when Meredith eked out a little gasp. He looked into her eyes, grinning as he waggled his eyebrows. "And I promise you at least fifty years of magical sex and fun and laughter together. Starting right now with a wild ride to ecstasy." He flipped Meredith around so she was astride him.

As Jack McKenna thrust up into his bride's pussy, she started to cry again, overwhelmed by the joy, the passion, the unbridled happiness of being Mrs. Jack McKenna.

Chapter One
Twenty Years Later

စာ

"*Eeeeek!* There it is again!" Meredith McKenna abruptly flew into the arms of Cristoval de Medina, her hunky next-door neighbor, plastering her ample curves against his hard muscled form. She further ensnared the scrumptious young Spaniard by wrapping her arms around his neck and her legs around his narrow waist.

Securing his hold on the pseudo-hysterical Meredith, Cristoval glanced around her small kitchen. "Where? I don't see it." His deep accented timbre seemed designed to set women's hearts aflutter.

"It just scampered across the floor." Whimpering, Meredith pressed her breasts harder against Cristoval's naked chest and buried her face into the crook of his neck and shoulder, inhaling his delicious male scent. "I think it went out through the crack at the bottom of the kitchen door."

"Ah, *sí.*" Cristoval nodded. "Mice can squeeze themselves through the tiniest spaces. I'm sure it's gone. Believe it or not, it's more afraid of you than you are of it." He laughed and then moved to set Meredith down.

"No!" Gasping, she locked her arms tighter around his neck. "Don't put me down yet. I'm...I'm still scared." She raised her head and gazed into Cristoval's chocolate-drop eyes, which were fringed with lush licorice-black lashes — the longest she'd ever seen on a man. She couldn't risk having him release her yet — not now that she'd finally mustered the courage to be a wanton woman. She might lose her nerve.

The night before, while jabbing an accusatory finger toward her reflection in the bathroom mirror, Meredith had spat, "That's it! I've had it. That chronic goody-two-shoes attitude of yours is ruining my sex life. Your reign as Queen of the Boring, Sniveling Good Girls is officially terminated as of this moment, do you hear me?" She paused. "Good *girl*? Hah! *Middle-aged woman* is more like it. You're turning forty tomorrow, remember?" she'd managed through choked laughter. "That's ten years shy of half a century." Bracing her hands on either side of the sink, she'd leaned closer to her reflection, narrowing her large blue eyes as she scrutinized every laugh line, wrinkle, sag and imperfection.

"Face it, missy" she'd said, staring herself down, "the bloom of youth has withered. Life is passing you by, and what the hell have you done about it? Nothing! You haven't had sex once since Jack left you three years ago. *Three goddamn years*, Meredith!" She'd poked her finger at the mirror again. "And it's nobody's fault but your own."

And then she'd straightened, elevating her chin and curling her lip into a wicked smile. "Well, your dry spell ends tomorrow morning when the new, improved, forty-year-old Meredith McKenna fucks that glorious young specimen of muscled masculinity next door. Got that?"

And that's why Meredith was feeling just a tad panicked now...why she couldn't possibly let go of this choice opportunity. If Cristoval just set her down and left, with no more than a quick smile and a friendly *adios*, she could lose her last chance to escape the suffocation of her tediously virtuous life.

Cristoval stared into her eyes for a moment before dropping his gaze to the pair of generous breasts heaving against his chest. Meredith watched him give her a languorous appraisal. And then he swallowed hard as his hands warily squeezed her ass cheeks.

Yes!

God, it felt so damn good to have a man's hands on her body again. She'd dressed in a thigh-high lavender silk robe with nothing underneath, to make things as simple...and accessible...as possible. Oh but she felt so liberated! So delightfully wicked! And so exceedingly glad that she hadn't chickened out and shackled herself in her utilitarian white cotton panties and sturdy bra.

"Thanks for coming to my rescue, Cristoval," she whispered before pressing her lips against his cheek.

"Anytime, Mrs. McKenna," he murmured against her ear.

"Please...call me Meredith." Her voice was soft and breathy. "I've been divorced for three years."

"All right...*Meredith*," Cristoval whispered as she daringly crushed her pussy close against the mounting erection in his jeans. Mmm, he felt nice and big. She moaned in anticipation and heard a reciprocal groan erupt from deep within his bronzed chest.

"I hope I didn't catch you in the middle of something important, Cristoval," she said, as if she didn't know. As if she hadn't meticulously orchestrated her seduction right down to the exact moment she knew he'd be walking down the corridor.

"No," he sucked in a ragged breath, "I was just coming back from my morning workout." His bulging biceps flexed as he held her, emphasizing his statement. Being encircled in all that bunching muscle made her pussy weep with joy.

Meredith allowed the curious fingers of one hand to travel down his sculpted, sweat-glossed chest, while the other hand trailed to his biceps. "You're my big, strong hero." She rubbed her thumb across his small, flat nipple and squeezing the muscles in his arm. He felt superb. How long had it been since she'd fondled an irresistibly sexy young man? *Way* too long. Oh yeah, she definitely liked the new improved bold and brazen Meredith.

Cristoval's impressive pecs flexed involuntarily.

"Am I too heavy for you?"

He shook his head. "Not at all. Just perfect." His fingers pressed into her ass cheeks, kneading and establishing even closer contact.

"Today's my birthday, Cristoval," Meredith said, drawing invisible patterns across his pecs with her finger.

"Happy birthday, *cara mia*," he whispered against her ear.

"Do you know what I'd like for my birthday?" She flattened her palms against his chest, sinking her fingertips into his flesh and relishing the distinct feel of firm masculine youth beneath her hands.

Cristoval glanced down at her crimson-tipped fingers digging into him and flashed a dazzling white-toothed grin. "I think I have a pretty good idea." He walked a couple of feet to the kitchen wall and positioned Meredith's back against it while he rubbed his substantial cock against her pussy. Meredith moaned. She'd almost forgotten what it felt like to be this turned on.

"Um...how old are you, Cristoval?"

"I just turned twenty-five. Why? Are you afraid I'm not man enough for you?" he teased, eyes glittering.

"Hardly." She ground herself against him, chuckling as she silently thanked God the kid wasn't still in his teens. It made the goody-two-shoes that still resided in her feel a smidgen less like a debauched cradle robber. "I'm forty today," Meredith admitted haltingly. "Do you think that's...old?"

Giving a husky laugh, Cristoval captured Meredith's full lips in a kiss, probing with his tongue until she gave him full access. His tongue's movements were insistent and aggressive as he plundered the recesses of her mouth. Oh yes, the boy knew how to kiss all right. And all Meredith could think about was that if he was this good with his tongue then he must be damned exceptional with other parts of his anatomy.

"Old?" Cristoval pulled back and fixed her with an intense gaze. "On the contrary, Meredith, you're perfectly ripe," he nibbled her bottom lip, "and juicy," he dragged her lip through his teeth, "deliciously sexy and in your prime. You've been driving me loco ever since I moved in last year."

"Really?" Meredith's eyes widened in genuine surprise. "But you never...I had no idea."

Cristoval grinned. "Because you were giving me unmistakable *hands off* signals."

"Hmm, I suppose I was." Meredith laughed quietly, thinking about the months that she'd so stupidly wasted, when she could have been happily fucking the hunky boy next door. Silly girl. "It's amazing what can suddenly happen to a seemingly unapproachable woman when she turns forty, isn't it, Cristoval?" She removed a strategically placed hair clip and shook her head, allowing her long cinnamon-brown locks to pool at her shoulders, thankful that the action came off without a hitch, just like in the movies. And then she tugged on the sides of her flimsy robe, baring her breasts for him.

"Ahhh...so beautiful," he said. "So sexy."

"Cristoval?"

"Hmmm?" His gaze was locked on her tawny, crinkling nipples as they brushed his chest.

"Fuck me."

In an instant Cristoval moved them to the oak kitchen table, where he deposited Meredith after sweeping the floral centerpiece aside. He opened the clasp and zipper of his faded jeans and they slid down his hips. Meredith watched in delight as his cock, unencumbered by underwear, sprang free. Oh dear Lord, the fun she could have been having with her very own Latin lover all this time!

"Oh no," he gritted through his teeth as he grasped Meredith's jiggling breasts. "I don't have anything on me."

"Condoms, you mean?" He nodded and she grinned as she dug into the pocket of her robe and produced a foil packet. "Well, what do you know? I just happen to have one on me." She offered an inviting smile as Cristoval sheathed himself and she spread her thighs in anticipation of her great big juicy birthday present.

Hot and horny took on a whole new meaning as Cristoval held her in his brawny arms. She was fully drenched in expectation of being filled for the first time in three years. It was a happy surprise that her pussy hadn't withered up or rusted or something equally as objectionable after being idle for so long.

As Cristoval feasted on her nipples, currents of pleasure crackled to her core, making her greedy for more. And when his stiff, eager cock thrust into her depths, causing the sweet slick friction of which she'd so long been deprived, tears of joy actually flowed down Meredith's cheeks. Oooh...he was *so* much better than her worn-out plastic vibrator.

Their brisk, brief and vigorous sexual encounter bordered on being rough—in a most agreeable manner. Mmm-hmm, there was definitely something to be said for an impromptu fucking session on the kitchen table. In broad daylight. With a twenty-something bodybuilding stud. Ole!

And when that remarkable cock of Cristoval's rammed deep into Meredith's pussy for the final plunge, she could have sworn that the table took wing and flew out of the kitchen, soaring high into the azure sky and fluffy clouds where her being splintered into a million shards of sheer orgasmic bliss.

"Oh, yes..." she heard herself murmur with a throaty chuckle. "Happy birthday to me!"

Chapter Two

ଽଠ

"This isn't a good idea, Meredith. I know you too well. All Jack has to do is crook his little finger and you'll be at his feet, like some vulnerable little puppy, lapping up stray droplets of attention and begging for more." Karyn Archer dislodged the medium blonde wisp of hair from her forehead with an exasperated swipe.

"Hardly. How many times do I have to tell you that I'm over Jack?"

"Yeah, right. One telephone call from the rat and you drop everything to have dinner with him."

"That's not true. You know I didn't have any plans for tonight anyway. When he called last week he literally begged me to come, Karyn. He said it's urgent. Honestly, the only reason I'm going is out of curiosity—and because I had nothing else to do."

"Hah!"

Patting a stray lock of long hair in place as she gazed into the vanity mirror, Meredith tsked. "For heaven's sake, Karyn, I'm a lot older and wiser now. At forty—"

"That's another thing," Karyn cut in. "This is a hell of a way to spend your birthday. You could be going out with any number of promising prospects instead of that lecherous ex-husband of yours. Like that adorable young toreador next door. You know, the one with the gargantuan package bulging in his tight jeans and the biceps that won't quit." Karyn waggled her eyebrows and licked her lips. "Ooh, what I wouldn't give to see him naked."

"Cristoval?" Meredith feigned a yawn. "Been there, done that," she chirped with a flick of her wrist. "And it's even bigger than we imagined." She grinned and waited for Karyn's reaction.

"You? Hah!" Karyn folded her arms across her chest and huffed. "Dream on, Miss World's Oldest Living Virgin."

Meredith laughed. "I may have been celibate for three years, but I'm most certainly not a virgin."

"Maybe not technically, but a three-year dry run qualifies you as Virgin Second Class in my book. Celibacy must have taken its toll if you're hallucinating about screwing the boy next door."

"So I guess that means you don't want the juicy details, hmm?" Meredith nailed Karyn with a challenging gaze.

Karyn's jaw dropped. "Oh my God, are you serious?" She looked incredulous as she did an almost classic double-take and then gasped. "You are! You and Cristoval really did it? Ohmigod, ohmigod! When? Where? How?"

"You sound like a reporter." Meredith chuckled. "This morning. Here in my apartment. Horizontally—on the kitchen table. There, I think that answers your questions." Stifling a grin, she turned back to the mirror and checked her eye makeup.

Karyn leaned against the wall and closed her eyes as she hugged herself. "The kitchen table," she whispered, stretching out the words. "Wow. I've never known anyone who's actually done that. And I certainly never expected the first to be you. No wonder you've had that shit-eating grin on your face ever since I arrived this afternoon."

"Oh yeah, that'll definitely do it. There's nothing like ending a prolonged bout of celibacy with a *wham-bam-thank-you-young-man* round of raw, wild sex."

Karyn nodded slowly, with a look of bafflement clouding her gaze. "But the last I heard, you and Cristoval had just exchanged brief nodding hellos passing each other in the hall. So how did you get from that to this so fast?"

Meredith felt the grin Karyn had so aptly described return in full force. "This morning I ran out into the hall, frantic because I'd seen a mouse. It just *happened* to coincide with the time that Cristoval returns from his workout. He was shirtless and sweaty and..." She gushed a dreamy sigh at the memory. "I told him what happened and asked him to come over to take a look." Closing her eyes, she licked her lips and moaned. "God, Karyn, what a glorious set of meaty pecs. Scrumptious. And he was wearing those wonderful tight faded jeans, the ones with the tears in provocative places. Interestingly enough, I just *happened* to have my short little silk robe on, without anything underneath."

"Hmm, imagine that," Karyn interjected.

"I know." The perfect picture of innocence, Meredith nodded. "Amazing coincidence that this was the one morning I wasn't wearing a ratty old T-shirt and sweatpants, isn't it?" Karyn chuckled at that. "Anyway," Meredith went on, "when the mouse scurried through the kitchen I screamed, jumped into his incredibly strong arms, and he held me up off the floor as if I weighed no more than a stick of butter. Can you imagine? Talk about a rush! And then...well, one thing led to another. Jeez, Karyn, the kid's really hung—and mega-talented. It was unbelievable."

"Wow. Happy birthday to you!"

Meredith nodded. "Yup, I figured I deserved something *really* special for my fortieth."

"Did he catch the mouse?"

Meredith looked at Karyn sheepishly and then glanced away, fiddling with the perfume atomizers on her vanity while another grin spread across her cheeks. "What mouse?" She shrugged.

"The one that—" Karyn stopped herself and gasped audibly, wagging an accusing finger at Meredith. "Oh my God. There never was any mouse, was there? You purposely seduced that poor unsuspecting half-naked youngster.

Woman, you are positively wicked!" She erupted with laughter.

"Men like to be heroes, saving damsels in distress. So I simply provided Cristoval with the opportunity to play the part." Meredith lifted a shoulder nonchalantly. "Conjuring up a mouse seemed like a perfect idea. And it worked like a charm." She winked.

Karyn wiped the tears of laughter from her cheeks. "And here I've been feeling sorry for you because you've been a goddamned celibate shut-in for the last three years. I've all but given up trying to talk you into getting out more, with the possibility of a little bit of sex in your future — and all the while you're orchestrating scenes with phony mice so you can fuck the stud next door. You slut!" She continued to laugh.

"Yeah, isn't it great?" Joining her in laughter, Meredith put her arm around her friend's shoulder. "There's something about turning forty that drives a single woman to desperate measures. I just couldn't ring in the big four-oh without doing something radical. Spontaneous, you know? Anyway, Karyn, you'll find out when you reach your fortieth in a few months."

"Yeah, but the guy who lives next door to me," she hiked a thumb toward her apartment three flights up, "is bald, has a big beer belly and reeks of stale sweat. Can I borrow Cristoval?"

Meredith laughed. "Sure. Maybe this time we'll fabricate a cockroach story."

Karyn's eyes brightened. "Ooh, *la cucaracha*! I like that." She twirled around like a flamenco dancer, clicking a pair of imaginary castanets as she sang.

"But only if you promise to stop ragging at me about my date with Jack tonight," Meredith added.

Karyn's jovial expression slumped into a pout. "That's not fair."

"Just because you're my business partner, missy, doesn't give you the right to interfere in my personal affairs."

"Maybe not," Karyn admitted, "but being your best friend for the last thirty years gives me carte blanche to do that and more." She stuck out her tongue and Meredith laughed. "Honestly, Meredith, what a sucky way to end your birthday, especially after starting the day off fucking a hunky young thing on the kitchen table." She gazed at Meredith thoughtfully. "Speaking of young…just how old is Cristoval, anyway?"

"Fifteen years our junior."

Karyn's eyebrow arched while she mentally calculated. "Twenty-five? Ooh, yum!"

"Yeah, I guess that makes me slightly less lecherous than if he were eighteen." Meredith laughed. "And as for my meeting Jack later, on the contrary, Karyn, seeing my ex tonight is the *perfect* way to finish celebrating the dawning of my," she cleared her throat, "shall we say…middle years?" She rolled her eyes and sighed, still not quite at ease with leaving her thirties behind. "I'm not a sweet, naïve, trusting little simpleton anymore. How many times do I have to tell you that I'm over Jack?"

"Uh-huh. Right." Nursing a smirk, Karyn folded her arms across her chest. "Just like you're over chocolate." She nodded toward the yawning box of Belgian chocolates on Meredith's nightstand.

"That's different." Meredith flicked her wrist. "I clearly wasn't in my right mind when I vowed to give up chocolate for my New Year's resolution. I mean, really, what's a few more pounds here and there on my already…ahem…" she patted her hips, "ample shape compared to the desolation and emptiness of a life void of chocolate?"

"Hey, you won't get any argument from me. You're preaching to the choir, honey," Karyn said with a resolute nod as she mimicked Meredith's hip patting against her own plump curves. "Frankly, I don't know what on earth you were thinking at the time."

"Oh yes you do." Meredith laughed. "That's when you and I got drunk on New Year's and decided we needed to go on a major self-improvement kick before we turned forty, remember?"

"Oh yeah." Karyn smirked. "Just like all those drunken good intentions we had just before we turned thirty...and just before we turned twenty. That does have a familiar ring to it. Well, those were all grandiose ideas that fizzled fast, weren't they? Guess that's what comes from guzzling all that cheap champagne." She bubbled with laughter.

"That and a bad-ass hangover." Meredith rolled her eyes in remembrance of the nasty day after. "This time I was supposed to give up chocolate and you vowed to give up pistachios. Ha!" She snickered. "Aren't we a pair? I'm *never* giving up chocolate again, damn it. It's my best friend...well, after you, of course." With a wink, she smiled before blotting her crimson lipstick and checking her teeth.

"Yeah, bullshit." Karyn crossed her arms over her chest. "Don't worry, Meredith, I have no delusions about replacing chocolate as your number one buddy. But then, you only come in second to my penchant for pistachios, so I guess that makes us even." She returned Meredith's wink.

"I guess it does."

The gleam in Karyn's eye was apparent as the corner of her mouth hiked into a knowing smile. "I know what you're trying to do, Meredith, and I'm not going to let you get away with it."

"What?" An expression of deliberate innocence blanketed Meredith's features. "I don't have any idea what you're talking about." Doing her best to hide a budding smile from her far too perceptive friend, she went back to fluffing her hair and checking her reflection.

"Trying to deflect me from what's important—your date with Jack—that's what."

"Don't be ridiculous, Karyn, I—"

"Give it up, Meredith," Karyn cut her off, brandishing an accusatory finger under Meredith's nose. "It's me, remember? I've known you since we were ten years old, which means that I'm painfully familiar with your lame attempts at subterfuge. Now enough talk about our food addictions. I want to know why the hell you'd ever consider, for even one minute, going out with the man who single-handedly succeeded in transforming you into a whimpering, depressed, self-doubting, chocolate-bingeing, pathetic blob of insecurities."

"Ouch."

Karyn pulled Meredith into a hug. "I'm sorry, sweetie, but those are the facts. You were a mess. I was worried to death about you for that entire first year after Jack dumped you for that college kid. I'd never seen you in such a state of hopeless despair. Have you forgotten about all of that?"

"Of course not. How could I? And I'll never forget how hard you worked to pull me through that awful time." Meredith gave Karyn a squeeze. She knew without a doubt that if it hadn't been for the loving, dogged persistence of her childhood friend, she may not have even been around to see her fortieth birthday — the depression had been that acute.

Karyn gave a watery smile and sniffed. "It's no more than you did for me after my rat-bastard husband skipped out on me with *his* teeny-bopper." Meredith suddenly erupted in laughter and Karyn blinked in surprise. "Oddly enough I really fail to see the humor in that."

"Sorry. I was just thinking that you and I probably hold the world's record for really shitty choices when it comes to men." Karyn rolled her eyes in agreement and laughed along with Meredith. "Honestly, you can stop worrying about me. Jack no longer has any hold over me. I'm completely immune to the man's charms." Meredith rearranged another errant wisp of hair as she tried to convince herself she was speaking the truth. She'd worked hard over the past months to steel herself against the scintillating charisma of her first and only real love. She just hoped that she'd come far enough to succeed

36

in her vital mission tonight. She drew in a deep breath and released it. "I know it's taken me a long time and a lot of heartache to learn my lesson, but believe me, I'm nobody's dopey little doormat anymore."

"I don't know about that." Karyn hiked an eyebrow. "First you spend a small fortune on insanely expensive sexy undies and then—"

"And I'll have you know that nothing is bigger than a size eighteen-twenty," Meredith interrupted. "I haven't been this small in years!"

Karyn nodded. "Yes, you've only mentioned that about fifty times this past week—and I've already told you how stunning you look, fifty-one times." She laughed. "Now stop interrupting me when I'm on a roll, okay?" Meredith saluted her compliance and Karyn continued. "Then, you primp and fluff for over an hour. And," she turned and pointed to the stack of clothes on Meredith's rumpled bed, "you've changed outfits at least a dozen times. Jesus, I'd hate to see what you'd be doing if you *weren't* over Jack."

Trilling a sigh, Meredith shook her head and laughed. "You don't understand, Karyn, this is the first time I've seen Jack in nearly three years and—"

"Yeah, since he dumped you and married that anemic-looking prepubescent floozy, Becky. The one who *pretended* she was pregnant so she could get her greedy little claws on your husband's fame, his name and his money. The money he earned only because *you* broke your ass working two jobs to put him though school while you guys were still engaged to be married. And then he had the audacity to go fucking around with God knows how many of his classmates behind your back." Karyn's shoulders slumped as she heaved a sigh. "And now that Becky's smartened up, left him and moved on, he's come skulking back to you so you can lick his wounds." She narrowed her eyes. "And his cock," she added under her breath.

"I heard that little aside," Meredith said, pointing a reproachful finger and smirking. "Jack's cock, as enticing as it may be, is definitely not going to save his sorry ass this time." She took a deep breath, doing her damnedest to blot the image of her ex's anatomy from her thoughts. Damned if the man didn't have the innate ability to charm the pants off her— literally. "Believe it or not, I'm not stupid, Karyn. And I haven't forgotten any of what Jack put me through. By now I'm *more* than familiar with his pattern. I'm fully aware that all I am to him is a warm, familiar place to store his overeager dick between bimbos."

"I don't get it." Karyn shrugged. "So why all the pains to look so ravishing tonight? Why torture yourself by agreeing to see him again after all he's done to you? For chrissakes, Meredith, this is the third time he's walked out on you and then come back begging your forgiveness."

"Fourth time, actually. Two broken engagements and two divorces." Meredith's eyes brightened as she studied her reflection. "Gee, you really think I look ravishing?" She smoothed her hands over her black dress and smiled.

"Too damned good for that bastard, that's for damned sure," Karyn said, shaking her head and hiding a grin. "If those big tits of yours were plumped up any higher they'd fall right out of your dress."

"Good. I want to make him drool." Meredith pirouetted as she gave herself another mirror check. "I want Jack to be so fucking hot for me that he'll need a fire extinguisher to put out his blazing libido." She giggled. "When he catches his first glimpse of me tonight I want him to look like one of those cartoon wolf characters with their tongues rolling out onto the floor and their eyes bugging out of their heads as a big *ah-oooogah* horn goes off in the background." Meredith gestured dramatically, illustrating the scenario. By working Jack into a lathered state of sexual need she'd definitely have the upper hand tonight.

Clearly, Karyn couldn't help but laugh. "And just what do you intend to accomplish by turning him on, hmm? I mean, you already know that Jack is intent on getting you into bed and screwing your brains out until you agree to take him back again, anyway. He knows how damned easy you are when it comes to him." Meredith turned sharply toward Karyn and gasped. "Oh don't give me that righteous indignation crap. One clit-quivering touch from Jack and you're spreading your thighs—you told me so yourself, many times. So why knock yourself out trying to drive him even crazier with lust?"

"It's absolutely crucial." A deep throaty laugh erupted from Meredith's lips. "Trust me, I didn't spend months in grieving celibacy, medicating myself with gargantuan doses of chocolate while I contemplated encasing my feet in cement and hurdling myself off Portland's highest bridge, just so I could let that philandering sonuvabitch stomp on my heart again. Quite the opposite, my dear friend." Meredith's lips curled into a deliciously wicked smile. "I have a plan."

"Oooh." Karyn's eyes widened in delight as she broke into a grin. "I like the sound of that—and that devious look in your eye." She rubbed her hands together briskly. "Come on, Meredith, spill your guts. What kind of fabulous comeuppance have you planned for that bastard?"

"Mmm, a deliciously wicked little payback scheme." Meredith sauntered to her nightstand, where she selected a chocolate hazelnut truffle from the box of candy, holding it aloft and eyeing it as if studying the facets of a fine diamond. "This former goody-two-shoes is going to give Jack McKenna a night that he will *never* forget." Closing her eyes in anticipation, she popped the creamy morsel into her mouth and moaned her pleasure.

Chapter Three

ഔ

Just as Jack promised when he'd called Meredith the week before begging her to have dinner with him, the stretch limo he had sent arrived promptly at eight. The upscale mode of transportation was a far cry from the barely functional used cars they'd owned when they were married. And that's when they could even *afford* a car. Giving herself a final once-over in the full-length mirror, Meredith smoothed her sleek black dress, double checked the contents of her beaded envelope purse for the umpteenth time and, sucking in a deep breath, left the apartment.

She sank into the limo's plush leather interior and noticed the elaborately ribboned long white box that held an envelope with her name. She opened the envelope and read the enclosed card. *Pity this one perfect rose that can never hope to equal your beauty. Love, Jack.*

Meredith smiled, remembering the wonderful way Jack had with words. Now an internationally acclaimed motivational speaker, his skill was clearly evident in anything he penned. She still had every one of those I'll-love-you-until-the-day-I-die poems and letters he'd written her, opening the box to re-read them and have a good cry every few months or so. Oh yeah, Jack had known exactly how to manipulate her. A poem here, a love letter there, a two-pound box of Belgian chocolates when she had PMS... But that was in the past. The new, more judicious Meredith breathed a sigh of relief. Now that he was world renowned, maybe she'd put Jack's love letters up for sale on one of those online auction sites. He'd positively hate that. And she'd start the opening bid at just a penny. The devilish idea tickled her.

As her gaze fell on the single long-stemmed red rose in the box, Meredith's brain blithely conjured up happier times, especially those first blissful years together when they couldn't keep their hands off each other. Even when all they could afford was a few cans of pork and beans and a box of crackers, they didn't care because they were so very much in love. When Jack got home from his university classes and Meredith was still at work, he'd meticulously set the scene for seduction. When she got home to their little apartment she'd often find it aglow with shimmering candlelight and perfumed with the mouthwatering scent of dinner cooking on the stove. And more often than not, there was a hot, scented, candlelit bubble bath waiting for her to slip into and relax for awhile as Jack finished his homework. Those were such incredibly happy times...

"Stop it!" Meredith chastised herself, hoping her voice hadn't been loud enough to reach the chauffeur's ears. "This is most definitely not the time to be thinking positive thoughts about Jack," she whispered. "He's not the same man anymore." If she didn't stop summoning pleasant memories, she'd *never* make it through the evening with her far too appealing ex-husband.

Meredith forced herself to snap out of it, to purge all blissful thoughts of him from her mind and to focus on the task at hand. She needed closure. And Jack was in serious need of payback. She forced herself to remember the way he'd taken advantage of her over the years as one frolicsome young plaything after another caught his eye. And each time, after the interlude had ended and he'd begged Meredith's forgiveness while pledging undying love, she had swallowed her pride and forgiven him. All but the last time, three years ago.

The first time he'd done this to her was after they'd been married just a few years. Jack failed Monogamy 101 miserably when faced with the temptation of a juicy little sprite employed at one of the coffee shops he frequented—Lisa the barista.

That was divorce number one.

Barely ten months later, Meredith's firm resolve to excise Jack from her life finally cracked amidst a plethora of pledges, promises and innumerous acts of contrition. After his divorce from the cappuccino goddess became final, Meredith and Jack remarried and remained entrenched in connubial bliss. Or so Meredith thought. And then Becky, the impossibly thin, unbearably young, pseudo-pregnant bimbo entered the picture. The final mortal blow to their relationship came when the immensely charming, handsome hunk Meredith had been making a fool of herself over since she was eighteen years old had unceremoniously dumped her to marry Becky.

That was divorce number two.

Groaning at the necessary but painful recollections, Meredith dropped her head into her hands and massaged her temples. As distressing as those memories were, she needed to keep them at the forefront of her thoughts, reminding her flighty brain of the importance of focusing on the task of the moment — payback...*payback*...PAYBACK!

By the time the driver opened her door in front of the swanky five-star Northwest Passage Hotel and Meredith placed one shapely high-heeled leg on the curb, her mind was calm and her thoughts entirely on her plans for the evening ahead.

She headed for the hotel's Lewis and Clark room where Jack was booked for a speaking engagement. She spotted him immediately after opening the huge gilded doors, surrounded, not surprisingly, by a gaggle of fans. Some were shoving their programs at him for his autograph, some were purchasing sets of his tapes, books and CDs and others were apparently just hoping for a chance to talk to the mesmerizing *Dr. Jack.* He was an amazing orator all right, she'd give him that. Jack had brought auditoriums full of people to sniffles and tears with his heart-wrenching stories and their impossibly upbeat endings.

God knows he'd used those same skills and tactics on her often enough in the past, wheedling his way back into her shattered heart after she'd promised herself to turn a deaf ear to his persuasive pleadings. Meredith felt her lip curl into a sneer, disgusted with her former naiveté.

She stood quietly at the back of the room, tucking herself into the shadows and studying Jack as he charmed his fans. Tall and still undeniably handsome, with the same thick, espresso-brown hair and winning smile, he hadn't changed much since she'd last seen him. Damn it, he hadn't even changed much at all since they were first married, except to get even better looking. She was hoping that maybe he'd developed a paunch, or that he'd gone bald, or that perhaps he'd developed jowls or had to wear reading glasses with bottle-thick lenses that made his eyes look small and beady. No such luck. The man was still more enticing than a hot fudge sundae — and that was saying a lot coming from a chocoholic. She sighed, feeling half-defeated already.

When Jack finally spotted her, gifting Meredith with that brilliant smile of his, she felt her traitorous heart skip a beat. *No! You will not get all stupid and let him get to you again!* She sucked in a deep breath and steeled herself against the palpable charms of the man she once believed was her soulmate. Her one and only.

Within a few minutes his publicity people had shooed the last of the hangers-on from the room. And then Jack walked toward Meredith — and her double-crossing heart beat a rapid tattoo with each step he took. The moment he was near enough, Meredith inhaled, breathing in the scent of him. God, he smelled so good. He smelled like…Jack.

"Aw, Meredith. *My* Meredith." He took both of her hands, stood back and appraised her from head to toe. His heated gaze lingered on the cleavage she'd made sure to frame with the perfect neckline and he smiled. "You're an absolute vision. Even lovelier than you were the last time I saw you, if that's possible." He reached up to finger her hair, twisting his finger through the locks as he gazed at her eyes. "God, how I've missed looking into those hypnotic lavender-blue eyes of yours. Happy birthday, baby." Leaning close, Jack drew Meredith into his arms and brushed his lips against hers. The light kiss and firm embrace were possessive...commanding. It felt comfortable, familiar...and entirely too inviting. "I've got a very special dinner planned for your birthday."

"I'm looking forward to it," Meredith responded as she gazed up into his eyes. They were hazel. She'd always been intrigued by the mesmerizing combination of green, brown and gray that changed with the light and with his mood. "I've missed you too, Jack. It's good to see you again." She'd expected to be more nervous and was glad she felt moderately calm and in control. The last thing she wanted was to come across like a skittish, love-starved ex-wife. That would spoil everything.

Curving his hand against the small of her back, Jack guided Meredith from the room, explaining that he'd made dinner reservations at Columbia, the hotel's famous skytop restaurant that overlooked the city.

Once they'd been shown to their table, Meredith was suitably impressed with the expansive views of Portland's city lights. After she and Karyn had moved from Chicago to Oregon—to get as far away from their respective ex-spouses as possible—Meredith had read about the breathtaking views here, though she'd never been to the restaurant before. Since the menu offered nothing, not even soup or appetizer, under twenty dollars, Columbia hadn't been among her first choices for dining out.

"Do you know why I chose this particular restaurant?" Jack asked, capturing her fingertips with his in a gentle grasp.

"Because they serve a mean cheeseburger?" Meredith laughed.

"Not quite." Jack's eyes twinkled with amusement. "I selected it specifically because it's on the fortieth floor with a view of the city skyline. Just like our wedding night, forty floors up in that fancy Chicago hotel suite twenty years ago...remember, Meredith?" His fingers slid up to cover her hand and he gave it a squeeze while gazing into her eyes.

Remember?! Of course she remembered. It was the most beautiful, romantic, perfect night of her entire life for chrissakes. How could she possibly forget? And how dare he have the audacity to bring it up now of all times. As Jack brought her hand to his lips, Meredith slid free of his grasp.

"That was a lifetime ago, Jack. We were children then. Babies."

"Ah...we had such lofty hopes and dreams back then, Meredith. If only — "

"Oh look," she said with a bit too much enthusiasm, immensely happy to see their waiter approaching. "Here come the hors d'oeuvres."

Over appetizers and flutes of pricey vintage champagne they talked about the prosperous speaking circuit, Jack's bestselling self-help books and sets of audio-visual programs, as well as the lucrative offer he'd just accepted to host his own TV talk show, *On the Right Track with Dr. Jack.* They also touched on Meredith and Karyn's thriving resale shop, Abundant Finds, which offered upscale clothing for plus-sized women.

They fell so easily into comfortable conversation that it was almost as if they'd never been separated. Half-listening as he regaled her about winding up his current speaking tour so that he could start on the production of his television show, she studied Jack's handsome face and the dark shadow along his strong jaw line. She silently admired the classic tailoring of his clearly expensive charcoal gray three-piece suit and the way it hugged his broad shoulders, concealing the muscles she knew were there. He'd always been a stickler for working out at the gym and had the mouthwatering results to show for his efforts. The sensual image of Jack naked and poised above her as he prepared to ram his big cock into her flitted across her mind, causing a slight tremble. Startled by the lusty thoughts,

Meredith shook her head, reminding herself to reset her train of thought.

"You're shivering. Are you chilly?"

"Oh...no, no, I'm just fine." Smiling, Meredith did her damnedest to stop picturing him naked. Or to think about that oh-so-satisfying cock of his. The great sex she'd shared with Jack had always been her downfall. His proud cock...the hard planes of his sculpted chest...the sensuous way his tongue would curl around—

"Anyway, as I was saying," Jack said. And, embarrassed, Meredith realized she had no idea what in the world he'd been saying because her thoughts had been focused on his sexual attributes...and her carnal appetite. "Marrying Becky was a foolish mistake," he continued. And now he had Meredith's full attention. "It was a rash and mindless decision. One that I regret wholeheartedly, especially because," and now Jack dropped his head in a hangdog expression, "because I know how much it must have hurt you, Meredith." He looked up at her with pleading puppy dog eyes. "And I wouldn't want to hurt you for anything in the world, babe."

Meredith realized her expression must have mirrored her thoughts when Jack quickly added, "But, honestly, what could I do? Becky was pregnant."

Planting both elbows on the table, Meredith rested her chin on steepled fingers and gazed at Jack, doing her best to conceal the contempt that had suddenly obliterated all thoughts of him hot, naked and pumping. "She was lying, Jack. To get you to marry her."

Jack raised a finger in objection. "Probably, but we can't know that for a fact. According to Becky, she had a miscarriage while visiting her mother in Wisconsin just after we returned from our honeymoon."

"Uh-huh. Right." It was especially painful for her to recall the whole fake pregnancy ploy Becky had pulled, considering how much Meredith and Jack had wanted to have a baby of their own. They'd talked and dreamed about being parents so often. They'd wanted twins, a boy and a girl. All the tests confirmed that they were healthy. There wasn't any medical reason why Meredith couldn't conceive, but the pregnancy they'd hoped for never happened. The recollection usually made Meredith teary, but tonight it had a decidedly different effect.

"You know, Jack, little Becky was still pooping in her diapers when we got married — the *first* time we got married, I mean." She gave a saccharine smile and sipped from her champagne, only to choke on it.

"You okay?"

The last of her sputtering coughs subsiding, Meredith nodded. She certainly wasn't about to tell him that it was fleeting thoughts of her own naughty, before-breakfast tryst with a boy who'd been no more than a child when she and Jack married that had caught in her throat. Of course, her situation and Jack's had one indisputable difference — hers wasn't a sneaky, behind-the-back extramarital affair.

Jack breathed a sigh. "I know how disappointed you are in me, Meredith. What can I say? I'm a flawed man. You already know that. Becky was just one of a meaningless string of distractions that meant very little to me."

"Like Lisa the barista you mean?"

Jack rolled his eyes. "I swear, Meredith, I've never had the soul connection with any of them that I have with the one and only woman I've ever truly loved. With *you*, Meredith."

Meredith's understanding smile hid the fact that the words *rotten lying scum-sucking low-life cheating bastard* seemed to flash like a bright neon green sign over his head.

"The only excuse I can offer is that I was young and — "

"The Becky incident only happened three years ago, Jack," Meredith couldn't help but interject. "You were forty." Her lip hiked in an insipid smile.

"You've got me there." Laughing, Jack winked and pointed a finger at Meredith, pistol fashion. "Let me amend that from young to inexperienced and weak." He paused expectantly, and she nodded in accord. "I admit that I got caught up in the lure of young flesh. Being constantly pursued by nubile young fans at my university speaking engagements was intoxicating, addicting. Almost like being a rock star. After those first few appearances on the TV talk shows, all of a sudden *Dr. Jack* was hot. I'd somehow become a sex symbol almost overnight and had women of all ages throwing themselves at me." He sucked in a deep breath. "It was tough. I'm only human, Meredith."

"Poor baby." Meredith averted her gaze, peering out at the multitude of lights dotting Portland's hills. "I remember a time when I thought our love was so strong, so real, that it could withstand any obstacle...any temptation," she recalled, her gaze still affixed to the glimmering lights while her thoughts were miles away. *Years* away. "A timeless love powerful enough to overcome any odds, including all the glitz and glamour." Then she turned back to face Jack, locking gazes with him. "And then you dumped me. Not once, not twice, not even three times, but *four* times—at least that I know about."

"It was only twice, sweetheart," he offered with an apologetic smile.

"Yeah, while we were married." Meredith's eyes narrowed. "You're conveniently forgetting the two times you broke off our engagement so that you could sow your wild oats with Amy and Cookie."

"Okay, okay," Jack said, raising a hand. "Point taken, but—"

"There are no buts. You did this to me *after* I had supported you by working two jobs so you could go back to school and take," she held out her fingers to count, "elocution lessons, drama, public speaking and all the other classes you said you needed to become a successful motivational speaker.

In fact, it was while you were in school that you dallied in your pre-marital oat sowing."

"You're absolutely right, Meredith." Jack bobbed his head up and down, nodding his agreement and looking just like one of those bobble-head toys on a car's dashboard. "You've always been an angel. My sweet, precious, hard-working guiding light. And I was a thoughtless bastard. I treated you horribly. Abominably. You certainly didn't deserve that. Any of it."

"You promised me the world, Jack — the moon, the stars and villas on the French Riviera. And all I ever wanted was your love. I would have been satisfied with that and nothing else." Hearing a distinct catch in her voice, Meredith felt tears rising to the surface and squelched them down. She took a deep breath and worked to regain her composure. "Well...*that*," she added with a smile, cognizant of the fact that she needed to lighten up a bit, "and the lifetime supply of chocolate you promised me." She indulged in a little polite, nervous laughter and Jack followed suit.

The waiter's arrival with their hideously expensive dinners of artfully prepared but miniscule portions of Pacific Northwest-style gourmet food interrupted their conversation. And it was just as well because Meredith needed to maintain her cool if she wanted her scheme to work. Being argumentative at the risk of alienating Jack just wouldn't be prudent.

Once the cool, efficient server had departed, Jack admitted, "You're right about everything, Meredith. All of it. What we had was pure and genuine and beautiful, and I spoiled it because I couldn't keep my dick in my pants."

He gifted her with an adoring gaze and Meredith marveled at the way the flickering candlelight made the flecks of color in his eyes sparkle. And when he brought her hand to his lips again, she allowed him to kiss it.

She breathed a lengthy sigh as cauldrons of inner turmoil roiled in her gut. The ravenous appetite that usually overtook her when she was nervous was curiously absent. Instead, she mindlessly picked at her food through dinner, barely eating or really tasting much of anything. Her plan had seemed so perfect, so simple...but adding Jack's magnetic presence to the equation threatened to skew the outcome.

Lack of appetite hadn't seemed to be a problem for Jack. He'd all but licked his platter clean. "What say we have dessert and cognac in my suite?" He leaned forward, his hand caressing hers. "We have a lot to discuss, Meredith, and after that," his lip curled into a beguiling smile and he shrugged, "who knows?"

"Right." Meredith returned the smile and then finished the champagne in her glass. "Who knows?" *She* knew — because she had it planned, every step of the way. And she'd be damned if she was going to allow her traitorous libido to get out of hand and louse things up now.

With a smile clearly designed to bedazzle, Jack offered Meredith his arm and led the way to his suite. Oh yes. He clearly had a night of carnal decadence in mind.

And Meredith wouldn't dream of disappointing him.

Chapter Four

ഇ

Meredith had promised herself that she wouldn't gawk when she caught her first glimpse of the Columbia's Astoria penthouse suite. That she'd be nonchalant, cool and collected, as if strolling through an opulent suite of rooms that dwarfed her entire apartment was an everyday occurrence—but gawk she did.

It was the kind of fairytale suite that she and Jack used to dream about back in their salad days. Its splendor even dwarfed that of the fabulous Chicago hotel suite they'd stayed in that one magical night twenty long years ago.

Contrary to common sense and better judgment, Meredith's thoughts drifted back once again to the early years of their marriage. She remembered several evenings when she'd come home from work so bone-tired she couldn't see straight and Jack had swept her into his arms and bedded her, ignoring her sleepy, half-hearted objections. He'd massage her sore muscles while painting lush verbal pictures of their future life of luxury together. While he spoke, incandescent hunger blazed so brightly in his eyes that it excited her beyond all reason. Because she knew the hunger wasn't for money…it was for her. And after soothing her muscles and tendons, Jack confirmed it by feasting generously on her weary, aching body until that certain area deep within her belly wound tightly with an almost unbearable coil of anticipation. He'd speak to her of gold and satin and diamonds and silk as he finger-fucked her. Then he'd lick her juices from his fingers as if her taste was the finest of gourmet treats.

Forcing herself back to the present, Meredith realized why Jack had chosen this ornately furnished suite with its massive gilded mirrors, exquisite furnishings, mile-deep

51

carpeting, yards of Italian marble and the other extravagant touches it offered. It was the epitome of their youthful dreams and aspirations come to life. He was letting her know that it was what she could have if she took him back again. But he'd missed the mark this time. It was never money and riches that she yearned for, not really. Oh sure, it was fun to think about being fabulously rich but she didn't need that to be happy. All she needed was Jack—body and soul. True and loyal and loving her forever. Alas, that had proven to be far more elusive than material wealth.

And that's exactly why she was here tonight.

"You've certainly come up in the world, Jack. The past three years have been very good to you."

Dropping his gaze to his feet, Jack shoved his hands into his pants pockets and shook his head. "Only monetarily, Meredith. I lost the only treasure of any real value through my own stupidity." When he raised his head again their gazes locked and Meredith sucked in a breath hoping that Jack hadn't noticed the pulse in her throat quicken. She watched his jaw muscle twitch as he studied her in silence, his commanding gaze boring into hers. She broke the spell by clearing her throat and strolling over to an ornately framed painting, feigning interest.

"Does this remind you of anything, Meredith?" She turned to find his arm waving in a sweeping gesture around the living room. "Remember those talks we used to have when we were just a couple of hungry, starry-eyed kids? The enchanting fantasies we shared? The trips we longed to take?"

"I remember...everything, Jack."

His expression was so fixed she began to fidget. His chest expanded with a deep breath and he finally looked away. "Take a look at this," he said, motioning to one of several rooms.

Meredith wasn't at all surprised to discover that the room Jack pointed out was the bedroom. Its focal point was the biggest most elaborate bed she'd ever seen. It was cloaked in yards of shimmering gold satin and topped with a veritable explosion of gold-trimmed and tasseled ecru linen, velvet and lace pillows of all shapes and sizes. The massive, ornately turned wrought iron bed would never fit in her bedroom at home but it was perfectly proportioned for this huge, stately room. Her eyelids fluttered shut briefly as she pictured herself with Jack, naked, sliding and rolling around its broad expanse as his talented tongue found its way to her inner lips, slipping inside to lave her needy clit. Stroking...lapping...bringing her to—

"Come on." Jack plopped onto the edge of the bed, bouncing as he patted the rich satin spread. "It's like a cloud."

Startled out of her imaginary revelry, Meredith blinked. Her seeming inability to keep the task of Jack's payback primary in her thoughts was really becoming a problem.

She watched him springing up and down like a kid and smiled. At that moment he looked for all the world like the carefree, spirited young man she'd married. Unable to resist the temptation to join in the fun, Meredith primly sat on the edge of the bed, loving the way it firmly supported her while allowing her to sink at the same time. She glided back a bit further. No doubt about it, the bed was an open invitation to bounce. And she did, tentatively at first and then laughing freely as her bottom connected over and over again with the golden satin, unmindful as her long hair flipped up and down with each bounce. She glanced at Jack and saw that his gaze was locked on her jiggling breasts. Good. She rebounded a few more times, making sure to give him a substantial eyeful of what he'd forfeited.

"Now that's the Meredith I remember." He grinned, tearing his gaze from her breasts with obvious difficulty. "Happy, fun-loving, ready to have a good time at the spur of the moment." In a move she hadn't anticipated, Jack scooped Meredith into his arms and held her close. She flattened her hands against his chest—his big, broad, warm, expansive chest—and pushed, with all the effect of trying to topple a brick wall with a toy hammer. He hugged her tighter. "I missed that joy of yours so much, Meredith. God, I missed *you* so much." He captured her mouth with his, seeking entry into her sweet depths with his probing tongue. She resisted at first. She really did. But the second their lips met and she felt his passion and hunger, she was lost. As they kissed they fell against the mattress and rolled until Jack was positioned atop Meredith.

"That was very sneaky, Jack," she managed through ragged breaths. And, oh God, it was hot and delicious and— Oh no, no, no. This wasn't good. This wasn't good at all.

He kissed the tip of her nose. "As they say…all's fair in love and war…"

"Yeah, well if you don't get off of me this instant I can guarantee you it's going to be war." She pushed against Jack to no avail. And he had the nerve to grin down at her as he pinned her in place while she struggled. Of course, the flood of hormones raging through her system, flushing her skin, prickling at each nerve ending and making the region between her legs all hot and balmy probably weren't helping to make her protests very convincing.

"Oh, sweetheart, I want you back," Jack said, securing her firmly against the gleaming satin. "Desperately. All the fame and fortune in the world can't fill up the void that's been with me ever since I was stupid enough to let you go." He kissed her again and she felt herself falling deeper under his spell. "I need you, Meredith." Another kiss. "I want you." Another kiss. "I love you. I cherish and adore you." Kiss, kiss, kiss. "I simply cannot live without you." This last kiss was more insistent, more forceful as he mashed his mouth against hers and pressed his erection against her thigh, evidencing the effect she had on him.

Willfully tuning out the drumming pulse beating in her ears, Meredith listened to Jack's declaration of undying love. The words she'd been yearning to hear for three long years had her breathless and her pussy drenching with need. She fought valiantly to keep logic at the forefront but the sweet pressure of Jack's cock nestled against her leg was too powerful a reminder of their sensational lovemaking sessions over the years. Oh, the undulating waves of wild, raw, shuddering, quaking, mind-bending joyous, rapturous pleasure. The way she'd suck his cock at the same time that he was eating her pussy.

She licked her lips, quickly losing the battle against those damned treacherous hormones of hers. And then Jack's hot wet tongue was in her mouth again, thrusting and urgent. He cupped her breast, pinching her nipple through the fabric. An impassioned moan erupted from somewhere deep inside her being. Her nipples had tightened almost to the point of pain and she craved his talented touch...ached for the feel of his mouth on her breasts, nipping, sucking, tugging. And then she felt his hand caress her pussy, gently at first and then clamping more firmly...rubbing, pressing... She trembled at the way he took command of her body, as if he still had the right. As if...

Oh what the hell. So what if she chose to indulge in a teeny bit of casual fucking before she got down to the business of payback? Would it really be so terrible? It was her birthday after all. Didn't she deserve to treat herself to a great big juicy birthday orgasm with the one man who knew precisely how to drive her wild?

Well, of course she did! Naturally she'd never be able to tell Karyn about it. Ever. Karyn would absolutely —

"Meredith...Meredith?"

"Huh?" It wasn't eloquent but it was the best Meredith could do, considering what she been pondering.

"You seemed to be a million miles away just then. What were you thinking about?"

"Love and war...and us." Meredith smiled, biting her bottom lip to keep from breaking out in a full-fledged grin. "Fucking each other senseless the way we used to when we were kids," she said huskily as she reached for his cock and squeezed it. "Getting all hot and sweaty and musky together." She stroked the length of his cock firmly. "Sending each other to the moon. Remember?" She licked her lips slowly, luxuriating in the way her blood simmered with need for him.

"Oh, baby..." With a primal groan Jack rolled onto his back, yanking her flush on top of him. He practically squeezed the life out of her as he wrapped his arms around Meredith and crushed her against the hard muscled planes of his physique. She soon found herself staring down into darkening eyes that gleamed with carnal intentions. She knew that heated look so well.

"I remember every luscious nook and cranny of your body," he said. "Each sensuous curve. Each hill and valley." His hand stroked up her back and sank into her hair. "And more than anything, baby, I remember eating your sweet little pussy. Licking that juicy all-woman taste of yours and holding you as you shattered with a wild, screaming orgasm." He assaulted her mouth with an expectant kiss and Meredith felt preliminary tingles rippling to her clit.

Oh yesss... She longed for just one last delectable, passionate romp. One final joining of their perfectly matched bodies. One last magical trip to paradise together. Meredith licked Jack's lips with a purr of excitement and he groaned low in his throat, the vibrating sound thrilling her. She'd keep it casual...not allow her heart to get involved this time...

Jack grabbed her ass cheeks, kneading and bearing her down determinedly against his cock. He knew just what to do, just how to position their bodies so that his cock pressed against her in just the right way, just the perfect position to—

"Oh *Jack!*" She squirmed against him shamelessly. God, Karyn was right. She *was* easy...but she *really* didn't want to clutter her mind with chastising thoughts at the moment. All she wanted was to give in to the spiraling current centered at her clitoris.

"Yeah. That's what I want to see, baby." He slid his hand between their bodies, resting it next to his cock and using his knuckles to rub firmly against that special spot between her legs. His hand labored at her pussy, moving in hypnotic little circles until she wanted to scream. "Come for me, Meredith. Let me feel you shatter in my arms again. It's been so long, sweetheart. So very long…"

Her body was obedient if nothing else. With both of them fully clothed, Meredith felt the familiar tightening between her thighs as the first waves of pleasure blissfully assaulted her clit. Stiffening as he braced her, Meredith clawed at Jack's arms and chest. And then, gazing deep into his eyes, her world exploded.

Before the last delicious wave of pleasure subsided, there was a knock at the door and Meredith gasped.

"Shit!" Jack spewed as she rolled off his body and they both sat up. "That must be room service," he growled, rising from the bed to answer the door.

"Room service? We just had dinner," Meredith said. She felt limp, sated and groggy. And she definitely didn't want to think about what she'd just allowed to happen.

She soon discovered the next step in Jack's ongoing quest to win her over, and she had to admit it was brilliant strategy on his part. Appealing to her deepest gustatory desires he'd pre-ordered two each of the fabulous desserts on the menu to be sent up to his suite. And now the luscious-looking desserts beckoned to her from silver trays and triple-tiered crystal plates. As an accompaniment, he'd selected a bottle of their finest aged cognac, which probably cost more than Meredith's new dress, undies and stiletto heels lumped together. Yup, Jack certainly hadn't forgotten that the best way to get to her heart was through her stomach.

"I suppose I'm glad this was delivered." Jack scratched his head and sucked in a deep breath. "Because I'd never be able to finish what I want to say to you with us on the bed together, happily fucking ourselves silly. You're just too damned alluring, Meredith." After brushing his lips across hers, he winked and led her to one of the plush brocade-covered armchairs in the living room, motioning for her to sit as he seated himself in the other chair. "First we'll have some dessert and cognac while we talk and then," his expression became devilish, "we'll finish what we started on that bed in there." He flashed his most winning smile, the one that had had never failed to make her melt, and she felt herself blush. "We've got all night, baby…and I want to spend it pleasuring you until you beg for mercy."

Oh yes…that sounded heavenly, simply divine— *No!* No, she couldn't allow herself to get sucked in again. A whimper escaped her lips as Meredith's emotions warred within. The intensity of his smile, his gaze and the lure of his sensual words had begun to thaw her heart while her brain labored to pack it in ice again.

There certainly wasn't any problem indulging in an evening of hot, casual sex, was there? No, of course not. As long as she kept her heart strictly out of it. Otherwise she'd be sunk—taken in by Jack's considerable charms for the umpteenth time. And she simply couldn't allow that to happen. She'd worked too long and hard to get over him, only to let Jack stomp back into her fragile heart again. Nope. Uh-uh.

"I know what a devoted chocoholic you are," Jack said, sinking Meredith's dessert spoon into the velvety chocolate mousse and then feeding it to her, smiling as she murmured her pleasure.

Chocolate. The magic word. Damn. He knew her far too well.

Chuckling as he watched her fully succumb to the overt delights of the dessert, Jack added, "Some things never change, sweetheart. That's why I thought a private little chocolate buffet would be a perfect complement to our celebration of your thirty-ninth birthday."

"Fortieth," she countered, rolling her tongue around inside her mouth and relishing the sumptuous taste of the sinfully rich mousse.

"You'll never be a day over thirty-nine to me, sweetheart." He scooped another bit of mousse onto her spoon and slipped it between her parted lips. "Remember years ago when you told me you couldn't picture yourself ever being forty? You thought it was ancient."

"Hell yes. I still do!" Meredith said.

"Nonsense." Jack laughed. "You're as fresh and youthful and beautiful today as you were when you were just a girl. Only better, because you're all woman now. Saucy, seasoned, scintillating and sexy as hell."

Oh, lordy. With the expert turn of a phrase, the mere butting together of a few simple words, the man was an absolute wizard at making a woman feel special, attractive, desirable. No doubt about it, Jack McKenna's magical tongue could mesmerize…in more ways than one. Oh, damn. Why oh why did she have to think about his tongue in *that* way now?

Jack dropped another bit of mousse onto Meredith's tongue, smiling as she savored it. And then she paused in her enjoyment a moment, struggling to remind herself why she was *really* here with Jack on her birthday. Little by little she could hear Karyn's adamant warnings hammering in the far recesses of her brain. And, damn it, Karyn was right. She'd be insane to let Jack back into her heart. She closed her eyes for a moment and heaved a sigh.

"So, Jack," she said, licking her lips and then clinking her glass of cognac against the one he presented, "exactly what is it that you wanted to talk to me about?" She sipped the liquid in her glass, enjoying the smoky silk sensation of the expensive liquor sliding down her throat.

Jack swallowed a forkful of raspberry-swirl cheesecake and then reached for Meredith's hand, clasping it in both of his. "I never stopped loving you, Meredith. While we were apart you were never far from my thoughts. You need to believe that because, as God is my witness, it's the truth." He rubbed his thumb along her wrist. "You have so much more to offer than any other woman I've ever known. Beauty, brains, class... There's an ever-present ache lodged deep in the pit of my soul when I'm without you, Meredith. You complete me."

Take me. Just take me now, she was temped to cry.

Doing her best to quiet her dancing libido as her tongue slid along the back of her teeth, capturing any lingering chocolate, Meredith studied him. What if Karyn was wrong? What if Jack had really changed this time after all? He certainly seemed different. Contrite. Sincere. *Anything is possible...right? It would be hugely unfair to exact retribution on a man who's repented and changed his ways...wouldn't it?*

"When we first met, you were a diamond in the rough," Jack continued. "My sweet, wonderful, adorable, naïve little goody-two-shoes." He chuckled and Meredith smiled, knowing he was certainly accurate about her youthful personality. "You were like a lump of clay ready for me to mold. A freshly erased blackboard ready for my chalk. A computer's blank hard drive waiting for my formatting."

Meredith wasn't smiling anymore.

"And through the years under my guidance and mentoring," Jack continued, "you've developed into a multifaceted polished gem, sweetheart. Since applying the self-help techniques I developed, you've matured...ripened into an incredible woman, level-headed, practical, intelligent and determined enough to build and operate a successful thrift shop for indigent fat women, entirely on your own."

The lenient, forgiving mental discourse that had been pleasantly floating inside Meredith's head abruptly took a nose dive and her face fell. Jack's *compliment* contained so many assumptions, inaccuracies and false statements that she didn't know which to attack first. But she had to keep her cool, couldn't risk blowing up at him now—not until her task was complete. She took a deep breath and mentally counted to ten before she spoke.

"What gave you the idea that our clientele is indigent, Jack?" She hoped her smile didn't appear too strained.

Jack shifted in his seat, lightly chuckling. "Well, after all, Meredith, it is *used* clothing. Who else would be interested?" She realized her expression must have darkened when he sat forward, bracing his elbows on his knees and clasping his hands together and then gifting her with one of his magnanimous *Dr. Jack* smiles. "Sweetheart, I'm not attacking your business. I know what a fondness you and Karyn have always had for digging through trash and going to yard sales and such. The natural progression would, of course, be to open your own little junk shop so you could sell all your special finds. And it was certainly brilliant of you to create a special niche by catering solely to fat women." He graced her with a smile that said he was perfectly pleased with his carefully chosen response.

Meredith cleared her throat. "Um...I think there's a bit of a misconception here, Jack." She felt her cheeks growing hot and calmly smoothed the hair away from her face, ensuring in the process that steam wasn't venting from her ears. That would be a dead giveaway. "First of all, Abundant Finds offers *upscale* vintage clothing, mostly designer wear, and we cater primarily to middle-class plus-sized women, not the poor or the homeless. There are a number of fine, charitable organizations and shops that serve that need. That is not our focus, however. Secondly, being plus-sized women ourselves, Karyn and I patently avoid the term *fat* in reference to us or our customers because of its negative connotation. We much prefer thinking of ourselves and our customers as BBW, which stands for Big Beautiful Women. Of course, I've told you this repeatedly over the years, but obviously you didn't pay attention."

"Now I've done it." Jack's head dropped. "I've gone and hurt your feelings when that's the last thing I wanted to do.

Sweetheart, you know I've never thought of you as fat. On the contrary, I love all of your plush, womanly curves. You truly are the quintessential big beautiful woman, Meredith."

Right. That's why each time you cheated on me it was with a twig. "Thank you." Meredith wasn't finished bristling yet. "Since my success is largely a result of your tutelage, I guess that makes me indebted to you." Meredith awaited his telltale response with bated breath.

First came that slow patronizing smile of his as Jack patted her hand. Caught up in all of his charm and magnetism earlier, she'd almost forgotten that particularly annoying look. "Indebted? Absolutely not, sweetheart. There's no thanks necessary, Meredith. Just seeing you happy in your *BBW venture,*" he hung invisible quote marks around the term with his fingers, "a direct product of my counsel, is thanks enough for me."

Meredith's eyes widened. *That arrogant bastard!* Oh, Karyn would love hearing this. She'd eviscerate him right where he sat. Jack had never shown a lick of interest in Abundant Finds, and he sure as hell had zip, zero, nada to do with the shop's success and popularity.

"I know how hard you've worked and how dedicated you and Karyn are to your shop. And if I asked you to give it all up and move with me back to Chicago, I doubt that you'd even consider it. Am I right?"

"You're right," she answered without hesitation.

"And I would never ask you to do that because I care too much about you. As I told you over dinner, Meredith, I was weak and immature when I succumbed to the lure of those other women. I've learned a lot about myself since we've been apart and I'm happy to say that I've finally matured. I'm a weak man when it comes to women and probably always will be. That's why I need someone like you, Meredith, a woman who's strong and understanding. Stronger than I am. A woman who will be my steadfast rock."

Meredith's brow furrowed and she shook her head. "I don't really understand what it is you're saying, Jack." She was used to Jack coming right to the point and now it seemed as if he were talking in circles.

His shoulders slumping, Jack breathed a weighty sigh. "Sure, I may be relatively famous but I'm not really all that different from most men. We're inherently weak, Meredith. Women possess the strength and resolve to be on their own, all alone, while men need...companionship." He gave her a doe-eyed look. "That's our aggregate defect, our greatest weakness. Our heads and hearts tell us one thing while our insatiable cocks are singing an entirely different tune."

"That's obvious." Meredith crossed one knee over the other and popped a tiny chocolate meringue cookie into her mouth.

Jack swirled the cognac in his glass and sipped from it. "When I got involved with Becky while on that cross-country speaking tour it was because I was so lonely. She just happened to be there when I needed a woman most." He shrugged. "I mistook my need to have a warm body next to mine for more than it was. There was never any real emotional connection there. I never should have married her, or Lisa for that matter. I should have realized that all I really needed to get me through those times was simply a brief affair. A mindless, meaningless interlude, after which I would come home to you — the woman I love — and we could have gone on with our lives together just the way we'd always planned."

What?! The little cookie caught in Meredith's throat and she hacked a choking cough. *No...Jack couldn't possibly be saying what I think he is...could he?*

"Are you all right, sweetheart?" Jack said, rising from his chair.

Meredith waved him back to his seat and nodded. "Fine. Cookie just went down the wrong way." She coughed again and then took a fortifying sip of cognac.

Jack polished off the rest of the cognac in his glass and gazed at Meredith expectantly. "So what do you think? It's a perfect solution, honey."

"Uh-huh," Meredith interjected with a slow nod because Jack was clearly waiting for some kind of response. "I think I understand. Do tell me more, Jack, darling." Folding her arms across her chest and forcing a smile, she gave him her undivided attention.

He sat forward in his seat with an eager smile. "This way, whenever I have to be away for an extended period you'll understand that no matter what brief, meaningless interlude might occur, I'll always come back to you, my sweet, beloved wife. You see, Meredith? I would never, *ever* be foolish enough to leave you again." Expelling a deep breath, Jack shot his cuffs, rolled his shoulders and moved his head to the left and right until his neck cracked. It was an automatic tension-relieving sequence of his that she'd often witnessed in the past.

Meredith sat back against the chair and pressed her lips together as she blindly surveyed the room. No, no, no, no, no. Uh-uh. Even Jack couldn't be that crass, that self-centered, selfish and egotistical. That much of a conniving, opportunistic bastard, that much of a rat-faced sonuvabitch... No, her thoughts had been so heavily focused on romping around naked in that gigantic bed with her well-hung ex-husband that she probably hadn't paid close enough attention to what he was saying, that's all. She plucked an ornate chocolate-robed petit fours from a small triple-tiered plate and popped it into her mouth, chewing while she slanted Jack a thoughtful look. This time she'd *really* pay attention. "So, Jack, if I understand you correctly, you're proposing that you and I get married again and—"

"Yes." Bright-eyed, Jack nodded eagerly. "As soon as we possibly can, darling, so I can make passionate love to you all night, every night for the rest of our lives. Oh, Meredith, sweetheart, I can't wait to finally make you my wife again."

"For the third time," Meredith noted.

"The *last* time, honey. That's what counts. This time we make it permanent."

"Okay," Meredith held her index finger aloft, "just give me a minute to sort this out before you interrupt again." She smiled sweetly and Jack nodded. "I'd be making a home for the two of us here in Portland and continue to operate the shop and play the happy homemaker — cook, clean, darn your socks and so on — while you jet around the globe, making VIP appearances and tending to your TV show, etcetera." She waved her hand. "And then you'll come back home again where we'll be happily engaged in matrimonial bliss. Hmm? Do I have it right so far?" With a mouthful of mixed berry tart, Jack smiled and nodded as if the scenario Meredith described had been as enticing as a crème-filled chocolate cupcake.

Sonuvabitch.

"Good." Meredith swallowed a bite of flourless triple chocolate fudge cake and used her spoon to gesture toward Jack. "And because you're weak and flawed and simply can't *bear* to be without a warm body at your side while you're away," Meredith sipped from her cognac and swallowed, "you would engage in a series of meaningless, trivial trysts." She gave a dismissive flick of her wrist. "And then, because you love me with every fiber of your being," Meredith paused to fix Jack with a wide smile and fluttering eyelashes, "you'd fly back to my arms as soon as you could so that we could screw like happy, horny little bunny rabbits — until your next trip."

Meredith dropped a tiny nut-studded, pastel-frosted cookie into her mouth and with a satisfied little hum washed it down with the remaining cognac in her glass, which Jack quickly refilled. Brushing a few crumbs from her dress, she sat forward, reaching for Jack's hand and enveloping it in her fingers as she met his gaze and smiled warmly. "So, Jack, dear, is that about it in a nutshell?"

"Yes. Exactly." Jack kissed Meredith's fingers back and front and then released them. He visibly relaxed as his spine and shoulders lost their rigidity and he sagged against the back of his chair with a relieved smile. "I have to admit that I was a little worried there for a while but I knew you'd eventually see the perfect logic behind this solution, Meredith. If only I'd thought of it years ago, I could have saved us both a lot of anguish."

Yup, no doubt about it…Jack McKenna *was* a first-class schmuck.

"Well…okay then." Meredith plastered a smile across her features. The realization that the payback plan she'd concocted for the evening couldn't possibly come close to gifting her dear ex-husband with what he *truly* deserved saddened her. Nevertheless, she'd just have to make do. She breathed a sigh.

"I just knew you'd understand, Meredith. You're so smart and sensible…and loving. So unlike most other women."

"Like, oh say, the itty-bitty size-two Becky, for instance," Meredith offered brightly.

"Oh please." Jack huffed and made a raspberry sound. "There's no comparison. Becky is self-centered, demanding and completely lacking in understanding when it came to my needs. And besides, she's not the svelte little thing she was when I married her. She's really let herself go and put on quite a bit of weight."

"Really?" Meredith asked, genuinely surprised—and feeling not at all sympathetic. "I didn't realize."

"Yeah." Jack nodded. "She continually rejected my attempts at mentoring and because of it she's miserable because she's up to a size four now."

"Disgusting." Meredith shook her head and tsked as she smoothed her hand across the lap of her size eighteen dress. "The woman's a veritable blimp."

Jack did a double take and then laughed. "Still got that great sense of humor, I see."

"Yes…I'm just a barrel of laughs." She tittered a half-hearted laugh. "You know, Jack, after you left me for the nineteen-year-old size-two I ate myself sick and gained nearly fifty pounds." Meredith's eyes narrowed at the painful memory.

"Don't worry." With an abject look of pity in his eyes, Jack patted her hand. "You'll lose it again, Meredith."

"I already have." Her tone couldn't have been more acerbic.

"Oh." Tugging at the knot in his tie, Jack cleared his throat. He inhaled a deep breath and was silent for a moment as he appeared to gather his thoughts. "You're a beautiful woman, Meredith, with a sumptuous, zaftig body that I adore but," he paused to scratch his head, "big women just aren't in vogue now. Please don't get the wrong idea. It's not that *I* care how big you are, because I don't, sweetheart. Believe me, my darling, you'd simply be so much happier being — "

"A size two?" Meredith asked through a smirk.

"Now don't be silly, Meredith." He laughed. "You'd be a stunning size four." Meredith blinked and her mouth puckered into a little O shape. "Or even a six with that broad build of yours. Personally, I've always found plump with plenty to grab onto in the bedroom a real turn-on. But *out* of the bedroom…well, you know how it is. A man wants the woman who's draped on his arm to be a svelte little thing." He chuckled. "Another inherent male flaw I guess."

Meredith was proud of herself for resisting the palpable temptation to shove the dessert spoon up Jack's left nostril.

"Once we're back together, Meredith," Jack proceeded to bury himself, "you can visit any of those fancy spas for a month at a time as often as you like so you can get fit. With that and my self-help techniques you'll lose a ton of weight and be camera ready in no time." He grinned.

Furrowing her eyebrows, Meredith slanted Jack a puzzled look. "Camera ready?"

"Sure. Once my talk show debuts the paparazzi will be hot on my tail. Our photos will be splashed across the media and I'm sure you'll want to look your svelte best." He smiled and winked.

"I'm sure *you'll* want me to look my svelte best," Meredith countered, and Jack nodded.

"Yes, darling, exactly," he said confidently, as if he'd made everything just peachy keen by his remarks. "And the great thing is that, unlike when we were starting out, now I've got all the money we need to make that a reality for you. Spas, health clubs, plastic surgery, liposuction, stomach stapling, special diets…you name it and I'll gladly foot the bill."

"Mmmm." Meredith nodded thoughtfully. "How exceedingly generous and considerate of you, Jack, dear. I'm truly a fortunate woman."

"*My* woman." A grinning Jack winked.

"Yes. Uh-huh. Well, getting back to your ex-child-bride, I take it she wasn't too keen about your meaningless extramarital affairs."

"That's an understatement." Rolling his eyes and shaking his head, Jack popped a cookie into his mouth and continued to talk while chewing. "Becky raised holy hell about it even after I explained to her that the trysts were completely insignificant—just something to help me over the hump until she and I could be together again. The woman was totally lacking in empathy."

Meredith's hand flew to her chest and she gasped in mock indignation. "How could she be so selfish? So insensitive? You poor baby." She shook her head sympathetically. At the same time she wondered how in God's name it had taken her more than twenty years to realize that Jack was a self-serving giant economy-sized asshole. "And that's why you divorced?"

Hiking a shoulder in a shrug, Jack nodded. "That and the fact that Becky started sleeping with one of the other speakers on the circuit. She'd actually argued that if it was okay for me to sleep around, then it was okay for her to do the same thing.

Have you ever heard anything so self-indulgent and immature?"

"Never." Valiantly resisting the dual urge to applaud with glee while she guffawed in Jack's face, Meredith's brows knitted and she tsked. "Oh, Jack, that *is* terrible." She shifted positions and crossed her leg over the other knee. Casually weaving her finger through a tendril of her hair and coiling it, she added, "And, of course, you feel safe in the assumption that I'd never react to your affairs with a fling of my own."

"You?" Looking at Meredith as if she'd grown two heads, Jack laughed. "Of course not, Meredith. You're not the type. You're a rock. You're too—"

"Yes, yes, I know," she interrupted. "Too sensible and understanding." And Jack nodded. Stroking her chin with her thumb and forefinger, Meredith gazed at him with a narrow-eyed smile, wondering how he managed to squeeze that big fat swelled head of his through doorways. "You'd feel secure if we remarried because you'd know I would always be there for you—the loving, devoted, monogamous wife. Right?"

"Exactly." Pointing and winking at Meredith, Jack chuckled a bit. "See what I mean? We're on the same wavelength. We've always had that special connection going for us. We're meant for each other, honey." He sipped from his cognac and breathed a contented sigh. "Of course there'd be no reason for you to go bed hopping. After all, you'd have what you always wanted—*me*," with a bright grin he slapped his hands against his chest, "as your adoring, devoted husband." Now he gazed at Meredith with a warm smile. "And with my substantial income you'd have all the security, luxuries and anything else money can buy. You'd be able to stay in lush suites like this one," he motioned with his hand like a TV game show model as he peered around the hedonistic hotel suite, "anytime you traveled. And when I'm away and you can't join me you'd have your nice little secondhand shop to keep you happy and occupied."

"How...magnanimous of you, Jack," Meredith said, almost choking on the words and gleefully picturing him sticking his swelled head up his ass. The surprisingly vivid image made her smile, almost giggle. She uncrossed her legs and sat up straight. "You make it all sound so...romantic. So idyllic. So happily-ever-afterish."

Jack was at her side in an instant, capturing Meredith's hand in his, sprinkling kisses along her palm and wrist as he knelt on one knee. Meredith willed herself not to cuff his head with the hand he was kissing. "Oh, darling," he said, his eyes glistening, "then the answer's yes? You'll marry me again?"

"Well, they say that three's a charm." Smoothing her fingers through his dark hair and proud of herself for not yanking it from its roots, Meredith looked down at Jack's hopeful grin and smiled. "What woman in her right mind could possibly resist such a fairytale-like proposal?"

"You've just made me the happiest man in the world." Jack dug into his pocket and retrieved a honking big emerald-cut diamond ring, which he slipped on her finger. Her gasp of surprise was spontaneous and he smiled. "That's the first of many diamonds to come, Meredith. But none will shine as bright as your incomparable beauty." He rose to his feet then drew Meredith into his arms. "Just imagine how wonderful it will be, darling. The two of us together. Forever."

"Oh believe me," Meredith said, splaying her fingers and watching the dazzling stone sparkle as she moved her hand, "I can imagine."

Jack's voice became husky at her ear. "And think of the two of us engaging in all that hot, steamy sex. You know we've always been great together, babe." He growled and nibbled Meredith's ear. "Speaking of hot and steamy," he gestured with his head toward the bedroom, "what say we begin our engagement with a round of passionate lovemaking?" He bent to cover Meredith's mouth with his but she ducked and backed away, leaving him with a look of surprise.

"Oh you naughty, impetuous boy," she teased through laughter, wagging a chastising finger in his direction.

Jack groaned. "Aw, not fair, Meredith," he whined through a deep throaty chuckle. "I've been itching to rip off that dress and get my hands on that soft, plump, curvaceous body of yours since I first laid eyes on you tonight. I want to feast on those exquisite rosy-pink nipples of yours and then tease that slick little clit with my tongue. I want to hold you in my arms as you quake and quiver in orgasmic bliss... Oh, baby, don't punish me by making me wait any longer."

Closing her eyes, Meredith summoned all of her willpower not to dwell on the erotic delights Jack had proposed. With two big steps he'd closed the distance between them and was about to draw her into his arms when she forcibly flattened her hands against his chest and pushed.

"Oh, don't worry, Jack," she cooed in a seductive tone as she drew patterns across his chest with her finger. "Now that we've had our little heart-to-heart talk I'm going to make sure this will be a night that you and your dick," she emphasized the word by cupping his three-piece combo through his trousers, "will never, ever forget."

Chapter Five

ℬ

Growling, Jack pulled Meredith roughly against him, attempting once again to mash his mouth against hers.

"Honestly, Jack," she broke away from him again, eyeing him with a slow, wicked smile. "You really *must* learn to be patient. I guarantee that what I have in mind will drive you insane with desire—and let you know exactly how much you mean to me. But we do this at my pace, my rules and on my terms or we don't do it at all. After all, it is *my* birthday, Jack." She winked. "Agreed?"

Flinging his arms out to the sides Jack cocked his head and gave a broad, hungry grin. "I'm all yours, honey. Do with me what you will."

"Hmmm." She tapped her finger against her chin. "Even if what I have in mind might be a little bit...*kinky?*" She punctuated her question by dropping her head back and moaning as she cupped her full breasts and then dragged her hands down slowly across them, down her midsection, over her hips, finally bringing her fingers to rest at the vee between her thighs. While she did her best to look smoldering Meredith felt almost cool and mechanical.

"Oh mama!" Jack ground out, swallowing hard as his eyes all but popped out of their sockets.

Meredith thought of the horny cartoon wolf with its hanging tongue and bugging eyes and almost laughed. "All we need is an *ah-oooogah* horn and we'd be set."

Jack slanted her a puzzled look. "What?"

"Nothing." She engaged in a throaty chuckle as she turned her back to Jack, moving her hands from her crotch to her thighs and then to her ass where she cupped her cheeks and squeezed. "Bet you'd like some of this tonight, wouldn't you?" She peered at him over her shoulder.

"You know it, baby." He grasped his crotch. "My cock must have swelled another two inches just watching my sexy fiancée fondle herself. Looks like my girl has learned some snazzy new techniques since we've been separated."

"Mmm-hmm," she purred, stepping closer to run a crimson fingernail along his jaw. "I've been fucking my twenty-five-year-old next-door neighbor."

Jack's face fell.

"In fact, we had the most delicious impromptu sex on my kitchen table just this morning."

Obviously stunned, Jack gazed at Meredith for a long moment before his lip quirked and he began to laugh. "Aw, you almost got me there, Meredith." He pointed at her and winked. "Love that quirky sense of humor. Imagine *you* ever doing anything like *that*." He laughed harder.

"Yeah...imagine." Meredith joined him in laughter. "Actually," she sighed, "I've been sitting all by myself reading sex manuals as I pined for you, Jack. All in the hopes that you'd come back to me one day and I could learn to pleasure you so much you'd never want to leave me again." She batted her eyelashes demurely and grinned. It was an Oscar-worthy performance and she was damned proud of herself.

Nodding, Jack beamed a condescending smile. "My sweet, darling Meredith. Always putting me first." He craned his neck to kiss her but Meredith dodged him.

"First rule." She backed up a few steps. "No touching or kissing unless I give you permission. Understood?" She began to unzip her dress, pausing until she heard Jack's answer.

"Understood." Jack bobbed his head enthusiastically. "It'll be damned hard but...yeah, I promise." He crossed his heart and held his hand aloft in a vow.

"Good." Fully unzipping her dress, she shimmied so it glided down her hips and pooled at her feet. Hands on hips, she stood in front of Jack in a saucy black demi-bra, a lacy scrap of matching panties and a black satin garter belt. Sheer stockings, heels and marcasite earrings completed her bewitching ensemble. Meredith did a slow pirouette, splaying her hands across her ass as she presented it to her former husband. "So, Jack, what do you think?"

"Oh God. You're fuckin' killing me, Meredith," he rasped.

"I wish," she mumbled, rolling her eyes skyward. Noting Jack's injured expression, she laughed. "Just kidding, darling. You know my quirky sense of humor." She winked and Jack's features relaxed. Blowing him a kiss, she crooked her finger, beckoning him to follow her to the bedroom. He was at her heels like an obedient pup. "I want you to strip naked, Jack. All except for that *adorable* custom tie you're wearing." She flipped the charcoal gray tie out of Jack's vest and bit the inside of her cheek to keep from laughing as she eyed the length of silk, liberally sprinkled with tiny images of Jack's smiling face and the title of his upcoming talk show, *On the Right Track with Dr. Jack.*

Working at breakneck speed, Jack tugged, fumbled and yanked until he was naked except for his silly vanity tie. After one longing look at his marvelous equipment, Meredith sighed and did her best to ignore the wetness pooling in her panties. She drilled home the reminder that Jack was a jerk and that she was on a mission. Pity. The man had such a sublime body. A body designed to satisfy a woman...to satisfy *her*. What a shame that his warped and twisted brain had to go and spoil it all.

"Get on the bed, Jack. Just plant yourself right in the center of the satin spread so I can feast my eyes on your gorgeous cock." Jack wasted no time, immediately hopping onto the bed. His jolly cock bobbed up and down as he settled against the mattress. Meredith almost laughed at the shit-eating grin on his face.

74

"You know, Jack, we never experimented with bondage when we were together." She saw his eyes widen in expectation.

"I'd *love* to tie you up, Meredith." He licked his lips.

"Ummm...no." She shook her head. "That's not what I had in mind. Actually, I thought it would be really hot to tie *you* up to the bedposts so we could play dominatrix and slave." She bent over the bed and spiraled her finger up Jack's erect cock, circling the swollen tip and then licking her finger. "Are you game for something a little different?"

"Hell, yes!" he said without hesitation. "Sex with us was always terrific but I never dreamed you'd do something this inventive."

"Good." Meredith gave a throaty chuckle as she walked around the bed. "Then from this moment on you will address me as Mistress. Any objections?"

Jack frowned. "No...I guess not."

"No *what*?"

"Huh? Oh. No, *Mistress*," Jack corrected. He looked like a big dopey dog slobbering in expectation of a beefy bone. Oh boy, she was going to *love* this.

"Turn over on your stomach so I can see your ass," she instructed.

Groaning as he adjusted his rigid penis, Jack complied, giving a surprised little yelp when he felt the stinging slap from Meredith's hand across one ass cheek.

"Jack, you were a *very* bad boy leaving me for that little blonde bimbo after all I'd done for you. Weren't you?"

"Hey," Jack countered, "let's not get carried away with this, okay? If there's any spanking to be done, I'm the one who's going to—"

"Address me properly when I speak to you," Meredith barked, cutting him off. "I asked you a question, now answer it!"

"Yes, Mistress," Jack said half-heartedly. "A very bad boy."

"I think maybe you should get a spanking."

Jack was silent for a moment. "If that'll make you feel better...Mistress."

Meredith had never been involved in BDSM, but she figured she knew enough from books and movies to wing it and turn in a believable performance. Rather than give Jack a series of gentle, playful slaps, she whacked his ass good, letting him really have it as she repeated that he was a bad boy. She was amazed at how great it made her feel...*smack!* ...how liberated...*smack!*...how vindicated...*smack!*...how —

"Ow! Jesus Christ, Meredith, that really hurts!"

"It's *Mistress*," she countered sternly, issuing another slap before taking a deep breath to control herself. This dominatrix act was becoming *way* too enjoyable.

"Uh, Mistress," Jack said, turning on his side to see her better. "Don't you think you're being a little too rough? You're not supposed to actually inflict pain, they're just supposed to be light, playful slaps." He rubbed his bright red ass and winced. "I think you left welts!"

"Hmmm...maybe you're right." Meredith tapped her finger against her jaw. "Perhaps I should have paid more attention to the spanking chapter in my sex manual." She gave an elegant shrug, walked to the other side of the bed and propped her high-heeled foot on the bedspread, giving Jack a bird's-eye view of her crotch. "Well, all right, Jack. I'll tone it down for you, although I must say that I'm disappointed in your lack of stamina and playfulness. I was *so* hoping this evening wouldn't be boring." She gave an affected yawn.

"I'm all for sex games, Mer — I mean, Mistress. But maybe we can try something a bit less," he paused to rub his stinging ass again, "sadistic."

"Okay," Meredith said, glancing around the bedroom. Her gaze alighted on the ornate gold-leafed desk against one wall. "Here's what we'll do instead of administering the rest of the spanking that you deserve." With that she walked over to the desk and picked up one of the three expensive golden pens emblazoned with the hotel's logo. The first was a ballpoint pen. She scribbled on a sheet of hotel stationery, wet her fingertip and brushed it across the ink. As it smeared she hiked her lip into a sneer. Discarding the pen, she selected another one, which was a gel-tip. After scribbling she wet her finger again and wiped. The indelible ink scribble remained intact and Meredith grinned. "Turn back on your stomach, Jack."

"What are you—" Jack halted in mid-sentence when he saw Meredith's warning glare and heaved a sigh. "Yes, Mistress." He rolled back on his stomach.

Meredith straddled his legs and wrote something in big letters across his crimson-tinged buttocks, straining not to giggle as she appraised her finished work. "There. That's better," she said."

"What does it say, Mistress?"

"*Dr. Jack is a very, very bad boy,*" Meredith read from her artistry. Jack groaned. "Oh don't worry, it will come right off in the shower," she lied. The evening had become more fun and enjoyable than she had anticipated. This was the first time she'd ever been the one in control in her relationship with Jack. The heady sensation of power almost made her giddy. She couldn't wait to see Karyn so she could tell her all about how she'd achieved *closure* with her ex-husband.

"You have my permission to turn on your back now, Jack." He did as she asked. "Would you like to see me take off my stockings and garter belt?"

Jack nodded eagerly. "Oh, *yes*, Mistress."

Meredith made a slow, seductive show of placing one high-heeled foot on the bed right in front of Jack's face, smoothing her leg from her ankle to thigh. Her fingers inched toward the front garter and she unhooked it. And then she stopped.

"Oh dear. I just realized that I have my panties on over my garter belt. Would you like to see me remove my panties so you can see my furry little pussy?" Her voice was a husky whisper.

"Oh Jesus." Jack gulped hard. "Yes. Yes, Mistress. I want to see that very much. I don't think I can hold out much longer."

Cupping his scrotum with her cool hands, Meredith smiled. She resisted the terribly naughty urge to flick him there with her fingernail. "You'll have to be a good, obedient boy and wait until your Mistress tells you that it's time to ejaculate." A strangled groan traveled up through Jack's chest and Meredith struggled to keep from laughing. She hooked the garter back on to her stocking and slipped her hands inside the elastic at the top of her panties, easing them down slightly. And then she stopped. "No...on second thought I think I might want to start with something else." She slowly dragged her hands back out again.

"Your bra, Mistress?"

"No, not that." She removed her foot from the bed. "I'll be right back." She strolled into the living room and returned with her long beaded envelope purse. Unclasping the latch, she peeked inside and withdrew a pair of red panties. "These are the cute little crotchless panties you gave me for Christmas three years ago." She spread the panties over her outstretched fingers to display the frilly slit. "Just before you left me for Becky. Remember?" Jack gave a slow, cautious nod. Meredith twirled them on her finger before dropping them onto Jack's abdomen. "Put them on," she instructed.

"What?!" Jack bolted upright to a sitting position. "You want me to wear your panties?" he said incredulously. Meredith nodded. "Aw come on, Meredith. I'm not into wearing women's clothes. If this is something you got out of that sex manual of yours it's way off."

"How many times must I remind you that it's *Mistress*?" Meredith tsked.

This time Jack scowled. "You know, Meredith, you're getting far too carried away with all this dominatrix crap. I'm getting real tired of this game. I think it's time for you to stop your teasing and playing control freak and just get into bed so we can fuck."

"I can see what you're saying and I appreciate that," Meredith offered, spouting directly from her recent course in assertiveness training. "However, and I say this with all due respect, Jack, if you want to satisfy little *Jackie*," she gave in to the unappeasable urge to gently flick his dick, "then you'll continue to play my game. In return I can guarantee you that what I do to you tonight will be forever etched in your memory." She folded her arms across her chest and tapped the toe of her shoe against the marble floor. "Well?"

With incalculable grousing, grumbling and groaning Jack put on the stretchy panties and it was all Meredith could do not to laugh hysterically at the ridiculous sight. Here was the staid, conservative, internationally renowned Dr. Jack, dressed in nothing but his dopey tie and her crotchless panties — with his mighty cock prettily framed and poking out of the frilly slit. "That's a good boy." She stroked his cock and kissed the tip. "You've made Mistress very happy."

A stream of air escaped Jack's mouth as Meredith's lips touched the head of his cock, causing it to twitch in response. "Honestly, Mistress. I'm about ready to explode. At least let me touch you...*please*." He reached out his hand tentatively and Meredith slapped it.

"Soon, Jack," she said, backing away from the bed. "Very soon." She picked up her purse again and drew out two pairs of sheer stockings, which she placed at the foot of the bed. "As you can see, I came fully prepared for our fun-filled little game tonight." Jack just gave her a puzzled look as she held one of the stockings in front of her, stretching it. "Yes, this will work just fine," she added with a satisfied smile.

With a gleam in her eye, Meredith looked at her bewildered former husband. "Okay, Jack. I want you spread eagle across the bed so I can tie you up and we can have some real fun."

"Couldn't we reverse roles for awhile?" Jack's voice was soft and seductive. "I'd love to have you spread out before me, nice and secure...and then lick you into an orgasmic frenzy." His tongue slid across his lips.

First came an involuntary whimper...followed by a trickle down her thighs. Meredith couldn't help it—he'd caught her off guard with the lusty scenario. The very idea of being bound and...*tortured* as she squirmed beneath Jack's skilled tongue had her tingling with desire. Clamping her thighs together, she took a few deep breaths to regain her composure. And then, chin elevated, she looked down her nose at Jack, determined not to give him the satisfaction of seeing her lose control.

"So," her voice was shaky and she paused to clear her throat, "shall Mistress take that as a refusal to cooperate?"

Jack rolled his eyes and tsked. "If I let you tie me up am I finally going to be able to fuck you...Mistress? I'm getting awfully anxious to shove my cock into that pretty little pussy of yours." He hungrily eyed her crotch.

"Oh, don't worry, Jack," Meredith assured. "You'll get fucked all right." She beamed a smile. "Real good."

His enthusiasm returning, Jack followed Meredith's direction. She secured the stockings snuggly around his wrists and his ankles, tying the ends securely to the wrought iron bedposts. Then she stood back to admire her handiwork. Nodding, she smiled. "Oh yes. Just perfect," she purred. "You know," she said thoughtfully as she got on the bed and kneeled between his spread legs, "I think I'm getting hungry again." Giving Jack a slow once-over, she licked her lips and moaned as she dipped her head and opened her mouth. Jack's cock sprang to attention so fast she half expected to hear it go *boing*!

"It's about time, Mistress," he said huskily, his eyes heavy-lidded. "You can eat me anytime, honey. This is all for you, baby." He focused on his eager cock, making it jerk.

Meredith stopped just short of wrapping her lips around Jack's thick cock. "Hmm...I think it would be so much more fun if parts of you were covered in chocolate first. Don't you, Jack?" Meredith hopped off the bed and slid her fingers up from one of his ankles, across his groin, up his chest and ending at his chin.

"Whatever floats your boat, Mer—Mistress."

"Be right back," Meredith said, scooting back into the main room of the suite. "Don't go anywhere," she called, giggling to herself. In a few moments she returned with the rolling dessert cart piled with the remaining desserts and the bottle of cognac.

"Now it's time to frost the cake," she said, doing her best to appear as if she were eyeing Jack hungrily. Actually, it wasn't difficult to pretend. Even wearing her crotchless panties and his silly tie, Jack McKenna was still one delicious specimen of manhood. "And then it will be time to lick the platter clean," she finished. Closing her eyes and moaning, Meredith licked her lips with an exaggerated flourish.

She valiantly resisted the urge to jump Jack's bones. At forty-three he was still sexy as hell and she knew so well the orgasmic ecstasy they'd share if she rode him to completion. But he'd irretrievably buried himself earlier with his crass suggestions of an open relationship—open, at least, on his part.

"Christ!" Jack cried in a strangled voice. "I'm so fucking hot I'm ready to combust." His cock twitched, giving credence to his statement. "Once I finally get my hands on you, Meredith, I'm going to fuck your brains out." She watched him eye her full curves with longing, finally resting his gaze on her breasts. "Please...take off your bra for me...Mistress," he said roughly.

"Only because you asked so nicely, my sweet," Meredith cooed as she unclasped her bra and tossed it on the corner of the bed. It was to her advantage to keep his cock happy until she was finished. Jack's eyes popped as her breasts sprang free and jiggled.

"Nobody has breasts like yours, Meredith." Her nipples involuntarily crinkled and darkened in response. "Oh, the dreams I've had about those big beautiful tits of yours, baby. Come on, Mistress," he coaxed, "rub them in my face." He growled as she leaned over him, dangling an enticing nipple over his mouth, and then his face dropped as Meredith got up from the bed and headed for the dessert cart.

God, how she longed to have him take her nipples into his mouth, teasing them with his tongue and teeth until she writhed, gasping in pleasure...but she'd get too carried away and her payback mission would be as good as dead.

"All in good time, Jack," Meredith said hoarsely. "First we need to get you all frosted so I can gobble you up." She winked at him as she brought over a goblet of chocolate mousse and plate of the raspberry cheesecake. Using her fingers, she plopped dollops of the desserts on Jack's chest, circling his nipples with the sweets while making sure to leave his vanity tie neat, clean and in place.

Methodically, she returned to the cart for the remaining confections, artfully arranging them all over Jack's anatomy. Except for his cock. That remained unadorned. Every now and then she'd seductively lick a smidgen of dessert off Jack or slide her finger up and down his rigid shaft, just to keep him in a heightened state of arousal.

"You look like a sexy abstract painting, Jack," Meredith observed positioning a chocolate meringue cookie atop each of his flat nipples. "But," pausing, she frowned and tapped her chin. "Something's missing."

"And I know exactly what it is," Jack offered with a lusty growl. "Your mouth on my cock." He grinned broadly.

"Hmmm." Meredith shook her head. "No, not that." She returned to the rolling cart and grabbed the bottle of cognac. Opening it, she poured a stream of it over Jack's red-lace-framed pecker.

"Hey!" he shouted, struggling against his bindings. "What the fuck are you doing, Meredith? It's getting all over the bedspread. Oh, shit! *Shit*! It burns!"

"The discomfort is only temporary." She smiled. "Aged cognac should make an excellent antiseptic agent. After all, you wouldn't expect me to slide onto your busy little cock after it's been God knows where, now would you, Jack?" She couldn't hold her laughter back any longer.

"Meredith, what's the matter with you? This is *not* funny!" Jack bellowed. "I'm telling you it really stings!"

"Hmm, the more bimbo germs the more stinging I guess." She returned to the cart, carrying her untouched mixed-berry tart. She poured a little bit of cognac on it and stirred with her finger. And then she began to paint on the bedspread between Jack's spread legs.

"Holy shit, Meredith!" Jack cried, straining to see what she was doing. "Are you fucking insane? You can't do something like that here in a five-star hotel. What if they charge me for ruining the bedspread?"

"You can afford it. You're rich now, remember?"

"What'll the staff think when they see this mess?" he whined.

"They'll think that Dr. Jack's been a bad boy," Meredith answered with a nonchalant shrug. "At least that's what it says here on the bedspread, just like it does across your tight little ass."

"For chrissakes, Meredith—"

"Mistress," she patiently corrected.

"Enough with the Mistress crap, Meredith!" he boomed in anger. "When you said kinky, I figured you meant something hot and sexy, not something fucking nuts!" He struggled harder against the nylon stocking bindings but they only grew tighter. "And cut this shit off of me. We're done playing your stupid little games."

"Oh," Meredith said innocently. "You mean you don't want me to eat you anymore, Jack?" She knelt on the bed next to him, leaning over until the tips of her breasts brushed against some of the chocolate mousse on his belly. Then she sat up and scooped the chocolate from her breasts, licking her finger and moaning with pleasure. "Don't you want me to suck the cognac off your cock now that it's been purged of all those nasty bimbo microorganisms?" She ran her fingertips across his semi-erect shaft. Like a good boy it immediately sprang back to attention.

"Yes," Jack said more softly, swallowing as he tried to compose himself. "That's what I've wanted all along, Meredith. Come on, baby, it's time we got down to business. It's time you stopped all this silliness and give me a blowjob. I fucking deserve it after all you've put me through tonight."

"After all I've put *you* through, huh?" She chuckled. "Honestly, Jack, your sense of humor is even quirkier than mine. But yes, I suppose it's time we got down to business as you suggested." Meredith leaned over Jack's cock, inching her mouth closer and closer, her tongue peeking out as it slicked across her lips. Then, peering at the wristwatch on Jack's arm she shook her head and tsked. "Oh gee, Jack. I'm sorry but according to your watch you're mistaken." She fixed her gaze on his twisted expression and shrugged. "It's *not* time after all. In fact, it's three years too late." She picked up her purse and pulled out a folded plastic bag, setting it on the bed.

"Meredith…Meredith, what is this? What kind of game are you playing?"

"The lowdown dirty kind, darling." Humming the tune from Aretha Franklin's song "Respect," Meredith skipped into the suite's living room, returning in a moment with her dress and stepping into it. She boldly sang out, substituting R-E-V-E-N-G-E for R-E-S-P-E-C-T as she zipped up the back. Then she glanced at Jack and smiled. "The name of the game is *Payback*, lover boy. Otherwise known as revenge, retribution, justice, etcetera. And I managed to invent it all by my little ol' self— without your tutelage or self-help techniques. Aren't you proud of me, dear?"

"Meredith!" Jack struggled harder against his bindings as his face turned a curious shade of tangerine. "Untie me this instant."

She paused to look at Jack, shook her head and tsked. "I feel it's only fair to tell you, love, that the harder you struggle the tighter those bindings will get." Meredith continued humming and singing as she removed the ostentatious diamond engagement ring Jack had given her and slipped it over his pinky toe. "You know...I don't think I'll be needing this after all, Jack." She patted his foot, gifting him with the same condescending smile he'd used on her earlier.

As she collected Jack's clothes, she removed his wallet and keys from his pocket and placed them on the nightstand. Then she bunched everything else together and crammed it into the large plastic bag. "There. Nice and tidy." She patted the bag with a bright smile as she surveyed the room.

"What the— No! Meredith, you can't do this." Jack thrashed back and forth. "You can't leave me helpless like this. You wouldn't dare!"

Meredith slanted Jack a saccharine smile. "You're right, Jack. Even after all you've done to me I can't be cruel enough to leave you completely exposed like this." She scavenged in the plastic bag and pulled out one of his socks. A few quick dabs of cheesecake made the cutest little white face against the black background. Meredith slipped the adorable little sock puppet over Jack's petered-out pecker, then stood back to admire her slapdash creation. "Oh yes...that's much better, don't you think?" She bent over Jack's face, kissed the tip of her finger and dabbed it to his nose. "It's been great fun seeing you again, Jack, but I really do have to run. I've got another hot and heavy kitchen table date with my neighbor in the morning and I need my beauty sleep." Then, plastic bag in hand, she turned to leave the bedroom.

"Meredith, wait!"

She paused at the doorway.

"Aw, I get it." Jack broke into panicky laughter. "This is all a big joke, right? Just to get back at me, right? Right, Meredith? You're not really going to leave me like this." He laughed again. She folded her arms across her chest and leaned against the doorjamb, disdain written across her features. "Okay, okay," Jack continued. "Very funny. You got me good. Ha-ha-ha. I forgive you. Now come on and untie me." Meredith didn't move a muscle. Jack's jovial expression morphed into a scowl. "Now you listen to me, Meredith. You're skating on thin ice here. If you don't untie me at once, I just may decide not to marry you again after all. Does that tiny brain of yours have any conception of the opportunity you'd be passing up to be the wife of a man as well known and successful as Jack McKenna?"

Meredith rolled her eyes and chuckled. "Oh, poor Jack. You really are clueless, aren't you? I never wanted your success...just your heart." She gave him one last look, smiled and blew him a kiss. "Maybe you'll get lucky and have some sexy little prepubescent housekeeper find you there, all trussed up and ready to perform for her." Flinging the plastic bag with his clothes over her shoulder, she left the bedroom. And before exiting the hotel suite, she called out, "Have a nice life, Jack," wincing at the highly imaginative string of profanity that the international babe-magnet, mega-successful speaker and about-to-be talk show host shouted after her.

Meredith pushed the call button for the elevator just across the hall. She could still hear Jack's vastly creative diatribe and for a moment, just the briefest interlude, she took pity on her poor, oblivious ex-husband and considered letting him off the hook because, damn it, she realized she still loved the big sexy obnoxious jerk. Her gaze lingered on the door of Jack's hotel suite as the elevator doors parted. With a fortifying breath, Meredith stepped across the threshold — and down into oblivion, because the elevator car wasn't there.

Chapter Six

ఐ

With a slow pirouette, Meredith surveyed her sumptuous surroundings and gaped, drop-jawed, at the wealth of gold, crystal, marble and a host of other fine-quality accoutrements. The area made Jack's luxurious suite look like a ramshackle hole in the wall by comparison. "This doesn't look like the hotel lobby," she mumbled to herself. "I must have taken a wrong turn after I got off the elevator."

"Ah! I see that you've arrived. Wonderful!"

With a sharp intake of breath, Meredith clapped her hand to her chest and swiveled towards the woman's voice. "Oh, you startled me." She gave a nervous laugh.

"Sorry," said the woman standing before her. The raven-haired beauty was so stunning, so faultlessly beautiful, that Meredith found herself staring. "It seems to be a nasty habit of mine. Delighted to have you staying with us, my dear." The woman extended her hand — the one without the foot-long cigarette holder. Awestruck by the costly array of glittering gems adorning the long fingers, Meredith clasped the proffered hand and shook it.

"You must be mistaking me for someone else." Meredith quickly released the woman's jarringly hot flesh. "I'm not checking in. I was just on my way out."

The woman shook her head from side to side causing her sleek chin-length bob to swing. "No, you're the one who's mistaken, dear. As a matter of fact, you're already checked in. I've seen to the arrangements myself." She absently flipped her bangs with the cigarette holder as she smiled.

Meredith laughed. "No, honestly, I'm not who you think I am," she explained. "I was just visiting one of the guests and when I stepped off the elevator I—"

"Watch out for that first step. It's a doozie!" The woman's pealing laughter reverberated throughout the opulent room as it sprang from her glossy blood-red lips. "Whoomp—splat!" Dramatically gesturing with her arms, she continued to laugh.

Her eyebrows knitting, Meredith balled her hands at her hips, resting her weight on one leg. Clearly the woman was either drunk or nuts. Probably some bubble-headed society matron who'd lost her way back to her event after a pee break. "I beg your pardon?"

"Oops." The woman's bejeweled fingers flew to her lips and her eyebrows arched high. "Evidently you don't remember yet." She gave a dismissive flick of her wrist. "No matter, it will all come back to you soon." She sauntered across the marble floor, the train of her skin-hugging red gown trailing behind her. Long sleeved, floor length and sequined, it looked like one of those preposterously expensive designer creations that upper echelon celebrities wore.

"Remember what?" Meredith said. "What's this all about?"

The woman studied Meredith's confounded expression and smiled. "Why, your unfortunate twelve-story fall down the elevator shaft of course."

"My what!?" Breathing an exasperated sigh, Meredith rolled her eyes. "If you'll excuse me, I'm not in the mood for dim-witted dark comedy." Tsking, she brushed by the woman and began walking. It had been a long, tension-filled evening fighting her emotions as she exacted retribution on Jack and she didn't have time to indulge some flighty, inebriated socialite.

"And just where do you think you're going, Meredith McKenna?"

"I don't really see where that's any concern of—" Meredith stopped abruptly and turned to face the woman in time to see her lip curling into a half-smile as the woman folded her arms across her chest. "Wait a minute... How did you know my name?"

"Well, that's what it says here." The woman flipped through the stack of papers that suddenly materialized in her hand, fastened to a glistening gold clipboard. "Born Meredith Annie Collins on...oh!" She stopped reading and looked up at Meredith, grinning. "Happy birthday."

Meredith's eyes popped wide. Okay, this was getting strange. Weird Woman not only knew her maiden and married names but her birthday too. And where the hell had that clipboard full of papers come from? Suddenly relief bathed Meredith's features. "Oh, I get it. Karyn put you up to this for my birthday, didn't she?" She laughed while craning her neck left and right. "Come on out, Karyn, I'm on to you. Very funny. Ha, ha." Her merriment was met with silence.

"Karyn Archer? Hardly," the woman said with a disinterested sigh. "Your dull, plump, pistachio-munching friend had nothing to do with this. I'm afraid she's not nearly that witty or clever." She returned her attention to the documents scrolling down the lines of data with her finger. "Let's see...yada, yada, yada...yup, here it is—married name McKenna. No doubt about it, it's you all right." Fixing her powerful gaze on Meredith again, she beamed a bright smile. "Married him twice, I see."

Still trying to fathom how the mysterious papers detailing her life had appeared out of nowhere, an awestruck gasp escaped Meredith's lips. "Where did you get that information about me? What in the hell—"

"Yes! That's it! Finally you understand," the woman interjected. The documents vanishing as quickly as they had appeared, she clapped enthusiastically as Meredith slanted her another bewildered look. "Yes, my dear Ms. McKenna, you're in Hell. H-E-Double-Hockey-Sticks. You've been damned here for eternity. Welcome!" the woman said in buoyant tones as she broke into a wide inviting grin and extended her hand to Meredith.

Ignoring the hospitable gesture, Meredith felt frozen in place, like one of the massive stone statues that lined the great gold-veined marble walls. Finally, she shook her head hoping to clear it. "I must be dreaming."

"Hmmm, I suppose some people might consider it a nightmare," the woman offered thoughtfully. "But no, dear, you're not dreaming. You're really dead, Meredith. As a doornail. As a dodo bird. As a—"

"Yeah, I get it, I get it," Meredith said, flicking her hands with a dismissive wave. "And this," she gestured to her extravagant surroundings, "isn't the Northwest Passage Hotel. It's Hell, right?"

"Exactly. Give the little lady a cigar!" With those words a stogie immediately appeared in the woman's hand and she held it out to Meredith, who ignored the ludicrous offer. With the shrug of one elegant shoulder, the woman tossed the cigar aside only to have it disappear into thin air before it had a chance to reach the floor.

Gasping, Meredith nodded in understanding. Okay…it wasn't the woman in red who was drunk, it was Meredith herself. Yes, she must have surpassed her limit sucking down all that cognac with Jack and now she was hallucinating. It was the only logical explanation. Meredith's head bobbed up and down and she started to laugh. "And I suppose you're, what? The Mistress of Darkness?"

"Ooh, I like that." The woman tapped a blood-red talon against her jaw. "Most people say *she-devil*, but Mistress of Darkness is so much more colorful, don't you think?" She glanced back at Meredith, whose expression was deadpan. "Well, in any case, just call me Dev." As she said the name, the room reverberated with the ovation of thousands of unseen disciples, giving Meredith a start. "And, sugar…" she reached out and lifted Meredith's chin with her cigarette holder, "you're wrong. You're not drunk and neither am I. This is the real deal, babycakes. Deal with it."

"You can read my thoughts," Meredith said as more of a statement than a question. Dev nodded. Oh God. She *was* dead. Really and truly dead. And by some hideous mistake in paperwork she'd landed in Hell instead of Heaven. Surrendering to an involuntary shudder, Meredith's chin quivered and one fat teardrop scrolled down her cheek.

"Oh, now don't be a crybaby, darling," Dev said, wrapping her arm around Meredith's shoulder and pulling her into a buddy-hug. "Why, in no time at all you'll be ready to begin your new way of life as one of my adoring minions and an eternal resident of Hell. It will be great fun...you'll see." Dev twisted her hand with a flourish. "Here, this will help you feel better." She offered Meredith chocolates that were suddenly resting in her palm. "They're Belgian...your favorite. Better take them quickly before they melt. I'm rather, uh, hot-blooded." She cackled.

Meredith took one confection from Dev's palm and studied it warily.

With a loud tsk, Dev coaxed, "Well, go ahead. It's not like it's deadly poison or anything. I mean, *duh*, you're already dead, Meredith." She erupted into gales of laughter.

Meredith popped the chocolate into her mouth and closed her eyes, enjoying the richest, creamiest, most exquisite truffle she'd ever tasted. A spontaneous moan of pleasure escaped her lips. "Oh my God, this chocolate is del —"

"Ahem," Dev interrupted with a laugh as she wagged her finger. "First rule...you'll need to work on finding more appropriate expressions here, dear. I'm not too keen on mentions of my chief competitor." She pointed heavenward and rolled her eyes.

Snatching the rest of the chocolates from Dev's open palm, Meredith shook her head and sighed. "This is all so weird and surreal. I mean, I don't remember dying. The last thing I remember is leaving Jack's suite and waiting for the elevator."

"Mmm-hmm." Dev nodded. "And then?" she encouraged, beckoning with her fingers.

"I...I can't remember." Meredith frowned.

"Here, let me help." Dev raised her arm high over her head and gave an elaborate swirl of her hand, before splaying her fingers and thrusting them in Meredith's direction.

As if a bolt of lightning had struck her, Meredith's body stiffened and quaked. A lifetime of memories flooded her brain, racing through her thoughts with implausible velocity. The memories slowed as they neared the present. After replaying her morning tryst with Cristoval, her discussion with Karyn and then the nasty little trick she'd played on Jack, Meredith saw herself stepping into the elevator — and screaming as she plunged into the dark abyss.

"Oh my God, I *do* remember."

Dev covered her ears and scowled. "Will you stop with the G word already?" She shuddered and then took on an eager, enthusiastic air. "Would you like to see what you looked like once you hit bottom?" Dev asked hopefully.

Meredith slapped her hand to her chest and gasped. "No!"

"Oh." Her buoyant expression sagging, Dev shrugged. "Too bad. They're wonderfully grisly images." She made a diving motion with her arm. "Whoomp — splat!" she repeated her earlier words and laughed.

Giving Dev a sideways glance, Meredith sneered and then shivered. "But why am I in Hell? I've never been a bad or evil person. On the contrary, I've spent the better part of my life as a boring goody-two-shoes type. There must have been a mix-up of some sort. I mean, shouldn't I be up there," she gestured upwards, "in Heaven?"

"Nope. No mistake." Stroking her fingers along her jaw in a contemplative motion, Dev slowly strode in a wide circle around Meredith. "But," she added, "I'll admit that there was some lively debate about your final destination—between them," Dev pointed skyward, "and us. But I finally won out. The evidence I presented was overwhelmingly condemning."

"I don't understand." Meredith heaved a weighty sigh. "What possible evidence could there be that would damn me to Hell for eternity?" She lifted her arms and let them fall, slapping at her sides.

Dev shook her head and smiled. "Payback is a bitch, darling." With a swoop of her hand, 3-D, bigger-than-life images of Meredith tying Jack to the bedposts and then leaving him in a compromising manner as she left the hotel suite played above their heads.

"I don't believe it." Meredith huffed a humorless laugh. "I've been sent to Hell for playing one admittedly sneaky and perhaps even a bit dirty little payback trick on the man who cheated on me umpteen times since we became a couple twenty years ago? The man who single-handedly turned my life upside down and inside out and practically drove me to dive off a bridge with an anvil clutched to my bosom?" She made a raspberry sound with her tongue. "Oh *puhleeze*. You have *got* to be kidding. Once. Just *once* in my entire life I do something purposefully nasty and I'm damned for it." She scraped her fingers through her hair. "And on my birthday no less! Shit. What kind of asinine judge and jury decided my fate based on this evidence, huh?"

"Shhh." Her fingers to her lips, Dev grimaced and glanced around quickly. "Only the topmost officials of both realms, darling," she said in a conspiratorial whisper.

"But all I did was—"

"Meredith, your seemingly innocuous actions had wide-ranging consequences. Some quite dire, in fact. Here, sit down and I'll show you."

"But there's no place to—"

Before she could finish her sentence an ornately carved, plush velvet upholstered chair instantly nudged Meredith's knees from behind and she fell back into it, rolling her eyes. Dev's chair looked suspiciously more like an elaborate gem-studded golden throne with blood-red upholstery. With a wave of Dev's hand, tubs of buttered popcorn appeared on their laps and Dev dug in immediately. A fully equipped bar manifested before them and Dev urged Meredith to soothe her jangled nerves with a little libation. Just the merest notion of a chocolate martini had skated across Meredith's mind before she found one ensconced in her hand. She didn't quite know whether to laugh or cry—so she did a bit of both.

"Keep in mind that while these events are in the future, with all things remaining as they are now, all of these scenarios will come to pass." Meredith nodded apprehensively. "Now this first clip," Dev continued, pointing to the image coming into focus, "takes place tomorrow morning. The cutie is Alicia Gonciarz, the greedy little hotel maid who finds Jack tied to the bed with your charming little sock puppet covering his crotchless-panty-framed pecker." Dev laughed. "Very clever. The little eyes, nose and mouth made out of cheesecake dabs added a definite panache." Meredith cringed a bit.

"And here," Dev said, "we see Alicia telephoning Ricky Scholl, her no-good sleazy but deliciously hunky boyfriend. He's a hotel security guard who doubles as a freelance photographer. She loves him…well, as much as any ruthless bitch can love a man, but she'd slit his throat in an instant if the price were right. Zipping ahead a bit, we find humiliating images of Jack plastered all over the supermarket rags. Oh that's a great shot of Jack's ass, isn't it, darling? Look how clearly your indelible ink message stands out." She tossed a handful of popcorn into her mouth and munched. "I'm going to love having Alicia and Ricky down here with me one day. Such a deliciously malevolent little pair."

Her eyes glued to the vivid telltale images of her ex-husband splashed all over the media, Meredith winced. "Oh no...that's terrible. I had no idea. If I had known anything like this would happen I'd never have—"

"And here," Dev cut her off, "we see Jack as the keynote motivational speaker in Seattle, his next stop on the tour. Listen..." Dev cocked her head and cupped her ear with her hand. "Hear the snickers as Jack takes his place at the podium?" She grinned while Meredith winced. "Then a trickling of guffaws as he starts to speak...first there's a heckler in the back of the room...then another heckler closer to the front...rampant chuckling...a couple of nasty comments... Then after he's struggled to get through his presentation, a sea of eager hands pops up. Ludicrous questions about the photo spreads in the supermarket rags...then another question about the hilarious animated images of Jack on the Internet...and finally we hear the room erupt in belly laughter. And here, after deflecting barbs and struggling in vain to maintain a shred of dignity, we see a defeated and beleaguered Jack McKenna leaving the stage. Take a good look at his face, Meredith. The man has been thoroughly humbled and humiliated." Dev reached over and gave Meredith a hearty slap on the knee. "Great job, kid. You've got real promise."

"Please stop. I don't want to see any more. This is making me sick." Flinching at the cruel images, Meredith rubbed at the hot spot Dev's hand left on her knee and then tossed back her chocolate martini. Another one immediately appeared in its place. "I never imagined there could be repercussions like this. Oh, poor Jack, I'm so sorry."

"His speaking engagements only go downhill from there. And the TV show...*phffft!*" Dev snapped her fingers. "*On the Right Track with Dr. Jack* never materializes after people laughingly refer to it as *Flat on Your Back with Dr. Jack*. The man's a veritable laughingstock. Before long the only offers Jack McKenna gets are from sleazy porn promoters who want to hire him for their seedy films or from the cheesy confession tell-all types of magazines. Even the supermarket rags have lost interest by now. Jack is old news. A has-been."

"How he must hate me," Meredith said softly, shaking her head back and forth slowly. Sure she'd wanted to get even with him, but never like this. Aside from being an unfaithful husband who couldn't grasp the concept of keeping his frisky dick in his pants, Jack was a good, decent man. He didn't deserve this. And to think he would suffer this fate due to her selfish need for reprisal had Meredith's stomach roiling.

"Oh yes, at first he hated you. Loathed the very mention of your name, in fact. And with good reason." Dev shrugged. "But, alas, the poor fool is annoyingly forgiving. Watch this..."

"That's Jack and Karyn." Meredith sat erect as she watched the unfolding images. "What's happening? Why is Karyn crying so hard? Where are they?"

"At the dinner following your funeral."

Meredith blanched. "Oh." Her hand went to her throat, resting there as she leaned back in the chair.

"It was tough at first," Jack said to Karyn. "I hated her for what she'd done to me—to my career. My entire life. But, dear God, Karyn, Meredith *was* my life, my heart, my conscience." His voice choked and a sob broke free. "I loved her, Karyn. With every fiber of my being and to the very depths of my soul I loved her."

"I know you did, Jack. And she loved you too, just as much," Karyn said as she patted his arm. "I've never known anyone with a bigger heart than Meredith, Jack. You do know that she never meant for any of this to happen to you, don't you?" Jack nodded. "It was all supposed to be a harmless joke, a prank, just to get even with you for—"

Their attention was drawn to the restaurant's entrance where some of the paparazzi who'd managed to get in were being ushered out by security.

"Look this way, Jack," one of them shouted, as he snapped photos while being ejected from the premises.

"Who's your pretty lady friend?" another called out. "Are you being a *bad boy* again, McKenna?" The restaurant's vestibule rang with crude laughter.

"What's the matter with you people?" Jack yelled. "We've just come from a funeral. Show some respect and consideration for chrissakes."

"Are you wearing your sock puppet today, Jack?" a third photographer shouted as his camera's flash went off.

Growling, Jack leapt to his feet and Karyn grabbed his arm. "No!" she said sharply. "That won't do any good, Jack. It won't bring Meredith back and it will only make matters worse for you. Now look at me and focus on what I'm saying," she instructed as Jack took his seat again. "I was telling you that Meredith never would have pulled that stunt if she had any idea that you were going to be hurt like this. Even after all you put her through, Jack, she still loved you. Although I did my damnedest to convince her otherwise."

"I know." Jack released a pent-up breath. "I know." He patted Karyn's hand. "I'm not going to claim to understand everything I did to drive her to such extremes but whatever it was, I must have..." his voice wavered, "I must have hurt her so deeply, Karyn. And now she's gone." He buried his head in his hands and sobbed. As she did her best to comfort Jack, Karyn's fragile hold on her composure crumbled and she cried too, dabbing her red eyes and dripping nose with tissues. "I've lost the only woman I ever loved," Jack muttered into his hands.

"And I've lost my best friend," Karyn choked out. "What will I ever do without her?" She sobbed a bit and then patted Jack's shoulder. "Time. It will take a lot of time but we'll get through it somehow."

"No." Jack shook his head slowly. "No, Karyn, you're wrong. It'll never be any better. She's dead...my beautiful sweet Meredith is gone from my life forever." After a moment he took a deep breath and looked up at her as another crop of news reporters started shouting inappropriate questions.

"Nothing else matters anymore," Jack said just above a whisper. "I fucking deserve whatever happens to me now."

"I've never seen Jack cry before," Meredith barely managed to say. By now tears were streaming down her face and she was hiccupping as she sobbed into the red silk handkerchief that had magically appeared between her fingers. "Look what I've done to them, all the grief and sadness and pain I've caused. Oh if only..." Her attention was drawn to a new set of images and she frowned.

"Here's to you, buddy," Karyn slurred as she tossed back a swig of whiskey straight from the bottle.

"Karyn looks terrible," Meredith said to Dev. "What's happening?"

"It's one year from today," Dev explained with a yawn. "Your loser friend is sitting next to your headstone *celebrating* your forty-first birthday." Dev chuckled.

"I never did get to fuck Cristoval on my fortieth, Meredith," Karyn said to the engraved chunk of polished granite. "I didn't even get to fuck the smelly old bald guy with the beer belly next door." She laughed and took another swallow and then she wiped her trembling hand across her mouth. "Seems as though I've found another best friend though. One I like even better than pistachios." Smiling, Karyn patted the liquor bottle. "Allow me to introduce my new best friend. He doesn't cheat on me, he doesn't give me lip and he's always there when I need him. What more could you ask, huh?" She laughed hysterically.

"Oh Karyn," Meredith whispered, shaking her head as she watched her friend. "Why are you doing this to yourself?"

"Because of you, of course." With an I-told-you-so grin plastered across her perfect features, Dev poked her finger repeatedly toward Meredith. "It's all your fault." Then she made a shame-on-you motion with her fingers. "Bad Meredith." And Dev erupted into giggles.

Expelling a monumental sigh, Meredith returned her focus to the dismal image of Karyn.

"I let you down, Meredith," Karyn said, lovingly stroking her hand along the headstone. "I lost the business you were so proud of—the one you and I worked so hard and long to build. As of yesterday, Abundant Finds no longer exists." She brought the bottle to her lips and drank again. "For some reason, it seems that our upscale clientele prefers not to do business with a drunk. Can you imagine?" She gave a meager laugh and then she started to cry. "I'm sorry, Meredith. I just can't do it alone. It was supposed to be *us*, you and me, friends and business partners forever. But then you left me. Why'd you have to go and die, Meredith?" She took another swig of whiskey and sobbed.

"She's never been much of a drinker," Meredith mentioned absently, reaching out to Karyn's image, wishing she could comfort her desolate friend. "Maybe a chocolate martini once a week or so but—" Rolling her eyes, Meredith trilled an exasperated sigh as another chocolate martini instantly popped into her hand.

"Drink up, darling," Dev encouraged. "We don't want poor Karyn to drink alone, do we?" Dev downed her own chocolate martini and smacked her lips with gusto.

Meredith thrust the glass toward Dev. "Here, I don't want—"

"Of course...what was I thinking?" Dev said. In the next instant Meredith's chocolate martini disappeared, replaced by a big glass of chocolate milk with a bendy elbow straw instead. A birthday sheet cake ablaze with forty-one candles floated before them, conical birthday hats appeared on their heads and party blowers were stuck between their lips.

Dev smiled brightly, admiring her handiwork as she blew, unfurling the rolled whistling blower. "There, that's better," she said, brushing her palms together. "We'll set an example for Karyn, showing her that she doesn't need alcohol to celebrate." Dev took a sip from her glass of chocolate milk

Growling in frustration, Meredith tore the party hat from her head. "Will you *please* stop it!" she said after spitting out the blower. "This isn't funny, Dev."

"Really?" Dev hiked her shoulders in a clueless shrug and took another sip of chocolate milk. "I thought it was rather amusing."

"...happy birthday, dear Meredith," Karyn was singing in melancholy tones overhead, immediately drawing Meredith's attention. "Happy birthday to you."

"Ooh, goodie, here comes the best part," Dev said excitedly as she wiggled in her throne chair and munched on another fistful of popcorn.

The next group of images began with the drunken Karyn behind the wheel of her car and Meredith gripped the arms of her chair in alarm. "Oh no. Please, God, no," she cried.

"Enough with the G word!" Dev grumbled.

Meredith watched in horror as Karyn drove along a dark road, her vision distorted by sheeting rain and blinding tears as she sobbed. Meredith covered her eyes with her hands, peeking out of a small opening between her fingers as Karyn's speeding car slammed head-on into a massive tree trunk.

"Wow, did you see that? What an impact!" Dev punched her fist through the air. "Wham!" She laughed and tossed another handful of popped corn into her mouth.

Working to compose herself after witnessing the horrendous accident that killed her best friend, Meredith turned to Dev. "You're a sick and twisted woman," she snarled. "Cold and cruel. How can you just sit there and laugh at the misfortune of others?"

"No, not sick or twisted, darling." Dev arched a perfectly shaped eyebrow and smiled. "Cold and cruel perhaps and, possibly, a teensy bit...evil." She held her thumb and forefinger an inch apart. "But, after all," she shrugged, "I *am* the Mistress of Darkness, am I not?" She smiled coyly, batting her eyelashes as she drained the chocolate milk from her glass. "And I have a certain image to uphold."

Meredith's head dropped into her hands and she groaned as her fingers raked through her hair. "You're right. I do belong in Hell. I was stupid and selfish and my actions have caused untold heartbreak to the people I love most."

"Now you're talking." Dev reached over and patted Meredith on the back. "That's what I like to hear. Just to further cement your conviction, take a peek at this." She gestured to the images coming into view.

"Oh, no more, please, Dev. I don't think I can bear watching another minute of pain and anguish."

Dev's head snapped toward Meredith, whose eyes widened when she caught the menacing expression on Dev's face. "I said watch!" Dev bellowed.

Swallowing hard, Meredith trained her attention back to the emerging images. As she watched the indigent street person foraging in a Dumpster for food, her eyebrows furrowed and she frowned. "Who's that?"

Dev just smiled.

"Hey, you old piece of shit," a man yelled from the back door of the restaurant. "Get your sorry, begging ass out of here or I'll call the cops."

Nodding, the bum backed away. "Sorry." He held his hands up in surrender. "I didn't mean any harm, mister. I'm just hungry, that's all."

"That voice…" Meredith said.

The next image found the tattered old man huddled and shivering in a doorway under a piece of cardboard. Leaning forward, Meredith strained to hear what the old man said just before he fell asleep.

"Goodnight, Meredith, my love," the old man whispered. "I miss you so much." He sniffled.

"Jack!" Meredith's hand flew to her throat and she gasped. "That poor old homeless man is Jack. Oh my G—"

Dev slapped a hand against Meredith's mouth, preventing another utterance of the G word, and wagged an accusatory finger under her nose. "Yes, it's Jack. Unable to continue working as a motivational speaker, he finds it almost impossible to get hired anywhere else. The in-your-face images of his bare ass boasting the declaration that he's been a bad boy along with pictures of his little pecker puppet spread all over the supermarket rags haven't exactly endeared him to the corporate world. First, the hotel's lawsuit wiped out most of his savings. Then he was sued by a number of calculating little bitches who figured they'd try to get their share of the pie."

Meredith screwed her features. "Sued for what?"

"Support. The bimbos claimed that he'd fathered their illegitimate children. All lies, of course, but due to his tarnished reputation," Dev fixed a piercing gaze on Meredith, "due to *you*, of course, Jack lost every case but one and was forced to pay child support for a little rug rat that wasn't even his. When he couldn't meet his financial obligations, he was thrown in jail. Needless to say, trying to get any job after that was difficult at best."

"No...that wouldn't happen," Meredith said, shaking her head in disbelief. "They'd need solid DNA evidence proving Jack was the father."

"A minor technicality." Dev sloughed off Meredith's logic with a flick of her wrist. "You're forgetting that my people are everywhere, Meredith. All it takes is a bribe here, a bribe there... The power of greed is amazing, and ruining Jack's life in exchange for a fat lump of cash didn't even make the paternity tester blink twice."

"All because of that dirty little trick I played on him..." Meredith gazed ahead with a blank stare.

"That's right," Dev agreed. "Because of your selfish need for payback, eventually your ex-husband lost everything he ever owned. He became a broken, battered old man, who blamed only himself for having hurt you so deeply. He died with your name on his lips. Here, let's play that clip again," Dev said with a flourish of her hand, and the image of Jack huddled in the doorway popped into view again, with a close-up on his wrinkled, weathered features.

"Goodnight, Meredith, my love. I miss you so much."

"And," Dev said, "as we fade to black, Jack McKenna breathes his last, still pining over the loss of the only woman he ever truly loved." She feigned an exaggerated sniff and wiped her eye. "Brings a tear to your eye, doesn't it?" A red silk handkerchief appeared in her hand and she blew her nose with a loud, cartoonish honking sound.

Meredith's shoulders slumped and her head drooped. "So what happens now?" Her voice was just above a whisper. "Do I start shoveling coal and stoking the fires?"

Dev cackled. "Jack was right, darling, you *do* have a marvelously quirky sense of humor. No, dear, as heinous as your little prank turned out to be, it's not something that would condemn you to such a gruesome eternity. In all actuality, we abandoned the whole coal-shoveling idea eons ago—terribly messy, you know—in favor of more high-tech retributions. But that's neither here nor there." Dev flicked her wrist. "No, your task, Meredith, will be to recruit new souls to the dark side. Naturally, you'll have a quota to meet and if you fail to do that, well, let's just say that there'll be some rather nasty consequences to pay." Dev shuddered.

"You mean, I'm supposed to go back to Earth and try to corrupt innocent, trusting people so that they become evil?"

"Delicious sounding, isn't it? Just imagine the fun you'll have."

"I'd rather be dead."

Dev threw her head back in laughter and then rapped her knuckles on Meredith's head. "*Hellooo?* You already are dead, remember?"

Staring at nothing in particular, Meredith sighed.

"Ah yes," Dev said, "you'll be mired in the myriad joys of inflicting humiliation, degradation, dishonor, mortification and ruination. What a rush! Of course, you'll find it easiest to sway lost souls—people who are already desperate, grieving, in a state of utter hopelessness. They'd be most likely to make a deal with the devil."

"No…please. I could never do that." Meredith's chin quivered as her eyes fill with tears. She had trouble killing bugs for heaven's sake. She couldn't begin to conceive of tempting good trusting people to sell their souls—damning them for eternity. She shuddered at the thought.

Dev tsked and rolled her eyes. "Ugh, these nonstop waterworks of yours are really getting tiresome, Meredith. Look, if you're not woman enough to prey on the dejected, forlorn sniveling wimps up there, then go ahead and shoot for a sure thing instead."

Meredith frowned. "What do you mean?"

"I'm talking about going after the greedy, money-hungry bastards who are already itching to sell their souls to ensure a cushy lifestyle for themselves. It's a cinch." Dev flicked her wrist with a shrug. "Piece of cake. Even *you* could handle it. Granted, it's not as much fun as snaring a selfless, bleeding heart, goody-two-shoes type—like you, for instance—" Dev gleefully waggled her eyebrows, "but you can work your way up to that in time."

No. No way. She couldn't do it. She'd rather scour sulfur pits twenty-four-seven. "Dev…isn't there any way that I can get a second chance?" Meredith raised her watery gaze to Dev's hardened one. "Something I could do to make up for the pain and devastation I've caused? Some way I can alter things so that Jack and Karyn don't have to experience those terrible fates you showed me? I deserve to suffer but at least give me a chance to make amends before you lock me away in some tar pool for all eternity."

An unholy yowl emanated from Dev. "Damn!" She shot up from her throne chair and fixed Meredith with a dark, ominous gaze. "I *hate* when the newbies ask that!" She narrowed her eyes as she stepped toward Meredith, menacing fangs sprouting from her mouth and hands extended with glossy, blood-red talons glinting in the light. And then Meredith glimpsed the pair of horns creeping out from just above Dev's bangs. The walls appeared to breathe as they reverberated with the tormented cries and angst-ridden wails of the damned. Dev's petrifying actions had a terrified Meredith slinking down in her chair, covering her eyes and whimpering.

All of a sudden, lightning flashed and thunder crashed throughout the room. The light was as blinding as the noise deafening and Meredith's trembled even harder.

Spinning on her heel and then stamping her foot with enough force to crack marble, Dev's resulting howl was akin to that of a wounded beast. "Yes, all right, already," she shrieked, throwing her hands up into the air as she looked skyward. "I know the drill. I'll honor the damned contract." The flashing light and clapping booms ceased immediately and Dev's shoulders slumped.

After a few moments of silence, Meredith finally braved a peek through her fingers. "What—what was that?"

"*That*," Dev said, hiking her thumb upward, "was a not-so-gentle reminder from the big guy upstairs. You know, the guy with the G name you so merrily keep invoking." Dev rolled her eyes. "My competitor and I have a pact when it comes to borderline cases like yours," she continued. "I get to keep them as long as they don't ask if they can try to rectify their mistakes. But if they ask then I have no choice but to give them a chance to redeem their souls." She clapped her hand against her forehead and groaned. "Damn! And here things were going so well between us before you had to go and open that blasted goody-two-shoes trap of yours."

Meredith sucked in a deep breath. "You mean I don't have to stay here?" Her face brightened. "I can go to Heaven instead?"

"Hah!" Dev gave her an incredulous look. "Wouldn't it be nice if it was that easy? Well, forget it, Meredith. You're going to have to earn your passage upstairs and, believe me, it's *not* going to be easy."

Meredith stood up and nervously smoothed her dress. "I understand. That's fine. I'll do whatever it takes to keep those awful things from happening to Jack and Karyn. Just tell me what I need to do."

"Hmmm." Dev gnawed on a fingernail as she circled Meredith slowly. A wicked chuckle bubbled in her throat, ultimately becoming full-fledged laughter. "Oh, wouldn't that be deliciously funny," Dev said to herself, and Meredith winced. "Yes, I have it," Dev said excitedly as she stopped her pacing and faced Meredith. "Here's what we'll do."

"Something tells me I'm not going to like this," Meredith muttered under her breath.

Dev nodded. "Perhaps not," she gave a dismissive wave of her hand, "but then, consider the alternative, dear. Have you ever tried to get your hair clean after spending all day in a tar pool?" She arched a brow.

Meredith sighed. "Go ahead. Let me have it."

"Good. We'll have a juicy little chat just like two high school chums," Dev said.

Suddenly they were sitting on swivel stools, sipping whipped cream-topped chocolate malteds as they leaned their elbows on the green marble soda fountain bar in front of them. Each was garbed in a short pleated skirt, knee-high socks, penny loafers and crewneck sweaters with white button-down shirt collars peeking out. Meredith noticed their hairstyles in the mirror behind the fountain. They both sported flips.

"I've always had a fondness for the 60s preppy look," Dev explained with a grin as she swung her feet.

Rather than fight it Meredith breathed another sigh and just kept sipping as she listened to Dev's proposal.

"The easy way would be to send you back to just before you pulled your nasty little trick on your ex-husband," Dev said.

"Meredith's eyebrows shot up. "You can do that?"

Dev looked at her as if she had holes in her head. "Well of course I can." She huffed a laugh and sipped from her malted.

"Great!" Meredith said.

"But I'm not going to," Dev said with a wicked smile. "No, what I have in mind will be so much more interesting...so ingenious...so terribly creative. But," she gave Meredith a warning look, "if you fail to change the future and save your friends from their cruel fates then you're all mine again. I have that clause in my contract with you know who." Sneering, she looked skyward and Meredith's gaze followed.

"Okay, I'm all ears," Meredith said. Her ears instantly grew to cartoon-like size and Dev laughed hysterically while Meredith gasped, slapping her hands against the giant protrusions on either side of her head. "*Dev!*"

"Sorry, darling. I couldn't resist." Dev snapped her fingers, restoring Meredith's ears to normal size. "Honestly, sometimes I just crack myself up." She laughed again and then settled down, taking a deep breath before she continued. "So anyway, you're going to go back to Earth and you'll remember everything that's happened—but you're not allowed to tell anyone what's going on. Understand?"

Meredith nodded. It sounded easy enough so far.

"You'll have to fix things without telling Jack or Karyn that you fell down an elevator shaft and went *boom* and then ended up in Hell after you died. And you can't tell them that you've seen their futures either. And if you attempt to divulge any of the aforementioned forbidden information, you'll choke on your words before they ever leave your mouth." Dev's hands flew to her throat and she gagged to illustrate her point. "Got it?" She asked with a strangled breath.

"Got it." Meredith nodded again. "So I'm going back before the time that I went to Jack's hotel suite?"

"Uh...no. The morning after."

"You mean I come back into the room and untie Jack before anyone finds him?"

"Uh-uh." Dev shook her head negatively. "Meredith has done her dirty work and now she's gone. She's outta there. She's taken a hike. She's nowhere to be found."

"Okay." Meredith swallowed a slug of her chocolate malted. "Now I'm confused. How can I do anything if I'm not there?"

"Well, *you'll* be there, but Meredith won't."

"Huh?"

"Remember that devilish pair I told you about? The sneaky little hotel maid who finds Jack, and her sleazy photographer boyfriend?"

"I think I understand." Meredith nodded apprehensively. "You're sending me back as the hotel maid."

Dev laughed. "Guess again, darling."

Chapter Seven

ဢ

"Get your ass over here right away," Alicia Gonciarz whispered into the phone. "Trust me, you'll make us a fortune with these photographs — but you've gotta make it fast."

"Come on, please," Jack called from the bedroom. "Untie me before anyone else sees me like this."

Alicia walked back into the bedroom and stood there primly. "I'm sorry, Mr. McKenna, but it's against hotel rules for me to do anything but call security in a situation like...uh...this." Her eyes scanned Jack and his embarrassing predicament and she couldn't help giggling. "Not that I've ever been in a situation exactly like *this* before." Focusing on Jack McKenna's scowl, Alicia cleared her throat and composed herself. "Um, sorry. I've already called security and they'll have a man up here as soon as possible."

"God damn it!" Jack shouted, struggling against his bindings to no avail. "I swear to God, I'll strangle that woman with my bare hands when I get a hold of her."

"What woman?" Alicia asked eagerly, hoping to get the name of the obviously vengeful woman who'd orchestrated the hilarious scenario. The more information Ricky gave the rags along with his photos, the more bucks they'd make. Hell, if they played their cards right, she and Ricky could be fucking themselves silly in the huge mansion they'd purchase in Beverly Hills. "Who did this to you, Mr. McKenna?"

"M—" Jack started to spit out and then, eyeing the attractive, shapely young maid, he stopped. "Never mind. It's not important," he grumbled.

Damn! Alicia's shoulders slumped. "Uh...I'll just wait in the other room, sir." She went into the main living area of the

110

luxurious suite and plopped down on one of the cushy chairs, sinking into the deeply padded brocade upholstery and imagining that she was a wealthy socialite guest instead of someone who was employed to clean up after them. "Fucking rich bastards," she fumed under her breath as she fingered the ornately turned gold-leafed wood on the arm of the chair. "They think they're so much better than anyone else." Her gaze rested on the door to the bedroom and she snickered when she thought of Jack's predicament. "Oh boy, you really must have fucked over some woman real good," she muttered under her breath. She snickered again and slowly nodded. "Yeah, you fucking deserve whatever happens to you, Jackie boy." She popped the chocolate truffle she'd palmed from the dessert cart in the bedroom into her mouth and savored it.

A short while later there was a light knock at the door and Alicia vaulted from the chair to peer through the peephole. She yanked the door open. "Hey, baby," she cooed, wrapping her arms around the handsome young man's neck and kissing him as soon as she'd pulled him into the suite and closed the door. "We gotta hot one in there. This is gonna make us a shitload of money, Ricky."

A hungry look in his eye, Ricky Scholl grinned and pulled his camera from the pocket of his security guard uniform. "Let's get this show on the road."

Alicia preceded Ricky into the bedroom. "Security's here, Mr. McKenna," she said, stepping aside so that Ricky could enter the room.

"It's about fucking time," Jack barked. "Get me out of this, will you?"

"Yes, sir," Ricky said. "As soon as I take some photos." He started clicking away.

"Photos!" Jack bellowed. "For what?"

"Hotel policy, sir. In case there are any lawsuits brought against the hotel." He snapped another photo. "The police will also want them for their records." He snapped more pictures as he rounded the bed, catching every angle of Jack's embarrassing predicament.

"Jesus Christ, is this absolutely necessary? If these photos got out I'd be ruined."

Ricky continued to snap as he zoomed in for close-ups. "Trust me, sir, these photos will be kept safe from prying eyes. It's just a precautionary measure for your safety and the safety of the hotel." He reached into his pocket and pulled out a jackknife, flipping it open.

Jack blanched as Ricky turned the large blade back and forth, the light glinting from its polished metal as Ricky approached the bed.

"Now let me get you out of this," Ricky said. Jack breathed a sigh of relief as the sharp knife easily sliced through the nylon stockings halfway between the knots at the scrolled ironwork and Jack's wrists and ankles.

The first thing Jack did after leaping from the bed was to yank the sock puppet from his penis and then he tore off the crotchless panties, tossing them aside with disgust. Then he covered his limp cock with a pillow. Alicia immediately grabbed up the two discarded items.

"What are you doing?" Jack said.

"I'm going to put them in the trash for you, sir," she lied. Dollar signs danced in her head as she imagined selling the telltale items to the highest bidder among their criminal cohorts. She could almost smell the seawater slapping against the shore of their oceanfront mansion now.

"No." Jack shook his head. "I'll take care of them. Leave them here." Nodding, Alicia deposited the items on the bed.

When Jack leaned over to pull the knotted nylons from his ankles, he heard the camera whizzing again and turned to find Ricky taking additional pictures.

"Additional evidence," Ricky said, clearly stifling a grin as he pointed to the *I've been a very bad boy* message scrawled across Jack's ass in indelible ink.

Jack muttered a string of obscenities as he grabbed the towel Alicia held out to him and started wiping the congealed desserts from his body. When he finished, he picked up his wallet from the nightstand... And then his shoulders slumped.

"How am I going to get out of here?" He looked around the room. "I don't have any clothes."

"She took everything?" Alicia asked, her hopes elevating again. Jack nodded woefully. "If you just give me your sizes, Mr. McKenna, I'll be glad to go downstairs to the men's clothing shop and bring you something. And, of course, I'll need your credit card." She smiled, imagining all the jewel-encrusted designer gowns she could snap up for herself from the hotel's boutique. And maybe she'd even have enough time to pick up a tux or two for Ricky. They'd be outta there before that rich bastard McKenna even had a clue about what they'd done. She licked her lips.

"Thanks. I'd really appreciate that." Jack opened his wallet and then, pausing for a moment, snapped it closed again. "On second thought just charge it to my room."

Alicia's expression fell. "Certainly, sir." Damn. She hadn't counted on him being quite so savvy. After jotting down his sizes, she turned to leave, giving Ricky an enthusiastic wink before she left the room.

"I just need to ask you a few quick questions before I leave, sir," Ricky said, taking a small spiral notepad and pen out of his breast pocket. "To document the event for the hotel's records." He was always careful to get as many details as possible for the editors at the supermarket rags, just the way Alicia had taught him. "Your full name and address?"

"Look," Jack held up his hand like a crossing guard, "I'd really rather not give—"

"Sure, no problem," Ricky cut him off. With a shrug, he walked to the room's telephone and reached for the receiver. "We'll let the cops handle it instead."

"Wait!" Jack said. "I don't want the police involved in this." He sucked in a deep breath. "My name is Jack McKenna. I live at—" He stopped abruptly, watching the young man's features contort as he clutched his chest. "Hey, kid...are you all right?"

"Yeah," Ricky said in halting tones. "Must be that chilidog I had for..." With a groan, he keeled over and hit the floor.

Alarmed, Jack scrambled to the security guard's side. He felt for a pulse—it wasn't there. "Shit! Hold on, kid, I'll get help."

Just as Jack picked up the phone, Ricky propped up on his elbows. "What happened? Where am I?" he asked in a groggy voice.

Jack slammed down the receiver and went to the young man's side again. "You passed out. It looked like you were having a heart attack. Are you okay?"

"Yeah, I think so." Ricky looked up at the face hovering over him. "Jack? Jack is that you?"

Jack nodded. "Yes. You're in my hotel suite, remember? After taking the photos you started in on your questions and then you collapsed."

With a bright grin, Ricky threw his arms around Jack's neck, pulling him into a hug. "Jack, sweetheart—"

"Whoa! Hold on a minute, kid," Jack said, trying to back out of the boy's embrace. "I'm not into that kind of stuff."

"But it's me, M—" Meredith choked on her name. Try as she might she couldn't get it past her lips. Each time she tried she gagged.

Wincing as he finally extricated himself from the young man's clinch, Jack backed away, fixing Ricky with a dubious look. "Uh...you're obviously disoriented. Maybe I'd better call a doctor."

"Jack, what's the matter? Don't you know me?"

114

Knitting his eyebrows, Jack nodded slowly. "Yeah, you're the security guard that the maid called after she found me."

Shaking her head to clear her thoughts, Meredith took a good look at Jack. He was naked with dried splotches of dessert clinging to his skin. Her eyes widened as the memories came flooding back. Then she looked down at herself, running her fingers over the security guard uniform she wore, gasping when she discovered that her breasts were gone and that, further down, she had a big wad of stuff between her legs. The wad twitched.

With a whopping wail, Meredith shot to her feet. "Holy shit! I've got a penis!" Her gaze was glued to her crotch as she grabbed it.

"Most men do." Unable to keep from laughing, Jack scratched his head. "Just keep it in your pants, okay?"

"And...and I've got a man's voice!"

"Whew," Jack cringed, "that fall you took must have really knocked you for a loop, kid," he said, shaking his head. "Here, why don't you lie down until you feel better." He motioned toward the bed.

Drop jawed, Meredith stepped over to the bed and sat on the edge. "Then it was all real...it wasn't a dream," she said, examining her new muscled body. After a moment, she rose from the bed and gingerly walked to the mirror above the dresser. When she saw the reflection of a striking young man staring back at her, there was a sharp intake of breath. As she touched her face she saw the young man do the same and she shuddered. "It's really me. I'm the photographer, just like she said I'd be." Her brows furrowed as she turned from side to side. She raised her arm and flexed the biceps, her eyes bulging along with the muscle. "Whoa! And I'm a hunk!"

Jack eyed the kid warily.

Alicia came back into the bedroom, her arms laden with several bags, frowning when she saw her boyfriend. "Ricky, why are you still here? Shouldn't you be off making your

115

report, hmm?" She motioned with her rolling eyes for Ricky to take a hike.

Meredith stared at the beautiful young woman, narrowing her eyes. "You're Alicia," she spat with disdain.

Alicia rolled her eyes. "Well, of course I am. What the—"

"He keeled over shortly after you left," Jack explained, grabbing the pillow again and covering his naked cock.

"Ricky!" Alicia gasped, returning her gaze to her boyfriend. "Are you all right?"

"I thought he was having a heart attack," Jack continued. "I tried to call a doctor but he wouldn't let me. I think he must have hit his head when he fell because he's rather...uh...disoriented." Jack stifled a chuckle.

"Uh, thanks, Mr. McKenna. I'd better get him out of here, downstairs to the main security area. I got you everything from underwear to shoes." She thrusted the bags at Jack, who clutched them. "It should be everything you need." She stood with her hand outstretched.

Meredith watched as it finally dawned on Jack that Alicia was waiting for a tip. "Oh, yeah," he said, taking a few bills from his wallet and crossing her palm with the money. "Thanks again. I really appreciate all your help."

Alicia nodded her thanks. "Come on, Ricky," she crooked her finger, "it's time to leave."

Meredith folded her arms across her broad muscle-bound chest and huffed, sneering at Alicia.

An incredulous expression across her features, Alicia walked over to Ricky and took hold of his arm. "Did you get all the photographs and information you needed?" she asked through gritted teeth as she tugged on him.

"Forget about it." Meredith shrugged out of Alicia's grasp. "I'm not doing this, Alicia. And neither are you."

"What are you doing, you idiot? Shut up," Alicia muttered under her breath. Wide-eyed as she returned her attention to Jack, and taking in his perplexed expression, Alicia erupted into nervous laughter. "Seems you were right, Mr. McKenna. Ricky must have got a good bump on the head." She laughed again and Jack chuckled. "I know you must be eager to clean up and get dressed after your awful ordeal, Mr. McKenna, so why don't you go ahead and take your shower while I take Ricky back to the security station."

"Sounds like a good idea." Jack nodded with a smile as he tossed the contents of the bags on a nearby chair. "Thanks again for your help." Selecting the underwear, Jack headed for the bathroom.

Breathing a sigh of relief, Alicia jerked on Ricky's arm again, but Meredith didn't budge.

"Jack, wait." Meredith took a step toward Jack as Alicia still clung to her arm. "We need to talk. It's all a scam. They…I mean *we*," she gestured to herself and Alicia, "were planning to sell those photographs to the newspapers and TV."

Alicia gasped. "Are you *crazy?*" Her eyes bugged in disbelief. "For chrissakes, Ricky, shut up!" She clapped her hand over her boyfriend's mouth.

"What?!" His mouth in a tight line, Jack looked from the maid to the security guard. "Hey, what the hell's going on here?"

"Nothing, Mr. McKenna. Nothing," Alicia insisted. "Ricky's just talking crazy because of what happened to him, that's all. Don't pay any attention to what he says."

"It's true, Jack. I'm not who you think I am. It's me, M—" Meredith's throat constricted. She made horrific gagging sounds as her hands flew to her throat and she choked on her name. Both Alicia and Jack gazed at her incredulously.

"See," Alicia said, thrusting her arms toward the choking security guard, "I told you. He's nuts."

Growling in frustration, Meredith cleared her throat and continued. "Please, Jack, you've got to listen to me." She patted her pants and pulled the camera from her pocket, shaking it toward Jack. "Here take it. He ..." Meredith rolled her eyes, "I mean *I* was planning on—" She stopped abruptly when Alicia dove for the camera, securing it against her abdomen as she grabbed it from Meredith and bolted from the room.

"I'm not going to let you fuck this up for me, Ricky," Alicia called as she fled the suite.

"Quick," Meredith flailed her arm toward the escaping maid, "we have to stop her. She's going to sell those photos!"

A look of panic etched across his features, Jack ran after Alicia with Ricky close on his heels. As they reached the suite's door, Jack stopped short. "Shit! I can't go out there like this," he motioned down to his nakedness. "I've got to put on some pants first."

"Don't worry," Meredith said, "I'll stop her. I won't let her ruin your life, darling. I promise." Meredith kissed Jack quickly on the lips before racing out of the room—leaving Jack with a look of astonishment as he wiped his mouth and shuddered.

Chapter Eight

ℰ

When there wasn't any sign of Alicia in the hall and no indication that the elevator had just departed, Meredith located the door to the stairs and jerked it open. The sound of feet hastily shuffling down the stairs echoed through the stairwell. "Alicia!" she called as she started running after the maid. "Alicia, stop!"

"Stay away from me, Ricky," a breathless voice responded. "You're crazy."

Rolling her eyes, Meredith swore under her breath. "You're right, Alicia," she said as she continued her descent. "Temporary insanity from that bump on my head. But I'm all better now. Trust me." She was amazed at how quickly she was able to bound down the stairs. Ricky's buff body was apparently in damned good shape. Before long she caught up with Alicia and grabbed her by the arm.

"Ow, Ricky." Alicia winced. "Let go, you're hurting me."

"Only if you promise to stay put," Meredith warned.

"Yeah, all right already, I promise." Meredith's grip slackened and Alicia wrenched her arm free.

"You can give me back the camera now, Alicia." All Meredith had to do was to yank the film from the camera, exposing it to the light, and Jack was out of danger.

Alicia didn't budge.

"Come on, I need it so I can give the pictures to my contact."

"I don't know…" Alicia eyed her boyfriend suspiciously. "How do I know that you're not going to go nuts on me again, huh?" She clutched the camera closed to her chest. "That was

119

Dr. Jack in that room, the famous guy who's gonna have his own TV show. Jeezus, do you know how much we'd make off these photos, Ricky? A shitload! I can't take a chance on you ruining this for us. Now I've got to get out of here in case McKenna comes after me or calls security or the cops, Ricky." She turned and started to walk down the stairs again at a slower pace.

"Tell you what." Meredith did her best to smile. "Let's you and me relax over a cup of coffee and we'll talk about this, okay? You'll see that I'm okay and there's nothing to worry about."

"Coffee?" Alicia said, scrunching her features as she turned around. "Since when do you drink coffee? See? That proves that you're still semi-nuts."

Meredith gave a nervous laugh. "Hey, I was just joking. Let's go get some," she paused, trying to size up the maid, "some shots," she added hopefully.

Still clutching the camera to her ample bosom, Alicia smiled. "Now you're talking, baby. Let's go back to our place, have some tequila, smoke some weed and do some serious fucking." She resumed her descent and Meredith followed. "That'll fix you all up."

Our place. Weed. Fucking. With an involuntary shudder, Meredith rolled the words around in her mind. So they lived — and smoked pot and fucked — together. But where? "Right. Sounds good. Uh, but you better drive, Alicia, because I'm still a bit disoriented from the fall." Meredith rubbed her head for effect.

Alicia's exasperated sigh reverberated through the cavernous stairwell as she stopped in her tracks and looked at her boyfriend. "We don't have a car, Ricky," she said as if speaking to a two-year-old. "We live in the city, remember?" She tsked. "We take the bus." She continued tromping down the stairs. "I thought you told me you were off coke. You start up again, Ricky? That why you're acting so crazy? You better not be back on that shit 'cause it costs too much money, you hear me?"

"Coke...you mean cocaine?"

"*Duh*," Alicia answered.

Meredith laughed. "I can assure you, Alicia, I most definitely haven't partaken in any cocaine. Perhaps my behavior is simply a sort of...uh, belated consequence of having previously used the drug."

"Do you hear yourself?" Raising one hand high in the air and then letting it fall, slapping against her thigh, Alicia looked at her boyfriend as if he'd sprouted a third eye in the center of his forehead. "Shit, Ricky, you don't even talk like you anymore." She sighed again. "Come on, baby, let's get out of here so I can take care of you."

* * * * *

Surprisingly, the neighborhood looked pretty good and their apartment building wasn't bad either. The apartment itself was another matter. It was so crammed full of stuff, including Ricky's barbells and other workout equipment, that there wasn't much room to move around.

"What in the world is all this crap?" Meredith wondered aloud as she absently fingered a multitude of items.

"This *crap*, as you call it," Alicia said, "is all the expensive stuff you were supposed to get to that fence so we could make some money off of it. But you've been dragging your lazy ass for weeks."

"Fence," Meredith repeated quizzically as she gazed at the stacks and piles of assorted merchandise. "You mean, like a person who specializes in the purchase and sale of stolen property from thieves?" She looked at Alicia whose features were twisted with incredulity again.

"There you go again," Alicia said, shaking her head, "talking all weird. You sound like a fuckin' encyclopedia, Ricky."

121

"You and Ricky are thieves too?" Meredith continued, ignoring Alicia's comment.

"Oh for chrissakes, yes," Alicia spat back. "Of course me and *Ricky*," she shoved hard against her boyfriend's chest, "are thieves." And then she laughed. "Now you got any more dumbass questions, you big jerk?" She eased by Meredith with a disgusted huff and left the room.

When Alicia returned she was wearing a cropped T-shirt and a scanty pair of panties.

Meredith blanched when she saw that the camera was conspicuously absent. "Where's the camera, Alicia?"

"Maybe if you're real nice to me I'll let you know," she purred and then rubbed her backside against her boyfriend. "You get the Sherlock and the weed and I'll get the tequila." Alicia headed for the kitchen.

"*Sherlock?*" Meredith mumbled, scratching her head and looking around the crowded room. Maybe it was some sort of *in* thing young people did nowadays, she speculated—smoke marijuana while watching old Sherlock Holmes movies. Maybe it enhanced their high. Meredith shrugged as she scanned the room for videotapes or DVDs. All she found were three long-overdue horror DVDs from a video store.

In a moment Alicia returned with a half-empty bottle of tequila and a couple of shot glasses. Shifting her weight to one foot, she indulged in a loud tsk. "Well why are you just standing there like a bump on a log? Do I have to do everything around here?"

"Uh...there's so much stuff piled around here that I couldn't find the movies...or the weed."

Alicia set the bottle and glasses down, rolled her eyes skyward and sighed. "What movies, Ricky?"

"Eh...the Sherlock Holmes movies..." By the disgusted look on Alicia's face, Meredith had a strong hunch that she'd just made an ass out of herself again.

"Ricky, I swear to God, if you weren't such a good fuck I'd be outta here so fast it would make your head spin." She walked over to an end table, opened the drawer and returned with a colorful glass Sherlock Holmes-style pipe and a bag of pot. "Are you planning to sit there in that ugly uniform? Come on, baby, strip it off for me and get comfy."

Swallowing hard, Meredith shook her head. "No, I think I'm going to leave it on. It's kind of cold in here, don't you think?" She rubbed her meaty arms. "In fact, maybe you should put on a sweatshirt or something."

Alicia wasted no time striding over to Meredith and unfastening the buttons on Ricky's security guard uniform. "You just wanted me to do it for you, huh, babe?" She gave a throaty chuckle. "Okay, I don't mind, Ricky."

And then Alicia grabbed Meredith's man-crotch and squeezed.

Wide-eyed and yelping, Meredith leaped back from Alicia. "Don't do that," she said in a strained voice.

"Quit fuckin' around, Ricky. You half scared the shit out of me."

"Yeah, well that makes two of us," Meredith said, crossing one hand over her crotch and the other over her chest.

Alicia gave her another one of those dubious looks. "You get a hit on the head and all of a sudden you're acting like a queer."

"No, I'm *not* a lesbian."

"Well of course you're not a *lesbian*. You're a man for chrissakes! At least I thought you were. What the fuck is the matter with you? Now either you strip down to your underwear or I'll get a knife and slice that fuckin' uniform off of you." Alicia directed a venomous glare at her boyfriend. "Of course...if you don't want the camera then you can leave your clothes on and just get the fuck out of here instead." Flipping her hair, she smiled wickedly.

Gulping hard to dislodge her heart from her throat, Meredith unbuttoned the rest of her shirt, shrugging it off to reveal a white sleeveless tank-style undershirt. She looked down at her masculine chest, closing her eyes and groaning with angst as she spied the shirt molding itself to an impressive set of bulging pecs. After a moment she kicked off her shoes, tugged off the socks and then removed her belt, unzipped her trousers and stepped out of them, leaving her in a well-fitting pair of briefs.

"Mmm, now that's more like it," Alicia said, stepping closer.

"I've, uh, I've got to go to the bathroom." Meredith backed away abruptly.

Throwing her hands up into the air, Alicia breathed a sigh. "So go already."

Meredith looked to the left and then to the right before choosing a direction — the wrong one.

"That way, lamebrain," Alicia said, giving her head a toss in the right direction.

Once in the bathroom, Meredith leaned against the door and took a series of deep breaths. "How the hell am I going to do this?" she whispered to herself. She stepped to the mirror and looked at the reflection, studying it carefully. "Ricky, you sure are some hunky piece of work. Look at that hard sculpted body. It's no wonder Alicia can't keep her hands off of you."

Looking in the mirror and seeing a buff young man staring back at her was unnerving to say the least. She lifted the undershirt high on her chest and gazed at the very masculine fleshscape before her. Meredith haltingly ran her fingers across the extraordinary set of pecs — her pecs.

Ricky's muscular body reminded Meredith of Cristoval de Medina's deliciously sexy physique, making her remember the tantalizing kitchen-table fuck that had started her day. Was that really just this morning? It seemed like a lifetime ago.

After examining Ricky's chest, her fingers traveled down across the washboard abs and then to the waistband of Ricky's briefs. Swallowing hard, Meredith hooked her thumbs in the elastic and tugged down. Even limp, the size of Ricky's equipment was enormously promising. Meredith tentatively wrapped her fingers around the dormant shaft, twisting her features with disbelief at the peculiar experience. Allowing her gaze to slowly journey from her groin, back up across her abs, to her chest and then up to Ricky's handsome face, Meredith found herself getting turned on. This was definitely *way* too weird!

Shit! The thing in her hands was swelling!

Gasping, Meredith let loose of Ricky's burgeoning cock as if it were a red hot steel poker and yanked the briefs back up over it, hoping that maybe it would just go away. After tugging the undershirt back down, she leaned over the sink and stared at her reflection. Yesterday afternoon she was carefully applying makeup to her feminine features and now she was eyeing her five-o'clock shadow. She shuddered.

"Ricky? You fall asleep in there or something?" Alicia's voice called out, breaking through Meredith's reverie. "Come on, baby, I'm feeling lonely here without you."

Meredith sucked in a deep breath. If she went out there chances were that she was going to have to have sex with Alicia. Her jaw dropped in horror as she felt her cock swelling further. She shuddered again. How in the goddamned hell could she get turned on by thinking of another woman naked? She felt the torturous cock expand yet again at the thought and groaned.

Apparently it was true—men's cocks really *do* have a mind of their own!

If she had her druthers she'd certainly rather be fucking Ricky than Alicia. Meredith choked out laughter at that thought. Hell...in her present condition she'd be fucking herself! Of course, in order to do that she'd have to masturbate—jerk herself off.

Ricky's eager cock grew bigger.

"Jeezus," she said, looking down at the enthusiastic penis bulging in her pants, "enough already! What's with you, anyway?"

"If you don't get yourself out here," Alicia called, "I'm gonna leave and take that camera with me, Ricky, you hear? I'll bring it downtown to your media contact myself!"

Meredith heaved a mighty sigh. "Yeah. I'll be right there," she called out in her deep voice. "You can do it," she whispered to her bizarre reflection. "Just stick that impatient thing between your legs into Alicia's vagina and pump." She swallowed and rolled her eyes at the ultra-weird mental image. "Remember, this is for Jack. You've *got* to do this for Jack!"

Chapter Nine

 හ

"That's more like it," Alicia said, patting the floor beside her. "Come on and sit down." She held out a tall double-sized shot glass full of tequila as she took a long pull on the Sherlock.

Meredith joined Alicia on the floor and tossed back the liquor in two swallows, closing her eyes as the fiery liquid coursed down her throat. God she hated tequila but she was definitely going to need a hefty dose of mind-altering assistance to get through this. Alicia shoved the pipe at Meredith. She looked at it as if it were an alien.

"You got some really decent bud this time, Ricky. Nice and fluffy."

As a former goody-two-shoes, Meredith had never smoked pot before, but she'd seen it done often enough that she had a rough idea how to do it convincingly. She finally took the pipe and brought it to her lips, taking a deep drag. And then she felt Alicia's fingers wrap around her dick.

Naturally, Ricky's cock didn't miss an opportunity to swell.

After choking on the smoke and passing the pipe back to Alicia, Meredith reached for the bottle of tequila and poured herself another shot, which she slipped more slowly this time. When Alicia pulled her cropped shirt over her head, Meredith began to sweat. She couldn't help glancing at the other woman's breasts. They were so huge and high and firm that Meredith couldn't imagine they were nature-given, especially given Alicia's slim form. From a purely clinical aspect, Meredith had to admit that Alicia's breasts were, indeed, beautiful.

"Suck my tits, Ricky," Alicia said, shoving one erect nipple at her boyfriend's mouth.

Meredith felt her eyes grow large as saucers as she spied the approaching nipple and she gulped.

Then Alicia was straddling her and tugging the undershirt from Meredith's chest.

Meredith drank the rest of the booze in her glass and reached for the pipe again, dragging hard. *I can do this...I can do this...I can do this...* She felt a curious kind of pulling, tickling sensation in her balls — well, *Ricky's* balls — and then felt it snake up into her abdomen area. While it was strange, it was clearly a sexual sensation, not too unlike the sensations she'd felt as a woman when becoming sexually aroused.

Alicia pressed her nipple against her boyfriend's mouth as she flattened her hand against Ricky's broad chest and moaned. It was quite a curious thing to have a woman writhing with passion in her lap.

Taking a deep breath, Meredith took Alicia's nipple into her mouth, wincing as she felt that cock between her legs grow even larger. Since she'd been on the receiving end and knew what she liked, she experimented and did the same to Alicia, sucking, nipping and tugging. Oddly enough, Meredith was rather enjoying it, but she didn't want to spend even a moment pondering what that might mean about her sexuality. Uh-uh. She'd much rather divorce her logical mind from this totally bizarre happening and just make the best of it. Alicia's impassioned moans were a definite indication that Meredith was on the right track.

A few squeezes on Alicia's breasts confirmed Meredith's suspicions that her tits were bought and paid for rather than a natural phenomenon. Funny...she'd thought about gifting herself with a breast lift and enhancement for her fortieth birthday and instead here she was fondling another woman's perky boobs while the persistent pole of foreign flesh between her legs was doing some sort of throbbing dance. The thought almost made her laugh out loud until, suddenly, urgent signals of need—the need to whip that pulsating sucker out and plunge it into Alicia's pussy—scrambled to Meredith's head. How odd. How very strange...but interesting and fascinating at the same time. *So this is what happens to men during foreplay.* As Meredith skated her mouth from one of Alicia's breasts to the other, she became aware of her clinical logic and curiosity rapidly being pushed aside by an army of raging hormones.

Sex. Must...have...sex...now.

"Fuck me, Ricky. Fuck me hard and fast the way you know that I like it."

That did it. With mindless urgency Meredith shoved off her briefs while Alicia shimmied out of her panties. "Jesus, will you look at how big this thing is?" Meredith blurted once Ricky's cock had sprung free, saluting the ceiling. She took it in her hands and marveled at it. "I mean, look at it...it's bulging and throbbing and—" She paused in her admiration to look between Alicia's spread legs. "Wow...so that's the view men get. I had no idea it was so beautiful. All pink and moist and glistening and—"

"Ugh!" Alicia growled. "For chrissakes just shut up and fuck me already!"

Swallowing a huge gulp, Meredith positioned herself over Alicia as the other woman squirmed in anticipation. Meredith grasped Ricky's cock, which was straining and warm to the touch and, with a deep breath, she plunged it into Alicia. Incredible. Abso-fucking-lutely incredible. It was like sliding into a wet silky sleeve that was warm and inviting and alive with sensation. Meredith pulled back a bit and then shoved in again even harder, feeling the slap of Ricky's balls against Alicia's dewy flesh. As she pummeled Alicia's pussy, she was vaguely aware of how far-fetched all of this was, but the hormones or testosterone or whatever the hell it was inside Ricky's body had all but taken over her brain, impelling her to appease The Cock.

129

Nothing was more important at that moment than driving to completion and shooting hot streams of cum into Alicia's pussy. And so she did.

Meredith felt Ricky's body tighten in anticipation of impending climax. The potent sensation captured her in entirety as the first powerful waves of release took hold. For a moment she thought she'd go insane with pleasure because it was almost too much to bear. And then she felt Alicia's inner muscles squeezing, pulsing against her cock as the woman exploded with her own orgasm. At the pinnacle of deliciously painful pleasure, while cum spurted firm and swift, Meredith heard Ricky's voice bellow from her mouth in a satisfied roar and then she collapsed atop Alicia.

Meredith was limp, sated and unmindful of anything or anyone else in the universe. Her only thought was that of the supreme, ultimate gratification that permeated every fiber of her being. She wanted to stay like this for eternity.

"Get off me you big baboon. I can't breathe!" Alicia was pushing and shoving. With great effort, Meredith rolled her leaden form off Alicia and to the floor.

"What an incredible opportunity," Meredith whispered a moment later as she stared at the rotating ceiling fan. "To know firsthand what having sex feels like from a man's perspective."

"Still talkin' crazy talk." Alicia tsked.

"I'll never forget this experience. Ever. It was great. Astounding."

"Yeah, it was great, Ricky." Alicia pulled herself up on her elbows and eyed Meredith. "All sixty seconds of it."

Meredith slanted Alicia a quizzical look. "Really? It seemed like so much longer. Like I was suspended in some amazing pleasure zone for hours."

"Get real, minute-man."

"Sorry," Meredith said. "I couldn't help it. It just felt so damned good." She chuckled at that, remembering how many times she'd heard Jack say the same thing. "At least you had an orgasm."

"That's only because you're such a sexy hunk of beef, Ricky." Alicia gave a throaty chuckle. "You might be quicker than a speeding train sometimes but that's one hot engine you've got doing the driving." She licked her lips and changed positions so that her face was opposite Ricky's flaccid cock. "Mmm and I like the way you taste too."

And then she licked the cock.

And the cock twitched.

And then all those blazing hormones started scorching Meredith's brain again.

Little by little as Alicia twirled her tongue, licking off the cum as if it were chocolate syrup, the thing with a mind of its own between Meredith's legs came back to life...ready for another round.

Meredith watched, amazed. "Ricky's got pretty damned good recuperative powers," she said. "Must be his age."

Alicia's busy tongue stilled and Meredith heard another tsk. "Come on, baby, what's wrong with you? Maybe you should see a shrink or something."

Meredith laughed. "I was just teasing. Just seeing if you were paying attention," she lied. "Now why don't you just go on back to what you were doing with that talented little tongue of yours." She pushed Alicia's head back down to her groin. Funny how a person's sex drive can force them to block out all sorts of things when necessary. Things like the fact that Meredith had a cum-covered cock and another woman was making it all tidy with her tongue. And that Meredith was thoroughly enjoying it. Yeah...if she ever made it out of this she probably would need a shrink. But for now... "Take it into your mouth and suck it, Alicia."

As Alicia sucked, Meredith felt the cock growing harder. She experienced a remarkable sense of power as it became rigid. As if it had the strength to batter down stone walls. Just that thought alone was responsible for releasing another sequence of insistent hormones throughout her system. She wanted to shove, to ram, to dominate, to conquer. The magnitude of those feelings were fairly foreign but exceptionally appealing nonetheless. *Gotta be the testosterone.*

Meredith watched Alicia giving the blowjob and got so turned on that she almost came. But she wanted to possess Alicia's mouth first—to show her who was boss. Meredith's hips bucked involuntarily and Alicia's eyes widened as the cock pushed against the back of her throat. Yeah. That was good—the way it looked, the way it felt, all of it. Meredith reached out and caught one of Alicia's dangling nipples in her fingers and she pinched. Hard. Alicia moaned and sucked the cock harder. Meredith pinched her other nipple and thrust the cock deep into Alicia's mouth. The woman moaned her pleasure and increased the pace as her mouth slid up and down her boyfriend's cock. These new macho sensations were fascinating and Meredith was determined to experience them all as long as she was stuck in a man's body.

From somewhere in the recesses of her mind—or Ricky's, she couldn't be sure—the overwhelming urge to spank Alicia's ass took hold. Without taking the time to think about it, Meredith clapped Ricky's big hand across Alicia's ass. In what seemed like an instant both Alicia and Meredith spiraled into orgasms, with Alicia swallowing every last drop of her boyfriend's cum and murmuring little mewing sounds of contentment.

Lord that was satisfying! Commanding. Controlling. Dominating. Me Tarzan, you Jane. Me Conqueror of the World, you Wench who Services my Mighty Cock.

Oh good grief, Meredith, get a grip!

If this was how the thought process worked inside men's heads, no wonder they could be such giant assholes sometimes.

As Ricky's happy-as-a-clam cock rested limp and replete against his groin, Meredith sensed the plucky feelings of manly bravado subsiding. Good. She needed to think clearly, without the intrusion of all those pesky male hormones. All she had to do was to get the camera back and destroy the film and then Jack and Karyn would be safe. Then she'd be out of there and, hopefully, on her way to Heaven—and even more hopefully, in her own body and not Ricky's.

She glanced down at Alicia, who'd curled up and snuggled against her boyfriend's side. She looked so sweet and innocent like that. Meredith wondered where the girl had gone wrong, how she could have become such a heartless, guiltless little thief. Maybe she'd been abused as a child. Maybe some bastard had forced himself on her. Meredith's womanly instincts surfaced and she pitied the poor girl. Without thinking, she gently stroked Alicia's hair. Eyes still closed, Alicia planted a kiss on Ricky's abdomen and purred. Meredith continued to stroke the girl's hair, plotting out the best way to retrieve the camera and be done with all of this. In the guise of Ricky she'd managed to give Alicia two orgasms— not bad for being a first time cock-thruster—so that should count for something. No doubt Alicia would be much more amenable to handing the camera over to her boyfriend now. She probably wasn't such a bad kid after all. She just needed some love and understanding. Someone to guide her to the light side. Someone who would take the time to—

"Your turn, Ricky." Alicia traced the outlines of Ricky's six-pack abs with her finger.

"Huh?" Meredith propped her head up. "My turn to what?"

"To eat me."

Meredith bolted up into a sitting position. No. Uh-uh. No way. She absolutely could not and would not do...*that*. "Uhhhhhhhh..." What the hell could she say? *Sorry, Alicia, the thought of sticking my face in your crotch and licking your pussy makes me gag?* Chances are she wouldn't get the camera with that line. "I've, uh...I've had a sore throat for the last couple of days. And a cough too." Meredith coughed for emphasis.

"We'd better wait until I'm better so I don't infect you with all those germs." She coughed again. There, that wasn't so hard. That sounded perfectly feasible and logical.

Alicia sat up and iced Meredith with a glacial gaze. "I just fucking swallowed for you, Ricky. I want your mouth on me now, mister." She leaned back, propping herself on her elbows and then spread her legs, lifting her knees slightly. Her fur-framed pussy lips were open just enough for Meredith to spy the primed orifice.

Did men get hot flashes? Because if they did, Ricky's body was definitely having one now. Not like a hot-sexy flash…more like a hot-sweaty-sick-all-over kind of flash.

"Alicia, baby, you know how much I love you." Meredith stroked Alicia's arm and shoulder. "You know that you mean the world to me and that I'd do anything to make you happy, but I just really can't do this right now. I promise—I swear to God—that I'll give you the best damned oral sex in the world tomorrow. As many times as you want. But I just can't do it right now."

"Listen, you big moron, I don't know what you're trying to pull but you know our deal. If one gets eaten, so does the other. Then and there. Not the next day."

"Yeah but—"

"But nothing. You still want your camera back, don't you?"

Panic flooded Meredith's insides. "Yes."

"Well, if you don't get your mouth down here and get to work in the next sixty seconds, you'll never see your fucking camera again. I'll sell those photos of Dr. Jack myself and make a bundle. I'll be living the life of luxury in that mansion in Beverly Hills we dreamed about. But it won't be you I'll be fucking. No, Ricky, it'll be my personal harem made up of our sexy pool boy, the hunky gardener, my personal butler and the muscular chauffeur instead."

Bitch. Cruel, heartless, selfish little bitch.

Meredith couldn't believe that she'd been making excuses for the girl and feeling sorry for her just a few minutes ago. Clearly, she didn't have a choice. Eat Alicia and get the camera or condemn Jack and Karyn to dire fates. She was fucked. As that bleak thought crossed her mind, the distinct sound of Dev's fiendish laughter permeated her senses.

And then Dev's voice followed. "Oh this ought to be good. I've got a batch of hot buttered popcorn in my lap and I'm ready to watch the show."

"This is *not* funny, Dev!" Meredith spat.

"What the fuck are you talking about, Ricky?" Alicia slanted Meredith a look of confused irritation.

Another string of wicked cackles and then Dev's annoying presence was gone. Alicia hadn't seemed to hear anything and Meredith realized she was the only one who could hear Dev.

"Nothing. Okay, Alicia, we'll do it your way but I want the camera first."

Alicia cackled. "What? Are you saying you don't trust me, Ricky?"

"Just give me the camera."

"How do I know you won't bolt?"

"You have my word."

"And you expect me to trust you?"

"Yes. Now give me the camera so we can...so I can..."

"Eat my pretty pussy?" Alicia flapped her thighs open and closed.

Meredith expelled a weighty sigh. "Yes."

Alicia popped up from her come-hither position and disappeared into the bedroom, returning a moment later with the camera. She set it on the coffee table and curled her lip into a half-grin. "It stays here until you finish. Then it's all yours."

Meredith nodded. "Deal." As she eyed the camera she smiled. She wouldn't have to stick her face in Alicia's eager crotch after all! Hell, she was a big, strong muscle-bound man and Alicia was just a little slip of a thing—aside from the huge fake tits. While they were impressive, they weren't much of a weapon. Meredith could overtake her easily. All she had to do was to grab the camera and yank out the film, exposing it to the light, and she'd be done with it.

Alicia stood arms akimbo, legs spread, looking down at Meredith. "Well? What are you waiting for?"

The heart in Ricky's chest thumped like a bongo. In the next instant, Meredith leaped to her feet and made a dash for the camera. Alicia slapped her hands over it first and clutched it to her chest. With relative ease, save for the cat scratches from a wild Alicia, Meredith wrenched the camera out of her hands.

"You sonuvabitch. I knew you were lying to me, Ricky." Alicia leapt up and clawed at Ricky's hair, grabbing a fistful and yanking his head back. Then she sank her teeth into her boyfriend's triceps. Meredith yowled in pain.

"I don't expect you to understand this, Alicia, but I love Jack," Meredith said, shaking her arm to dislodge the hellcat, "and I can't let you hurt him. He doesn't deserve it."

"You what?!" Alicia gasped, flipped herself around, landing in front of Meredith and then she punched Meredith hard in the gut, eliciting a loud, masculine *ooph* from Ricky's lungs. "That's for not telling me you're gay, Ricky—and for cheating on me. I hope you like the way McKenna sucks your dick, because I sure as hell won't be doing it again."

The punch hurt like hell, knocking some of the wind out of her, but Meredith maintained her grip on the camera. She turned it over, searching for the little door where the film rested, wrestling with Alicia all the while. After Alicia jumped on her back Meredith finally realized that it was a digital camera. It took considerable effort to shrug Alicia off, and when she did, she gave the woman a shove, making Alicia topple backwards over the coffee table.

"You fuckin' bastard," Alicia growled as she scrambled up from the floor. "If I catch you, Ricky, so help me I'll rip your balls off and feed them to the crows."

Camera in hand, Meredith leapt over the piles of stolen merchandise and worked her way to the door of the apartment, racing out, down the stairs and out the door of the building without looking back.

She had probably run more than a block before she remembered that she was stark naked. It was all that swinging and flapping of that thing between her legs that finally clued her in.

Shit! Shit, shit, shit!

Already attracting the unwanted attention of gawkers and disrupting traffic, Meredith slipped into an alley and pressed herself into the shadows. She was breathing heavily but not nearly as much as if she'd been in her own body. Hell, if she'd been in her own body she'd probably be dead by now after barreling down all those flights of stairs and running like a race horse for a block nonstop.

Oh. She forgot. She already was dead.

Shit.

Meredith turned her attention to the camera, trying to turn the damn thing on so she could view the pictures and then delete them. Ricky's fingers were so big, thick and cumbersome it was hard to maneuver them over the tiny buttons and levers. Finally the device whirred to life and Meredith pressed the review button. Nothing. No pictures. She wasn't an expert on digital cameras, not having purchased one yet, but Karyn was a photo buff, always showing Meredith her latest pictures in her camera's viewfinder. Meredith remembered Karyn talking about putting in a new memory card to store more pictures. Yes…that was it. The pictures were stored on the camera's memory card. Now Meredith just had to figure out how to access it.

After what seemed like an eternity she found the menu item that allowed the user to switch between the camera's memory and the removable memory card. She switched it to memory card mode. Nothing. Just a blank screen. Frustrated beyond belief, Meredith opened the compartment that housed the memory card. The chamber was empty.

Alicia! That conniving little bitch had already removed it.

And that meant Meredith had failed…she'd failed Jack.

All the pent-up fear, disappointment, hope and despair came crashing out of Meredith in a gush of tears. There she stood, six-foot-whatever of naked solid muscle and she was bawling like a baby.

And the sobbing noise emanating from Ricky's vocal chords wasn't very pretty.

"Stop it. Stop it right now," Meredith chastised herself as she hiccupped and gulped for air. "Standing here blubbering isn't going to help Jack or Karyn." She swiped Ricky's meaty paws across her eyes and down her cheeks. She had to get that memory card from Alicia before the bitchy little larcenist sold the pictures and skipped town.

With a deep cleansing breath, Meredith bolted from the alley and broke into a run—disregarding the flapping thing between her legs.

That's when she heard the police siren.

Chapter Ten

໓

"Officer, I can explain," Meredith said as she stood spread eagle with her hands up against a brick wall.

The cop snickered. "This ought to be good. Muldoon," he called to his partner still in the squad car, "get over here."

Meredith peered over her shoulder to see the tall skinny cop who'd stopped her and his roly-poly sidekick exiting the car. "I live just down the street," she explained, "with my girlfriend and she kicked me out after we had a fight."

"And so you decided to prance around the city in your birthday suit, huh?" Muldoon said. "Yeah, sounds logical to me. What about you, Kravitz?"

"I say this guy's strung out on dope."

"No! No, I'm not on anything. Honest. She locked me out, officers. All my clothes are in the apartment. I was just…just trying to find something to cover myself with when you showed up."

Kravitz nodded. "In the alley? You figured you'd roll some poor old bum and steal his clothes." He huffed. "What a prince."

"Look, this is serious." Meredith growled in frustration. "I'm going to be completely honest with you because time is of the essence. My girlfriend and I are criminals. We took compromising photos of a celebrity and we were planning to sell them to the highest bidder. But I had a change of heart and tried to talk her out of it. That's when she kicked me out. If we don't stop her she'll skip town and the guy's life will be ruined." Meredith turned to look at the cops, covering Ricky's cock, which had shrunk to the size of a cashew, with her hands. "Please, you have to help me get those photos before someone's life is destroyed."

The cops looked at each other, devoid of laughter. "Full name and address," Kravitz said, flipping out a small pad of paper and a pen.

"I'm Ricky and she's Alicia. Um…" What the hell were the last names Dev had mentioned? Meredith drew a blank and frowned. "I don't remember the last names and…" she looked skyward and gulped, "I don't know the address. But I remember which building it is."

Muldoon shook his head. "Doesn't know his name or address. What, are you just outta kindergarten or something? Or are you just trying to be funny?"

"It's complicated," Meredith said. "Dev, help me here, please," she whispered, looking skyward again and then, realization dawning, shifting her gaze down to the ground. "Just give me their names and address."

"You've got to be kidding, pumpkin," Dev's chuckling voice oozed. "I'm not the good guys, remember? You're on your own…and I'm enjoying every agonizing minute of it."

"Damn," Meredith mumbled.

"See," Kravitz said, "he's talking to himself. I told you he's on something. I say we haul his ass in."

And that's when Meredith started to cry again. Fat, wailing, unattractive sobs that shook her big manly body.

"Aw Jesus Christ," Muldoon said. "Knock it off."

"Please, officers, I know it sounds strange and I know it seems like I'm drunk or on drugs but you have to believe me. I'm telling you the God's honest truth and we're wasting precious time. For God's sake, *please* help me."

The cops looked at each other. Muldoon yanked a handkerchief from his pocket. "Here, quit crying and clean yourself up." He turned to his partner. "Maybe we should check his story out."

Kravitz shrugged. "Why not. It's a slow morning anyway."

"It's just a few buildings away," Meredith offered hopefully. "That one, I think." She pointed. "No, wait. It's that's building. Yeah, I remember the ornately turned scrollwork flourish embellishing the wrought iron gate."

"You hear that?" Muldoon said. "He's a queer."

"I am not," Meredith protested. "And I'm not a lesbian either."

"Naw, I just think his brain is fried," Kravitz offered. "I'll escort nature boy here on foot, you can follow in the squad." Kravitz jangled a pair of handcuffs and Meredith blanched.

"Cuffs? You're going to handcuff me?" Her chin quivered and she cried harder.

Muldoon and Kravitz exchanged rolling-eye glances.

"He seems harmless enough," Muldoon said.

"I won't cause any trouble," Meredith said. "I promise." She wiped her eyes and blew her nose then extended the handkerchief to Muldoon, whose lip curled.

"That's okay," he said before getting back into the car, "you keep it."

They'd only gone a short distance when Meredith gasped and pointed. "That's her! That's Alicia, standing at the curb!" Meredith broke into a full run with Kravitz right on her heels.

"Hold it, kid," Kravitz was shouting. "You can't go running around the streets of Portland like that with your dick hanging out."

"Alicia! Alicia, stop!" Meredith screamed, well, with Ricky's deep voice it was more of a bellow. "I need that memory card."

"Just stay away from me, Ricky," Alicia yelled back. She reached into her purse and then braced her arm close against her side, her hand outstretched.

Meredith was less than a hundred feet away from her now. She heard Kravitz yelling something in the distance but her adrenaline was pumping so hard and fast she couldn't focus on whatever it was he was saying. The only thing that mattered was getting the card with Jack's photos.

"I'm warning you, Ricky. Don't come any closer. Don't make me hurt you."

Meredith hesitated only a fraction of a second. Whatever Alicia was holding looked too small to be a gun. It could have been a small knife, in which case Meredith knew she could overpower her easily. But whatever it was, she sure as hell wasn't about to wimp out now and risk Jack's future. She kept advancing toward Alicia.

"I've got the cops with me, Alicia. They know everything. Give up the memory card."

"You're not gonna fuck this up for me, Ricky, cops or no cops."

Meredith was close enough now to see the tears streaming down Alicia's cheeks. A few more feet and she'd be close enough to grab her. And then she heard a couple of pops and felt something hot invading her chest.

Her gaze dropped to Alicia's trembling hand then and she saw the petite derringer, still pointing at Ricky. Well sonuvabitch. What do you know about that...it was a gun after all.

It was getting hard to breathe, but she kept on running. And then she heard another pop and felt liquid fire burning in her lungs. It felt like she was moving in slow motion, almost like running through a sea of molasses. Ricky's body was buff and strong and in shape—his body wouldn't let her down. Not now. It couldn't. She *had* to save Jack and Karyn. Nothing else mattered. She watched as a late-model sedan came to a screeching stop at the curb. The passenger door swung open and Alicia scurried in. The car burned rubber, fishtailed and then raced out of sight.

No. *No!* She was so close. It wasn't fair! Meredith tried to scream out Alicia's name again but nothing but warm liquid came out of her mouth. Meredith saw the squad with Muldoon at the wheel speed by, siren blaring, in hot pursuit. Kravitz caught up with Meredith, holding his side and gasping for breath, just as she fell to her knees on the pavement.

"I'm getting too old for this," Kravitz wheezed as he got down on his knees and supported Meredith. "Damn it, kid, I yelled out that she had a gun. Why didn't you get down when I told you to?"

Meredith had been so intent on getting the memory card from Alicia that she never heard Kravitz's warning over the pounding pulse in her ears. Kravitz seemed like a nice man. She wanted to tell him it wasn't his fault. She wanted to explain everything to him, the whole sordid story, but she felt herself drifting in and out of consciousness. She slumped to the side and Kravitz cradled her, holding Ricky's injured body in his arms.

She heard him talking on his phone or radio or whatever it was. Something about backup. Something about an ambulance. She did her best to point in the direction of Alicia's getaway car and then she managed to gurgle out the word *please*.

After that, everything went black.

* * * * *

It was the steady beeping that roused Meredith. Or maybe it was the voices. She didn't know where she was...or whose body she was in. She had tubes sticking out of her and it hurt to breathe. She must be in the hospital. This time, unlike the time she'd stepped into a nonexistent elevator car and plunged several stories before landing, Meredith knew she was dying. She could feel it. Sense it.

And she'd failed. She remembered that. Alicia still had the memory card with the photos.

"His name is Richard Scholl. Goes by Ricky. He's one of the security guards at the Northwest Passage Hotel downtown where you're staying."

That was Kravitz the cop. Meredith recognized his voice.

"Yeah, I recognize him. But why does he want to see me?"

Jack. That was Jack's voice! Meredith tried to call out his name but it just came out as a moan.

"Claims he was trying to stop his girlfriend, Alicia Gonciarz, the hotel maid who found you, from having some compromising photos of you published. Ever since we brought him here a couple of hours ago he's been asking for you."

Meredith sensed it when Jack neared her bed. She could feel him, smell him. She opened her eyes and looked up at Jack. He looked drained and tired and stressed. And it was all her fault.

"Is he going to make it?" Jack asked. Meredith didn't have to see Kravitz or the doctor she'd heard in the background shaking their heads *no*, because she already knew she was going to die. She just needed to hold on long enough to talk to Jack. If she could just explain...just apologize...

"Hey, Ricky. It's me, Jack McKenna. I hear you've been asking for me."

"Jack," Meredith whispered with great difficulty. "So sorry...love you...Meredith."

She saw Jack's eyebrows knit. "What about Meredith, Ricky? Do you know where she is? Is she all right?"

"That your wife?" Kravitz asked.

"My ex-wife. I've been trying to contact her ever since...well, for the last few hours."

"It's...me...I'm M—" The admission choked in Meredith's throat. Damn. Dev had stuck to her guns and wouldn't allow Meredith to tell Jack who she really was, even now. She felt a fat tear escape and trickle down the outside of her cheek. Crying made breathing more difficult. She had to stay calm. She swallowed hard and tried again.

"She...sorry...loves...you.　　　　　　　Loves...Karyn. Meredith...so...sorry."

"Ricky, how do you know about my ex-wife and her friend? How did you know she did this to me?"

"Did what?" Kravitz asked.

"Nothing," Jack said. "It's not important."

"Apparently it is," Kravitz said, "to the kid, anyway." Kravitz hiked his thumb toward Meredith. "Important enough to risk his life."

"Gentlemen, you're overtaxing my patient. I'm going to have to ask you to leave."

Meredith's pain-riddled chest burned with panic. "No! ...Stay."

"It's okay, kid, we're not going anywhere," Kravitz said. "You just settle down now and try to keep as comfortable as possible."

"Alicia..." Meredith whispered.

"Don't worry. We called in plenty of backup and caught her and the driver."

A pleasant sense of elation blanketed the pain in Meredith's chest. "Memory...card?"

"It's at the bottom of the Willamette River. Muldoon said she was one helluva feisty little firecracker." Kravitz chuckled softly. "Near beat the hell out of him while he was trying to cuff her. During the scuffle the memory card flew out of her hand and off the Burnside Bridge. Trust me, nobody'll be seeing those pictures now, kid, so you can rest easy."

"Thank...you...God...Jack, Karyn safe..." Meredith's eyelids fluttered closed.

"Ricky," Jack said, "what about Meredith? Please, Ricky. Is she okay? Has anyone hurt her?"

As she looked up and Jack and saw the concern in his eyes—the love for *her* in his eyes—Meredith's entire being filled with a soothing comfort unlike anything she'd ever known before. "Meredith okay...happy...never better."

And when she closed her eyes this time, she was aware of her spirit lifting from Ricky's body. The next thing she knew, she was floating near the ceiling of the hospital room and looking down at Ricky, Jack, Kravitz, the doctor and a flurry of medical people scurrying around. The monitor she'd been hooked up to had straight-lined, with a steady, uninterrupted tone.

Ricky was dead.

She was dead.

Jack was safe.

Karyn was safe.

And Meredith had never felt happier or more content.

Chapter Eleven

ॐ

Meredith held out her hands and studied them through the fog-like mist surrounding her. They were *her* hands, not Ricky's! She latched on to a hunk of hip and pressed her thumb and fingers into the ample flesh, delighting in the suppleness where Ricky's hips had been slim and unyielding. It was probably the only time she could ever remember actually being happy to feel that excess padding. Next she fastened her hands to her breasts, squeezing them just to make sure they were really there. And finally, clamping her hand against her crotch, a squeal of unbridled joy tripped past her lips at the confirmation that there wasn't a pulsing cock there instead of a nice soft pussy. *Yes!* She was back in her own wonderfully soft, round and curvy female body.

"I'm all woman again. Thank you G—"

Her words were cut off when a strip of duct tape clapped across her mouth.

"I'm profoundly disappointed in you, Meredith. I had such high hopes for you."

At the unmistakable sound of Dev's voice, Meredith froze. Something had gone terribly wrong if she was still stuck in this hell hole with the Queen of Vexation. She took in the familiar surroundings as the haze cleared and tore the tape from her face, wincing at the sting. "What am I doing back down here? I thought I was going to—"

"Don't say it," Dev commanded, jabbing an accusatory finger at Meredith. "Do *not* let me hear the H word come out of those lips."

Four pieces of duct tape promptly slapped across Meredith's lips in crisscross fashion. She ripped them off, grumbling in frustration. "Stop doing that!"

"Only when you stop invoking those infuriating words." Dev folded her arms across her chest, thrusting her chin into the air like a stubborn child.

"Okay, Dev, I've *really* had enough of your immature fun and games. I thought you and I were finished...so why am I here instead of..." Meredith silently hiked a thumb heavenward. If she had to spend much more time with devil-woman and her warped sense of humor she'd probably go insane.

"Standard technicalities, darling." Dev strutted leisurely, circling Meredith as she dragged from a ruby-encrusted cigarette holder. Meredith watched as the train from Dev's killer red-beaded gown swept the marble floor. "There are particulars which must be tended to before your reprieve is final. That is...*if* it's final. I haven't decided if I want to let you go just yet."

Before Meredith had a chance to open her mouth in wailing protest, a resplendent bolt of lightning flashed and thunder roared overhead. With a narrow-eyed glare, Dev angled her face up and shook a fist into the air.

"Damn! I was just teasing her. You never let me have any fun anymore!" She took another drag from the jeweled holder and curls of smoke streamed from her nose. "Sometimes this job really sucks," she grumbled, returning her attention to Meredith. "I need a drink." A quick flick of her wrist and her fingers encircled the stem of a glass containing a six-olive martini, which Dev promptly guzzled.

"So that means I made it?" Meredith asked cautiously. "I'm getting out of Hell?"

"Yes, yes, yes," Dev answered with a dismissive wave and monumental sigh. "And whatever you do, don't gloat. Gloating will definitely extend your stay."

Meredith breathed an audible sigh of relief. "So what happens next? What do we have to do?"

Flitting the empty glass from her hand and off somewhere into thin air, Dev paced. "As I said earlier, Meredith, I'm truly disappointed in you. I was looking forward to having you stay on. We could be best buddies. Just like you and Karyn—except better, because I'm not dreary and tedious like your tubby dishwater-blonde friend. And look at the tantalizing opportunities I can offer you. Think about it. How many other women do you know who've had the chance to experience sex from a man's point of view, hmm? Be honest now, wasn't that fun?"

"It was...different." Meredith rolled her eyes at the memory, recalling how she'd just barely avoided having to eat Alicia's pussy. "I admit that it was an eye-opener but it's not something I'd want to repeat any time soon."

"Don't you see? That's the beauty of it, Meredith. It wouldn't have to be anytime soon...you'd have all eternity. Ooh, here's a thought." Nodding in contemplation, Dev tapped her chin. "What about something like this for a change?" She gestured dramatically and an erotic scene unfolded before them. Meredith recognized her kitchen-table lover, Cristoval, herself in Ricky's body and Alicia—all naked, moaning and writhing together. "See, this way you'd be experiencing sex while in a man's body but with the added enjoyment of adding another sexy man to the mix. Giant turn-on, take it from me."

Meredith didn't want to watch but she felt compelled to look as Ricky fucked Alicia doggy style while Alicia sucked on Cristoval's cock and he teased her nipples. The grunting, the groaning, the facial expressions, the perceived pleasure of it all had the soft flesh between Meredith's thighs drenching.

"Or maybe you'd like to be in Cristoval's body instead." With a snap of Dev's fingers the change took place. Now Meredith was no longer merely a voyeur, she was a participant in the action—inside of Cristoval's body and experiencing everything he was feeling as Alicia sucked his cock. As the sensations built, Meredith found herself getting carried away with the lusty desire that coursed through the man's system. She didn't want this and yet she did. She struggled to bring her focus back to what was important—getting the hell out of Hell.

"Delicious, hmm? The best of all worlds!" Dev said, beaming a bright smile. Her expression clearly suggested that she thought Meredith would share her glee at being confined together for eons, engaging in all sorts of bizarre sexual adventures.

"Dev," Meredith ground out, Cristoval's body close to climax, "please put me back in my own body."

"A foursome, hmm? Why that's perfect, Meredith. Now you're getting in the spirit."

"No, I—"

Before Meredith could voice her protest, Dev twirled her finger and the setting changed. Meredith found herself naked, in her own body, being sexually ministered to by Cristoval, Ricky and Alicia. Mouths on her breasts, one cock in her pussy, another in her mouth and fingers kneading her clit. As much as she didn't want to enjoy it, it was wild, wet and wonderful. Sinfully pleasurable. Except for the fact that, with a snap of Dev's fingers, the scenario went up in a poof of smoke...the split second before Meredith corkscrewed into a rip-roaring orgasm. Damn, that was evil.

"And why limit it to just four?" Dev said.

Meredith clapped her hand over Dev's outstretched arm before she had a chance to zap up a multi-partner orgy. "No more. I appreciate the offer, Dev, but—" Dev's hand shot up, clenching a big red stop sign and Meredith sighed.

"All right, maybe hammering some broad with your very own ten-inch cock or participating in a multi-ménage isn't exactly your thing—although I can't imagine why not," Dev said. "But that's not your only alternative. Stay here with me,

Meredith, and I'll make every sexual fantasy you ever dreamed of come to life. Just imagine…the actual men of your innermost fantasies…" She snapped her fingers and three gorgeous, well-muscled specimens of manhood appeared. As if they'd stepped right out of Meredith's secret fantasy life, one was garbed in a brief leather loincloth, one wore a torn T-shirt and jeans that just begged to be ripped from his hard body and the last wore sexy, chest-baring pirate gear and a patch over one eye. Meredith's personal fantasy men — in the flesh. Their hair, eyes, features, bodies and costumes were exactly the way she'd so often pictured them as she'd pleasured herself with her fingers or a vibrator. Meredith watched them looking at her with their hungry, predatory smiles and she swallowed hard.

"Perfect sex…" Dev said with a wave of her hand and immediately three of Meredith's most delicious covert sex fantasies were being played out right in front of her. And there she was at the center of each mouthwatering scenario, having the most marvelously equipped and skilled lovers seeing to her every need…her every whim. Worshipping her entire body as if she were a goddess. Everything they did was perfect, exactly how she wanted it. An involuntary moan escaped Meredith's lips. She found her gaze locked on the intensely erotic scenes and felt her knees buckle as her clit quivered and her pussy trickled.

"Stupendous orgasms…" Dev said, gesturing with a grand flourish. Meredith's heartbeat raced as she watched herself succumbing to the lusty bliss of pre-climax with each lover. One lover rammed his thick, long cock into her, positioning it so that each time he plunged in and out it abraded her clitoris. The second lover plunged his magnificent cock into her hard and fast while he expertly fingered her clit. The third lover pinched and plucked her rigid nipples while his teeth and tongue worked their magic on the tender, swollen nub beneath her pussy lips. And then suddenly the sensations of each orgasm transferred into Meredith's body, so that she was not only watching but actively experiencing three separate, mind-boggling orgasms at once. *Three!* The passion, pain and pleasure were so intense, so all-encompassing, so jarring that Meredith screamed and fell to her knees. Her hands flew between her legs, frantically clutching at her crotch through her dress as wave after powerful wave of shuddering vibrations pulsed through her. It was too much. Inconceivable ecstasy ripped through her being with such magnitude that Meredith was certain she'd die — again. She wanted it to stop. She wanted it to last forever. Such sweet relentless torment.

When the final quaking jolts subsided, Meredith realized she'd been crying. Tears of joy…tears of rapture and supreme sexual satisfaction.

"And that's just for starters," Dev said, joining Meredith on the floor and sitting cross legged as cigarettes popped into their hands. "Stick with me and your clit will remain in a constant state of heightened quivernation. Oh…*quivernation*…I like that word. Don't you? I just made it up. I'll have to add that one to my sex dictionary. Quivernation. The state of being in continuous quivers. To quivernate." Dev nodded, clearly quite pleased with herself.

Feeling more limp, lethargic and sexually fulfilled than she'd ever been before, Meredith lazily studied the lighted object in her fingers. "I don't smoke."

"Why? Afraid it'll kill you?" Dev laughed. "Go ahead, darling, live dangerously. There's nothing like a good smoke after a perfect fuck." She drew in a deep drag and elbowed Meredith, encouraging her to follow suit. When Meredith just sat there, Dev rolled her eyes and snapped her fingers, replacing the cigarette with a candy version instead. "Guess you'll just have to take baby steps."

Meredith frowned. None of this was making any sense — but then not much had since she'd fallen down that elevator shaft. That was the best damned experience she'd ever known. Not the elevator shaft — the triple orgasm. Nothing, not chocolate, not *anything* could ever begin to touch the unparalleled sensation of that phenomenal experience. She wanted more of it. She wanted to see her fantasy hunks in the flesh again. Touch them. Lick them. Fuck them. She wanted to spiral into...into *quivernation* and stay there, dying a thousand pleasurable deaths from the utter overdose of bliss.

But this was Hell.

And Meredith had a sneaking suspicion that there was more to life in Hell than orgasmic ecstasy and doing lunch with the Mistress of Darkness. Nope. There was a monumental catch somewhere, she was sure of it. Maybe she'd be in the throes of passion with one of her fantasy hunks only to have him morph into a slimy green toad just as he was tonguing her clit. And then she'd hear Dev's depraved cackle in the background, enjoying Meredith's horrified reaction. Or maybe all her fantasy men would get some dreaded penis malady that turned their stunning cocks into shriveled pinto beans. Or maybe...

"So what do you say? Is it a deal? Could you envision yourself spending an eternity ensconced in a permanent cloak of sheer sexual perfection? Having all the Belgian milk chocolate your heart desires, without ever gaining an ounce or getting zits or worrying about developing diabetes? Having the power to change your appearance any way you like—the look...the age...the shape...the height...the weight...the color. Having an unlimited stable of handsome, rigid and ready sex studs eager to satisfy your every whim? You name it and it's yours. Whatever you wish for, whatever you yearn for...it would be yours. Just like that. All you'd have to do is to wish for it and it would become a reality." Dev cuddled up to Meredith, squeezing her into a buddy hug.

"This isn't something I offer to just anyone, Meredith. A deal like this is only for the cream of the crop. Like you. I see vast potential in you, Meredith." Dev brought her lips to Meredith's ear and whispered, "You have the ability to rise up in the ranks of Hell and be among my inner circle. A ruler rather than a minion. All you have to do is to agree. Just say yes and it will be done." And then her voice became even

153

quieter as if it were a mist of thought floating across Meredith's mind. "So easy...so perfect...so simple...you can have it all..."

Ahhhh...such sweet, palpable temptation. Dev painted such an idyllic picture. Everything and anything that Meredith could ever desire. Maybe she could do it. Maybe whatever price she had to pay would be worth it. Sound, logical reasoning warred with lust and yearning deep in Meredith's soul. It was almost as if she had a tiny cartoon devil whispering of untold gratification and excess in one ear and an angel whispering in the other, reminding Meredith that this was Hell. And Dev was the Devil...Satan—or his wife or whatever. And Satan was an evil trickster.

Meredith shuddered. "And what exactly would you expect of me if I agreed to remain here, Dev? You make an eternity in Hell sound like my idea of..." By now she knew better than to say the H word. "Of the upper dominion," she said, carefully measuring her words. "And I know it can't be like that. Come on, Dev...what's the catch? Because I know there is one."

Dev dropped her arm from Meredith's shoulder and chuckled. With a snap of her fingers they were both sitting at a gilded mahogany desk with a sheaf of papers unfurled before them.

"You don't have a thing to worry about. Everything's in the contract, Meredith. Right at the bottom in the fine print. Trust me, it's nothing you need to bother yourself with." A feather quill pen appeared in Meredith's hand. "Now all I need is your signature and your new life of incalculable pleasure within this glorious domain can begin. Just a tiny prick of your finger and we'll have all the blood we need to make your signature official." As Dev spoke the words, Meredith felt a stinging sensation in her finger and looked down to see a trickle of blood.

"I'm a stickler for detail," Meredith said, flipping through the lengthy document until she reached the last several pages.

"Whew, that's an awful lot of fine print, Dev." She squinted. "And it's so small." Meredith held the paper close and then again at arm's length, trying to focus.

"Presbyopia." Dev shook her head and tsked. "Pity."

"What?"

"It's an age-associated progressive loss of focusing power," Dev explained with a shrug. "It happens about the time people turn forty and that's why they need reading glasses. Of course…" she studied her crimson nails and blew on them, "you won't have to worry about that or any other age-related woes once you sign the contract." She smiled and patted Meredith's shoulder.

"Mmm-hmm. Just the same, I think I'll read it first. Can I have a magnifying glass or something?"

Dev patted her dress, as if searching for the object. Then she opened the desk drawer and felt around inside. "Sorry, dear. Looks like I don't have one handy. Believe me, Meredith, the fine print is nothing to worry about. Just a few teensy stipulations, that's all. Now go ahead and sign it before the blood dries and we have to prick your finger again."

"Cute, Dev. Anything else I think about immediately pops into view whether I want it to or not. But when I need something to decipher miniscule writing on this contract, all of a sudden you come up empty."

Scratching her head, Dev chuckled a bit. "Yes, I suppose it does seem that way. As perfect as I try to make things down here, occasionally things do go awry. However, I promise you that I'll have the person in charge of miscellaneous office supplies punished. Maybe a red-hot poker in the eye or an afternoon spent licking up excrement from my Hell hounds." She flicked her wrist. "I'll think of something. In the meantime, please do accept my apologies for not being able to accommodate you, Meredith. Now why don't you sign before you give yourself a nasty case of eyestrain."

Meredith set the quill pen down, ignoring Dev's insistent urgings and worked to focus. "Let's see...non-rescindable...quota of one hundred fresh souls converted each month..." Meredith looked up at Dev who smiled innocently.

"No big deal. It's just that little turning-souls-to-the-dark-side thing we touched on earlier," Dev said sweetly.

Meredith went back to reading. "Memory of friends, family and loved ones forever erased..." Her head popped up and her eyes widened. "What does this mean?"

Dev shrugged. "Nothing really. You're simply no longer burdened with memories of people you knew while living on Earth, that's all."

Slanting Dev a perplexed expression, Meredith asked, "You mean I won't have any recollection of Jack or Karyn or my parents or grandparents or anyone else I ever cared about? For all eternity?"

"Uh-huh." Dev nodded. "Once you're a permanent resident of Hell there'll be plenty to keep you occupied. We don't want you to get mired down in lovesickness or longing for past relationships. Makes things much easier that way. You'll see."

"Having all thoughts of Jack obliterated..." Meredith shuddered. "Oh no. I can't agree to that." Without waiting for Dev's reaction, she continued to read aloud. "Where was I? Oh yes... Deep, tender, ineffable feelings of affection and solicitude toward any person, pet or object, such as that arising from kinship, recognition of eye-catching qualities or a sense of underlying oneness—otherwise known as and henceforth referred to in this document as *love*—shall be excised from all residents of Hell." After a long pause, Meredith slowly raised her head. "You don't allow people down here to feel or experience love—is that what this means?"

Dev laughed. "You're looking at me as if that's a bad thing. Love is nothing more than a weakness, a flaw of the human heart and soul. Our residents are much stronger and better adjusted because they never have to deal with the pain that love inevitably involves. Once it's expunged from your soul you'll never miss it. I promise you."

"I'd be like an empty shell," Meredith whispered, shaking her head. "Devoid of all the characteristics that make me who I am."

"And then we take that empty shell and fill it with all the things that truly matter, Meredith. All of the potent qualities that will help you to succeed as a perpetual dweller of the Underworld. All extraneous concerns and interfering feelings are eradicated, leaving you free and unencumbered to focus on the primary objective—worshipping and obeying your new lord and master. *Satan.*" The last word hissed through Dev's lips as if she were the cunning snake offering Eve that fateful apple.

Meredith's system jolted with a disquieting shudder, alerting her sluggish senses back to a state of logic and reason. How could she have been so brainless as to forget where she was and who she was conversing with? How could she have been so weak as to have allowed herself to be tempted by Satan's smooth-as-silk words? To consider, even for a millisecond, the prospect of signing away her soul? To live an eternity without love and without even the memory of past love would be a hell in itself. All the perfect sex she could ever imagine...but devoid of emotion or romance or love or compassion or any of the other basic feelings that made her human.

"I think I'll pass."

Dev's face fell. She looked so lost and forlorn for a moment that Meredith thought Dev was going to cry. She almost felt sorry for her. The poor thing seemed lonely, in need of companionship. Friendship. *Love.* Meredith wished she could help...wished she could make Dev see the error of her ways, but—

Snarling as she thrust her arms into the air, Dev's expression morphed from one of human sadness to one of

157

grotesque malevolence. Her flawless porcelain skin took on a gnarled, reddish appearance and her attractive features grew warped and hateful. And then a set of horns fully sprouted from her head while a tail slapped back and forth beneath her dress. The transformation was so alarming that Meredith felt herself tremble right down to her toes. In fact, she almost peed in her pants.

All goody-two-shoes feelings of reaching out to help Dev find love and companionship dried up like a chunk of year-old beef jerky.

"Fine!" Dev bellowed, blowing hot sulfur-tinged breath that blew the hair back from Meredith's face and made her gag from the fumes. "Have it your way." And then she grabbed Meredith by the throat, lifting her off the desk chair and into the air until her feel dangled beneath her.

Meredith cringed as Dev's malicious features drew closer and the putrid breath grew stronger. When Dev's mouth opened again thick, sharp, yellowed fangs had replaced the pearly-white teeth there just a moment before. And the tongue… Meredith shivered again. It was forked, worm-gray and bubbled with what looked like pockets of pus. No doubt about it…this was, indeed, the epitome of the term *scared shitless.*

"Go ahead and keep your precious bleeding heart and your hopelessly good soul with its oozing feelings of love and forgiveness crippling your existence," Dev spat. "But when you're stuck sitting on a lump of cloud mindlessly strumming a harp for infinity, remember that it was your gross stupidity that put you there." Dev lifted Meredith higher and her mouth opened wider.

"Oh my God…please don't hurt me," Meredith begged.

And then Dev bellowed. An unholy desolate sounding wail. "God, God, you and your God! You dim-witted, sniveling, sympathetic, empathetic humans disgust me. So you want God, do you? You want Heaven, hmm? Well, too bad because they don't want you."

Meredith was bawling like a baby now. "But I don't want to stay here," she choked out. "You said I could leave. Please, let me go. Oh God, please help me. *Please,* God, get me out of here!"

Just as Dev began to mimic Meredith's whining pleas, a profusion of pale golden light permeated the room, cloaking Meredith with a profound sense of peace.

"Shame on you, Dev," a calming, echoing voice said. "You know better than to ignore the rules."

Spittle flew out of its mouth while the thing that used to look like Dev cackled. With the passing of each second, the demon grew more grotesque and frightening. "Interfering sons of bitches," Dev barked while shielding her eyes from the light with one hand as she continued to hold Meredith aloft with the other. She focused her attention back on Meredith. "Just remember, darling," she warned with demonic intonation, "one false move on your part and I'll haul your ass back down here so fast that it will make your head spin—literally. And next time there won't be any fun and games. It'll be straight to the tar pits for you where you'll bubble and boil and writhe in agony forever. Instead of *quivernation* you'll be in a constant state of *suffocation.*" With that, Dev drew her arm back and threw Meredith so hard and fast that she spun like a top.

Just when Meredith was certain that she'd hit the wall and burst into bloody smithereens, the same soothing voice she'd heard a moment before said, *Don't worry, I've got you.*

And then she felt herself enveloped by strong, masculine arms—and a pair of wings.

Chapter Twelve

ઈ૭

Floating in the midst of the comforting glow, Meredith felt safe and secure for the first time in so very long. The stench of sulfur had finally vanished from her nostrils and she knew she was free of Dev's clutches — hopefully forever. In Hell she felt as if she'd been in a drugged stupor, shrouded in temptation and nearly incapable of logical thought. Now, wrapped in the firm grasp of her winged rescuer, she breathed an enormous sigh of relief. She felt so free and happy that she almost burst into song. She glimpsed up into the face of the being that held her as they flew. As he looked down at Meredith and smiled, she saw that he was more than handsome, he was beautiful. Nutmeg-brown eyes, long black hair, a grin that warmed her heart and a superbly muscled body. And he was black.

"I always thought angels were pale, delicate, fair-haired creatures," she noted, immediately sorry for thinking out loud and making an ass of herself. It was such a ridiculous sounding observation. The last thing she wanted to do was insult this glorious being who'd whisked her out of Hell. "I'm sorry. That was a stupid thing to say." Meredith squeezed his forearms gently. Wonderfully firm and beefy, her robust angel was far from frail. "It's just that with all those muscles you look more like a warrior than any angel painting I've ever seen."

"We come in all shapes, sizes, ethnicities and colors." He chuckled. "Male and female. And there's no need to feel bad, Meredith. I know what you meant. We're usually portrayed as willowy blond Caucasians in artwork so it's a natural assumption."

Meredith could listen to his voice forever. It was strong yet lyrical and quite compelling. "Thanks for understanding. Do you have a name? What should I call you?"

"Lysander."

Meredith repeated the name and smiled. "What does it mean?"

"It's Greek for liberator."

"How appropriate." Meredith laughed softly. "Lysander, are you taking me to Heaven?"

"Not exactly."

"Oh..."

Lysander chuckled. "Don't worry, little one. There's nothing to fear. We're going to the Corridor of Souls. It's a place of decision and preparation just inside the Gates of Heaven."

"Decision...you mean as in judgment?" Meredith really didn't think she could handle any more stress today. And having a panel of heavenly beings decide her fate ranked right up at the top of her *Things That Make Me Really Panicky* list. "They...they won't send me back down to Hell, will they?"

"I already told you that you have nothing to worry about, Meredith. Just try to relax. We're almost there." Lysander's voice was so hypnotic that Meredith immediately felt the tension leave her body.

A short while later, Lysander's great wings flapped gently as they descended. Once they'd floated down through the last cloud, Meredith caught a glimpse of the gates. *Pearly* was actually a fairly good description of the massive structure. The vertical rods appeared almost translucent at some angles, with a look of rich, creamy mother of pearl. The depth and luster of the material was magnificent, unlike anything Meredith had ever seen. Ornate horizontal supports of gold and silver made up the lush scrolled framework. Standing within arm's reach of the gates, Meredith looked up. The gates rose so high she couldn't see the top.

The entire area was bathed in soothing lavender light and when Meredith looked down at her feet she saw that, rather than standing on a cloud, she was standing on luminous rays of lavender.

"Lysander Triple Eight Seven," the angel said to the gates, "with Meredith Annie Collins McKenna McKenna, case file eight zanillion thirty."

The colossal gates opened inward gracefully and Meredith's gaze flitted from one captivating element to another. An infinite city of light had materialized before her, with even the roads, walkways and buildings constructed of colorful translucent rays. There was radiance above, below and to the sides — never blinding, but soothing, joyful and inviting. Engaging sounds of love, laughter and happiness permeated Meredith's senses. And she longed to be a part of it all. As if she were an impatient child on Christmas morning, Meredith fidgeted, yearning to skip into the city and explore its many wonders. Lysander's hand resting gently on her shoulder captured her attention.

"Patience. Your time will come, Meredith. Follow me."

Just inside the gates, Lysander stepped to the right, entering what appeared to be a long hall of pale blue light. The light swirled in a clockwise direction as they walked but there was no sensation of dizziness. The end of the hall opened into a large area filled with compartments, almost like a series of small offices, but they were composed of blue light. It fascinated Meredith how the light could be translucent and yet it was impossible to see into each private cubicle — a seeming impossibility. As she took in one extraordinary feature after another, she almost felt as if she'd stepped right into the pages of a magical storybook.

The door to one of the rooms opened and Lysander led Meredith inside. The walls of light were adorned with picture frames that glowed with a sort of fluorescent radiance — like neon signs, only softer. Meredith gasped when she saw that each frame displayed moving pictures, like those from a video camera only more real and three-dimensional. They were all favorite scenes from Meredith's life, from her earliest memories onward.

"Oh, this is phenomenal," she whispered with reverence. "Awesome in the truest sense of the word."

"I'll return when it's time to escort you again, Meredith," Lysander said, lifting Meredith's hand to his lips and brushing a tender kiss across her knuckles.

A salient rush of joyous contentment saturated her spirit at the touch of the angel's lips. "Thank you so much, Lysander...for everything."

And then Lysander was no longer in the room.

"You've had quite a difficult time of it, my dear, haven't you?"

Startled, Meredith turned toward the voice and saw that it emanated from a crinkly-eyed, pink-cheeked older woman sitting behind a pearly desk. She was attired in a flowing garment of pastel blue from head to toe. Even her magnificent wings were a subtle shade of blue.

"My, my," the old woman's eyes sparkled as she smiled, "you're the spitting image of Katie when she was your age." Meredith cocked her head in confusion. "Oh forgive me, dear. I'm referring to your grandmother. I was her guardian angel, just as I am yours. My name is—"

"Annie," Meredith breathed with awe. "Just like my middle name."

"Indeed." The old woman nodded and smiled.

"Oh my God..." Meredith just stared silently for a moment. "Grandma Kate used to tell me about her guardian angel when I was little. She's the one who gave me my middle name—after you. But I thought it was just one of those elaborate yarns she was always weaving. At least, that's what my mom said." A maze of happy recollections whooshed through Meredith's mind. The wondrous tales of *Annie the Angel* that her grandmother had spun were the highlight of their visits together. She remembered the special glint in her grandma's eye whenever she regaled Meredith with a story. And now Meredith was actually standing before the lead player in Grandma Kate's heavenly tales. "How...how did my grandmother know about you?"

"Some people are more attuned to the spirit world than others and your grandmother was one of them," Annie said. "Katie could sense my presence from the time she was a small child and we'd spend hours chatting together. The family was concerned about her insistence that she and her guardian angel were conversing. They worried that perhaps Katie was a bit batty or that she'd conjured up some demon," Annie paused to laugh, "but she and I knew better. After a time Katie learned it was best to keep quiet about our chats and then the hubbub died down. It's much the same for many children who have what's referred to nowadays as an *invisible friend*. It's usually their guardian angels they're connecting with."

Squinting as she struggled to evoke a distant memory, Meredith said, "I had an invisible friend for awhile when I was little but I can't really remember much about it now. Was...was that you?"

"None other." Annie winked. "My but we did have fun." She extended her hand, gesturing to the gilded chair that appeared in front of the desk. "Do sit down and make yourself comfortable, Meredith, while we sort through things together."

"Is Grandma Kate here too? Can I see her?"

"Yes, she's here and she sends you her love, but I'm afraid you won't be able to see her until you come back to stay."

"Come back?" Meredith cocked her head. "I don't understand. Where am I going?"

"Back to your life on Earth," Annie said and Meredith's eyes widened in surprise. "Well, after all, that's been your heart's greatest desire, hasn't it? To go back and make amends to Jack...to try to patch things up between you. Right?"

Meredith nodded slowly. "Yes...well, until I caught my first glimpse of Heaven, that is. Now I want to stay here, Annie. Can I?"

"No, dear. Not yet." A knowing smile in place, Annie shook her head from side to side. "Naturally every soul feels that way after their first glimpse of Paradise. That's why you'll forget most of what you've seen once you go back—so you can fully concentrate on living, on fulfilling your destiny. Believe me, Heaven will be here for you when the time is right and, Meredith, it's even more magnificent than you can begin to imagine. But now it's time to focus our attention on getting you back to your earthly existence."

Stiffening with apprehension, Meredith gripped the arms of her chair. "When you say back to Earth, do you mean as myself? As a woman? In my own body?"

"Absolutely." Annie laughed and nodded. "While there are occasions where we need to send a soul back to Earth in an alternate guise, this isn't one of them."

"Whew!" An audible gust of breath escaped Meredith's lips as she wiped her brow. "That's a giant relief. What about Jack and Karyn—will I get to see them again?"

Annie's eyebrow shot up. "Indeed. And I'm afraid you'll have to work quite hard to rectify that wicked little bit of payback that you exacted on your ex-husband."

Meredith felt her cheeks flush at the memory. "But I thought his future was no longer in jeopardy because the photos won't be published—and Ricky's dead and Alicia's in prison."

"All true," Annie said. "And don't think we didn't notice that you worked diligently to set things right. Sacrificing yourself to save Jack while you were in Ricky's body was selfless and brave—and that earned you some big points. But it's not Jack or Karyn's lives we're concerned with at the moment, dear. It's yours."

"I see," Meredith said, although she didn't. Swallowing hard, she slumped down in her chair and worried her bottom lip. Life and death and Hell and Heaven…it was all so complex, so complicated. "So what am I going to be facing? Are you sending me back before or after I left Jack tied up? Will he remember what I did or not? Am I going to remember any of the stuff I went through in Hell or up here? What will—"

"Whoa!" Annie held up her hand and laughed. "Slow down. All of your questions will be answered. But there are no absolutes. What eventually happens will happen naturally of your free will, without any interference from me or from that devious creature who's so eager to make you a part of her dark domain." Sporting a sour expression, Annie pointed downward. "From this point on circumstances are entirely up to you and Jack and Karyn."

"That's good. I promise I'll work very hard to make amends."

"There's one thing you should keep in mind." Annie wagged a finger at Meredith. "Granted, Jack has an exasperating weakness for the ladies, but he's inherently a fine man, a good soul, Meredith. And he loves you deeply. In fact, he'd readily give up his life for you, just as you did for him. You and he are true soulmates." Annie's hand moved in a broad, sweeping gesture as she motioned to the frames on the walls. Each frame was alive with happy scenes of Meredith and Jack together. And the sensations of love, joy and romance were palpable. "Remember?"

Meredith bubbled with merriment as she scanned each frame. "Oh yes. Yes, Annie, I remember. And I want all of that with Jack again."

Resting her elbows on the desk, Annie leaned forward and shoved her fingers together so they were intertwined. "Of course, there are certain particulars, some difficulties that you'll need to overcome." She gazed at Meredith silently for a moment. "The passage of time in Heaven and Hell is unlike that on Earth. After you died the second time—in Ricky's body—you were supposed to be sent here directly. But according to the rules between the dominions, Dev retained the right to do her best to tempt you to remain with her. When she decided to exercise her option, we had no choice but to let her snatch you away. We were unable to interfere until you called upon us to save you or until your prearranged time there had lapsed—whichever came first. Fortunately, you finally called out to God before the allotted six-month enticement period passed."

"Oh boy." Meredith took a deep breath and smiled. "You scared me for a minute there, Annie. I'm glad I called for help when I did, because it's still the same day everything happened. Or no...I think it's the day after." Meredith shrugged. "In either case I can easily deal with a missing day."

"In Earth time, Meredith, more than four months have passed since the morning you were shot and died while in Ricky's body."

"What?" Meredith bolted from her chair. "But that's not possible. It seemed like I was only down there a matter of hours."

"The devil's greatest tool is temptation. It's alluring...intoxicating...fascinating. And you were tempted mightily with the most potent of her carnal offerings. You were steeped in her persuasive command for quite a long while before you called out to us, my dear."

Remembering the bounty of sexual enticements that Dev had conjured up for her, Meredith growled in frustration. "Sex...all because of sex..." She sank back down in her chair, dropping her head into her hands and recalling the tantalizing fantasy lovers, the outstanding sex, the astounding orgasms. And she remembered feeling drugged. Yes, somehow that demon trickster had managed to put her into a senseless stupor all the while she worked her evil ways.

"Oh good grief, what have I done?" Meredith groaned. She felt as if she'd slipped down a greased ladder almost overnight, from the dull-and-boring-goody-two-shoes rung to the depraved-and sinful-sex-fanatic rung. "I'll make up for it, I swear. I'll never allow myself to have sex again for as long as I live. I'll become a nun."

She whipped her head up when she heard peals of laughter coming from Annie. Her sweet old guardian angel had tears streaming down her face she was laughing so hard — and she was slapping the desk to boot!

"Annie!" Meredith's voice was indignant. "How can you sit there and laugh about the horrendous mess I've made of my life? I honestly don't see anything funny about it whatsoever!" Her chin quivered and one fat tear trailed down her cheek.

Wiping her eyes with the back of her hand, Annie got up and came around to the front of the desk, perching her ample butt on the corner. She took Meredith's hands in her own, smoothing her thumbs over the knuckles. "Oh, I'm truly sorry, dear. But I overheard your thought about sliding down the greased ladder and it just cracked me up."

Meredith slipped her hands from Annie's grasp and folded her arms across her chest. "And here I thought angels were supposed to be kind and compassionate."

"Oh, we are, we are...but that doesn't mean we don't have a delicious sense of humor." She winked. "You see, dear, you have it all wrong. There's nothing at all wrong with sex. After all, who do you think created it, hmm? Contrary to what Dev would have you believe there's much more going on up here than harp playing. Why, just this afternoon I—" Annie cleared her throat. "Well, we won't go into that now. But I can assure you, Meredith, that God created sexual union as a beautiful, mystical experience. While the passage of semen into the vagina is clinically necessary for conception, the joy of foreplay and intercourse, followed by the blissful rapture of orgasm, is most definitely not. It's the icing on the cake so to speak. Along with love, sexual pleasure is one of God's greatest gifts to mankind—and womankind." Annie drew Meredith up from her chair and into a reassuring hug.

"Well, I'm glad to hear that," Meredith sniffed against Annie's garment, "because I'd probably suck as a nun, anyway." She gave a little laugh.

"Yes, dear, I'm afraid you would," Annie agreed, patting Meredith's back and chuckling.

"Okay," Meredith broke the embrace and wiped her eyes. "So now what? It's been more than four months since Jack and Karyn last saw me. Do they think I'm dead or what?"

"They don't know what to think although the likelihood of your death looms larger with each passing day. They're both frantic with worry. And there've been a number of changes in their lives since the day this all started. But you'll find out about all of that once you go back."

Changes? Like what? Ugh. Meredith didn't have the energy or inclination to think about any of that now. She sat down again and frowned. "Where do I tell them I've been all this time?" She huffed a laugh. "Heaven and Hell?"

Annie shrugged. "If that's what you think is best—although I rather doubt anyone would believe you. Just be aware that the memories of your experiences after falling down the elevator shaft will gradually fade until barely anything is retained."

"How long will it take before the memories disappear?" Meredith couldn't imagine ever forgetting what she'd been through. Especially the part about inhabiting Ricky's body.

"It varies with the individual, dear. Sometimes a few days, sometimes a few months, sometimes longer. You'll probably always retain a few snippets, but in time you'll just think they're parts of dreams you've had."

"I suppose that's for the best." Meredith nodded slowly. "If I remembered everything it would be awfully hard to focus on regular everyday life again, wouldn't it?"

"Exactly." Annie slanted Meredith a cautionary look. "One word of warning, just to be sure that you don't find yourself ensnared in Dev's clutches again." Meredith shuddered at the thought. "In the future," Annie continued, "don't let things build up inside until they reach a boiling point and you resort to drastic measures. I mean, we got quite a kick out of your revenge on Jack...up to a point. He certainly deserved to get a good scare and you deserved to see him squirm, but you allowed things to go too far. Everything would have been all right if only you hadn't left him there in the hotel room all trussed up with that sock puppet on his penis." Annie covered her mouth, tittering. "Very funny, but walking out that hotel room door was a definite no-no."

Meredith nodded solemnly. The humor she'd felt while plotting and exacting her revenge on Jack had long subsided. All she had to do was to remember those bleak, horrid scenes of Jack and Karyn in the future to wipe any traces of a smile from her face. "I understand."

"And for heaven's sake, Meredith, that doesn't mean you should return to being a lackluster goody-two-shoes stick in the mud, either. Just find a happy medium, dear. You can have great fun, oodles of sex and as much chocolate as your heart desires — as long as it doesn't hurt anyone else — or hurt you." She scooted off the desk and linked her arm with Meredith's, tugging her from the chair. "Lysander's on his way here to guide you back home again, Meredith. Remember, dear...everything will be fine. I'll be watching over you, just the way I've always done — except that now you'll be aware of it. Talk to me whenever you need to. I'll always hear you and help in any way that I can." She hauled Meredith into a mighty hug and squeezed hard. "Goodbye dear...until we meet again."

"Annie...wait! There's still so much I want to ask you." Meredith reached out her hand but she was being whisked away, in the arms of Lysander again. Her guardian angel was out of sight and soon, so were the Gates of Heaven.

170

"Don't worry, little one," Lysander whispered in her ear. "You have all of the knowledge that you need. Just follow your heart."

Enveloped in his magnificent arms again, Meredith felt safe, warm and cocooned. She heard herself purr when her mind wandered, wondering what it would be like to make love with an angel.

"Glorious," Lysander whispered against her ear.

A small gasp escaped her throat as Meredith realized that he had heard her thoughts. Before she could say anything, Lysander brushed a kiss across her temple and Meredith closed her eyes, quickly slipping into the solace of dreamless sleep.

Chapter Thirteen

ഇ

"I'm telling you, Jack, if she's alive she'll be here," Karyn said, munching on a mini-pretzel.

"How can you be so sure? I hate sitting here twiddling my thumbs for hours waiting when I could be out there looking for her instead."

"Then stop twiddling and have a pretzel." Laughing, she pushed the bowl toward Jack, who ignored it. "Look, turning forty is a big deal for women, Jack, especially if we're single. It's one of those unpleasant milestone occasions where we need to rally and support each other. I was there for Meredith's fortieth and I know she'll be here for me. We made a pact."

"Maybe we should be downstairs waiting for her at her apartment." Being idle was driving Jack nuts. It was passive and nonproductive and definitely not his usual method of operation. He was a man of action, used to taking charge and being in control. Meredith's disappearance had changed all that. For the past four months he'd felt practically immobilized, gripped by aching sensations of loss and fear. He didn't want to use the word *grief* because that would mean that Meredith might be dead, and he refused to accept that. She *had* to be alive...she just had to. It was his discovery that Karyn had been paying Meredith's rent and utilities during her absence that made Jack's blood run cold. Irresponsibility simply wasn't one of Meredith's traits. She would never run off willy-nilly, sticking Karyn with her bills. Unless...

Karyn tsked. "Trust me, she'll be here."

Jack swirled the liquid in his glass, staring into his martini and shaking his head. "Something awful must have happened.

I feel it in my bones." And he did. It was weird...like some sort of intrinsic soul connection or something with Meredith. It sounded bizarre and new-agey, not at all like his usual rational thinking, but there it was nonetheless. He'd given up talking to Karyn about the feeling because each time he mentioned it she'd start blubbering and telling him how sweet he was. He couldn't take that. He didn't deserve her sympathy or encouragement. Whatever had happened to Meredith, he knew without a doubt that it was because of him. Sweet? Hardly.

"How could she just disappear off the face of the earth like that?" Jack continued. "Without a trace." He shoved his fingers through his hair. "I just don't understand it. It doesn't make any sense."

"Yeah, I know. You've been singing that same tired old song for the last four months." Karyn chuckled and grabbed another handful of pretzels. "Knock it off, already, you're ruining my birthday."

"Oh, right." Jack folded his arms across his chest, leveling a narrowed gaze at Karyn. With four months of near nonstop crying taking its toll, the woman looked like she'd been dragged through sewer water, wrung out and left to dry. "And like you haven't been tied up in knots and bawling like a baby ever since she disappeared yourself."

Karyn dismissed him with a flick of her wrist. "You know, Mr. Sensitivity, if you would have taken the time to show Meredith one iota of your feelings for her when you were still married, she never would have had to resort to such drastic measures. But, no, you were too busy fucking prepubescent floozies to think about what it was doing to your loyal, loving wife. Not to mention," Karyn slapped the table just as Jack opened his mouth to respond, "all that *open marriage* crap you told me about. I mean, what the hell were you thinking when you made that proposition to her, Jack? You were damned lucky Meredith didn't have a baseball bat in that purse of hers because, sure as shit, she would have cracked you over the head with it."

Jack sat back in his chair and let his head fall back. After staring at the ceiling of Karyn's kitchen for a few moments he heaved a sigh. "You're right. This is all my fault. Every time I cheated on her I was toying with her emotions like she was a goddamned yo-yo." He looked Karyn in the eyes, which was hard to do, knowing that the anguish etched across her features was entirely due to his actions. "And every time I think about what I said to Meredith that night," he winced at the recollection, "I'm just as amazed as you are that she didn't bash my head in. She should have. I was a selfish prick and Meredith deserved — *deserves* — much better." He didn't want to refer to Meredith in the past tense. Because she wasn't dead. She couldn't be.

Karyn's shoulders slumped and her eyes glassed over with tears. She reached for Jack's hand and squeezed it hard. "Oh, hell. Just put me out to pasture and shoot me," she said, laughing. "I'm sorry, Jack, you didn't deserve that at all. I'm just edgy…antsy. Believe me, after spending all the time we have together these past few months, I know how this is tearing you up inside. I know how much Meredith means to you. I'm sorry…really. Forgive me?"

Jack patted her hand and smiled. "Forget it. There's nothing to forgive." He was silent for a moment, lost in thought. No meaningless clandestine affair…no temporary cock gratification with any other woman…nothing in this entire world was worth losing Meredith forever. He'd castrate himself before he ever hurt her like that again. "I'd give anything in the world for the chance to make things up to her." And the chance to glove his cock in that soft, sweet, wet pussy of Meredith's one more time.

"Well, when she walks through that door with my birthday pistachios you can get started." Karyn beamed a bright smile.

Jack chuckled. "How do you know she's getting you pistachios?"

"That's part of our pact. I bring her Belgian chocolate on her birthday and she beings me—"

The sudden buzz of the doorbell gave them both a start. Wide-eyed, Jack and Karyn exchanged glances, gulping as they sat frozen like a couple of statues. The bell rang again and they jumped out of their chairs.

"Jesus, do you think…"

Suddenly panicked, Jack's mouth went dry. "God, I hope so."

They raced to the living room, scrambling to unlock and open the door. Finally, it swung open and they stood with gaping stares.

"*La cucaracha?*"

"What?" Jack and Karyn said in unison.

"Sorry. I forgot my English. I understand there is a cockroach here, eh?"

Jack's expectant smile sank as he eyed the muscle-bound kid across the threshold. "Do you know this joker, Karyn?"

"I am no joker, *señor*. Allow me to introduce myself." The young man took a deep bow. "I am—"

"Cristoval! What are you doing here?" Karyn said. "He lives next door to Meredith," she explained to Jack.

"*Sí*. Meredith sent me." He grinned and then gave Karyn a wink. "She said you'd know why, Karyn." His smile grew wider.

With a chorused gasp, Jack and Karyn poked their heads into the hall on either side of Cristoval, looking left and right, and then Karyn looped her arm through Cristoval's and yanked him into her apartment.

"Where is she?" Karyn said, wrapping her hands around his biceps and jiggling his arm.

Jack joined in, shaking Cristoval by the shoulders. "Where's Meredith?"

"She's—"

"Have you seen her? Is she all right?" Karyn said, tugging harder.

"You actually talked to her?" Jack asked.

"*Ai, ai, ai!* Just a minute! *Por favor!* You're making me dizzy." Karyn and Jack stilled and Cristoval shook them off. He thrust the large burlap bag he held at Karyn. "First, these are from Meredith. Five pounds of pistachio nuts for your birthday. She says to let you know that—"

"When did you talk to her? What did she say?" Jack interrupted, grasping the young man's arms.

"I am *trying* to tell you!" Cristoval gazed at his arm pointedly until Jack got the message and let go. "Yes, I talked to Meredith. Now just let me finish before I forget what she told me to say, okay?" He nailed Jack with a frustrated glare.

Jack raised his hands in surrender. "Sorry. Go ahead."

Cristoval brushed his arms where Jack had clutched him. "Karyn, she said to tell you that she just returned and not to worry because she is fine. She asked me to bring you the bag of nuts and said that she'd come and talk to you just as soon as she finds Jack. And, uh, she said that I am supposed to keep you company until she gets here. She suggested that I help you with that big cockroach you saw in your apartment—the same way I helped her with the mouse on her birthday." Cristoval waggled his eyebrows and then glanced at Jack. "But I see you already have someone else searching for your cockroach, no?"

"No! That's Jack. Meredith's Jack. Oh my God, Jack," Karyn squealed as she threw her arms around Jack's neck. "She *is* back!"

Confused, Jack hugged Karyn back as he tried to make sense of everything. "I don't get it. What's all this about mice and cockroaches?"

Karyn stepped back and scratched her head. "Uhhh…well. Cristoval is our, uh…exterminator. Right, Cristoval?" She looked at the kid with what Jack thought was a pleading expression.

Cristoval shrugged. "*Sí*, that's it. I am the exterminator." He took another bow. "And I'm *very* good at what I do." He did the wiggly eyebrow thing again as he looked at Karyn.

Jack slanted the buff young man a cautionary look, which Cristoval met with an angelic smile. "Is Meredith downstairs in her apartment?"

"Yes, but I think she was on her way out to go look for you when she came to talk to me."

"We've got to catch her!" Jack bellowed as he turned toward the door. Karyn was next to him in an instant. Shoulders crunching together as they reached the doorway, they became wedged between the doorjamb, thrashing about like a couple of slapstick comedians. With a final thrust, Jack jerked free and ran into the hall. "Meredith!" he yelled as he raced toward the carpeted wooden staircase.

"Wait for me!" Karyn screamed as she bolted after Jack.

Stopping just as he reached the stairs, Jack growled, "Hurry up for chrissakes!"

"Hey…what about me?" Cristoval called.

Turning around and jogging backwards, Karyn aimed a finger at him. "You stay right where you are, Cristoval. Don't you dare leave! I've been waiting months for you to come get rid of that *cockroach* and you're not leaving until you've done your job — thoroughly." She winked, turned forward and sped up to catch Jack.

"I look forward to it, *cara mia*!" Cristoval yelled as he blew her a kiss.

"Jack, you're going too fast!" Karyn said as she scrambled down the first flight of stairs behind him. "I'll kill myself if I try to run down three steps at a time like you."

Waiting impatiently for Karyn to catch up, Jack snarled. "Come on already! Move those short little legs of yours. We've got to catch her before she leaves."

Karyn grinned. "Thanks for saying my legs are little." Jack just rolled his eyes. "Maybe one of us should be taking the elevator." Karyn gasped out between ragged breaths as she scampered down the stairs, trying to keep up.

"Go ahead," Jack said. "Who's stopping you?"

"Never mind," Karyn said. "That damn old thing is so slow that we'll make better time on the stairs. Besides," she paused to suck in some air, "the elevator's so noisy that we'll hear it if Meredith tries to use it."

"Just one more flight, Karyn. We're almost there."

"At least she lives downstairs and not up. If I were racing up three flights I'd be having a coronary by now." As they turned the corner and galloped past the landing, Karyn's shoe caught on a bump in the carpet and she screamed out something that sounded like the call of a sick moose as she began to plummet forward.

"Shit!" Jack yelled as he braced himself to catch her without falling headfirst down the stairs as she plunged into him. Soon the two of them were tumbling, slipping and sliding down the last dozen stairs until they came to a stop in a tangled heap, half on and half off the stairs.

In the midst of their groans, moans and growled swearing, Jack heard laughter.

"Trying to recapture your youth by playing tag down the stairs, hmm, Karyn? Next thing I know you'll be running with scissors." The familiar laughter pealed again.

Scraping the hair out of her eyes, Karyn looked up. "Meredith? Is it really you?"

"In the flesh," Meredith said, beaming a smile. "Are you okay? Looks like you and Cristoval took quite a tumble."

"It's not Cristoval, it's—" Karyn growled in frustration. "Damn it, Jack, you weigh a ton. Get off of me before you break every bone in my body."

"Me? You're the one sitting on my face." Meredith stood there stunned as Jack's voice came from somewhere under Karyn's hips. "I can't move until you haul your big—"

"Jack..." Meredith's hand flew to her throat. "My Jack?"

Jack groaned as he and Karyn untangled themselves, sliding down the last few steps on their bellies. "Guilty as charged," he said, getting to his feet and pulling Karyn up with him.

Jack's hair was rumpled, with a hank of dark brown coiled haphazardly over one eye. It had been years since Meredith had seen him in jeans and a T-shirt—his standard uniform was a three-piece suit. Seeing the way his impressive physique filled out his clothes, it was no wonder she'd mistaken him for Cristoval before she'd seen his face. Jack looked so damned sexy it took her breath away. Without wasting another moment she rushed to his side and he yanked her into his arms, squeezing and kissing her with such intensity that Meredith alternately wept and laughed with joy.

She broke their kiss and pulled back just enough to study him, frowning when she noted the dark circles under his eyes and the overall weary expression—not to mention the fresh rug-burns on his cheek and chin from that slide down the stairs. "Oh, Jack, you look like hell," she said, cupping his face. But as exhausted and bedraggled as he appeared, he still looked good enough to eat—and she hoped she'd get a chance to do just that.

Jack nodded. "Yeah, lack of sleep will do that to a guy after nearly five months." Huffing a humorless chuckle, he clutched her upper arms and tugged her closer. "Where the hell have you been, sweetheart? We've been worried sick about you. For chrissakes, we were afraid you might be dead."

"It's a long story." Oh, it felt so good to be in Jack's arms again. And she wanted more than anything to fully unite with Jack…to feel him inside her again, filling her.

"I want to hear every word, Meredith." Jack rubbed his hand up and down her spine.

"Me too," Karyn chimed in as she ran up and joined them in a three-way hug.

After a few loving moments of crushing each other breathless, the three finally separated just enough to give each other some breathing space.

Meredith jangled her keys. "Instead of standing out here in the hall entertaining my neighbors," the three of them laughed as two doors in the vicinity immediately slammed shut, "let's go into my apartment so we can be comfortable." Once they'd gone inside and closed the door, Meredith turned to Karyn and smiled.

"Happy birthday, you young whippersnapper." She planted a big smooch on Karyn's cheek.

"Thanks. I knew you'd be here for me," Karyn said through a watery smile. "I just knew it."

"Of course. We have a pact. So…did you get the birthday present I sent up?" Meredith winked.

"Mmm, I certainly did. And I really can't wait to sample it." Waggling her eyebrows, Karyn giggled like a teenager. "Thanks, Meredith. You have my undying gratitude."

"I've never seen anyone get so excited over a bag of pistachios," Jack said, shaking his head.

Karyn and Meredith looked at each other and burst out laughing.

"I don't get it." Jack looked perplexed "What's so funny? You're missing for months, Meredith, and all you two can do is stand here making a big deal over a sack of nuts."

Exchanging another glance, the two women laughed even harder.

When their giggles finally subsided, Meredith wiped the tears from her eyes. "I'm sorry, Jack. I think it must be giddiness because we're so happy, that's all." She breathed easier when Jack gave a semi-satisfied shrug. "Before I caught you two engaging in those remarkable stairway acrobatics, I was just on my way to try to find you, Jack." Closing the distance between them, she traced his features with her hand and Jack stilled her fingers, kissing them when they reached his lips. "Oh, darling," her voice cracked, "there's so much I have to say. So much I have to apologize for. I never should have—"

"Shhh, shhh. There's nothing to apologize for," Jack said. "Not a thing." He squeezed Meredith close again, holding her so tight that she had trouble breathing but she didn't mind a bit. "Aw, baby, I thought I lost you. It's been hell."

"Absolute hell, Meredith," Karyn agreed solemnly.

"It has." Meredith sucked in a deep breath and exhaled slowly. "It has, indeed."

"Sweetheart," Jack said, "what happened? Where have you been all of this time? I've had private detectives and law enforcement agencies scouring the country trying to find you."

Meredith closed her eyes for a moment. "To Hell and back," she whispered. "God, you'll never know how happy I am to be standing here with the two of you." As they hugged again she luxuriated in the warm, secure feel of their arms and sent up a silent prayer of thanks to Annie for her safe return.

"Same here, honey," Karyn said, smoothing her fingers through Meredith's hair. "So, were you kidnapped or were you sick or did you just run away or what?"

"Uh...I was—"

"Why didn't you call me?" Karyn continued. "Do you have any idea how frantic we've been?"

"I'm sorry." Meredith took Karyn's hands in her own and squeezed them. She felt directly responsible for the agony she'd caused them by her disappearance. At least, thank God, things weren't as bleak as they could have been...if she had stayed dead after that fall down the elevator shaft and hadn't been able to rectify the results of her wicked payback scheme. An involuntary shudder took hold. "I couldn't call, Karyn. Believe me, I would have contacted you if it were at all possible."

"But more than four months, Meredith," Jack said. "Nothing. No word. Not a trace..."

Wringing her hands, Meredith looked from Jack to Karyn and back again. She had to say something, but what? How could she possibly tell them what really happened? They'd never believe her. She wouldn't believe it if the situation were reversed—if one of them had been missing and then told her they'd been to Hell and back, then to Hell again before going to Heaven and then finally back home again. Meredith had to bite the inside of her cheek to keep from laughing at the sheer absurdity of it all. As much as they cared about her, Meredith wouldn't blame Jack or Karyn one bit for calling the men in the white coats to put her in a straitjacket and lock her away in a padded cell if she tried to tell them the truth.

"Did you have an accident?" Jack asked. "Was it amnesia?"

"Amnesia!" Meredith practically shouted as she broke into a grin so wide her cheeks ached. "Yes, that's it!" Why hadn't she thought of that before? It was a perfect explanation.

"I don't understand." Jack scratched his head with a pained expression. "All the hospitals were checked...they were on the lookout for amnesia victims. We had your photo spread all over the place, newspapers, TV, flyers posted all over. How could they not find you?"

Meredith was surprised and pleased that Jack had gone through so much trouble trying to find her. And here she thought he'd never want to see her again after that nasty trick she'd played on him. As he stood there with a quizzical expression, she realized it wasn't a rhetorical question and Jack was actually expecting an answer. She smiled and shrugged. "I don't know."

"What hospital were you in?" Karyn asked.

Meredith looked to the left and right and then just smiled and shrugged again. "I don't know. I can't remember."

"Well, how long ago did the amnesia clear up," Karyn asked, "and how did you find your way back home if you didn't know where you were?"

All these questions! As much as she loved Karyn, Meredith wished she'd just shut up. She licked her lips nervously. "Uh...I don't really know what to tell you. The last thing I remember is stepping into that elev—uh...I mean stepping into the street...yeah, that's it...stepping into the street after I left Jack's hotel," she babbled. "And then, bam!" She gestured with her hands, crashing them together. "I must have been hit by a car or something and, next thing I know I'm in some medical facility without a clue as to who or where I am."

"Oh, you poor little thing," Karyn whispered. "That must have been so frightening."

"Was anything broken?" Jack asked.

"You mean bones?" Meredith blinked and Jack's eyebrow shot up as he gave her a *well-what-else-would-I-mean* look. Leave it to Jack to be so thorough. "Nope. I don't think so." Sighing, she shoved her hands through her hair and started to pace a bit as she tried to piece together a believable story. "All the rest is terribly vague. I just remember bits and pieces. I wasn't aware of the passage of time and until late last night I had no idea how much time had elapsed. Then...uh...then I just," she snapped her fingers, "snapped out of it. And before I even realized that I'd left the hospital, I was in my own bed— and that's where I woke up this morning." Meredith licked her lips again swallowed hard and studied their expressions. Jack nodded slowly as he rubbed his jaw and Karyn's lips were pursed into a little O as she nodded. She hoped to hell that they bought the story.

After a few moments of silence, Karyn patted Meredith's shoulder and said, "Well, I'm sure you'll remember more later, sweetie. We don't want you to tax yourself now, do we, Jack?" He shook his head in agreement. "In the meantime I think you should just sit down and relax." She grabbed Meredith's hand and led her to the sofa. Like a mama hen she plumped the pillows and cushions and gently tugged Meredith into position, propping her feet on another pillow that she set on the coffee table. And then she turned to Jack, giving him a push that seated him next to Meredith.

"Have you had anything to eat?" Karyn asked.

Meredith nodded. "Comfort food. A big bowl of oatmeal and the rest of my open four-month-old box of Belgian chocolates." She laughed.

Karyn grinned. "Good. Are you taking any medication?"

"Um...no. No drugs."

"Even better," Karyn said, trotting off to the kitchen. "I'll be back in a minute, so if you two want to do any necking, feel free. I promise not to peek...too much."

Before Meredith had a chance to respond, Jack's lips were on hers. She opened to him as his tongue probed and they engaged in a kiss so sweet, so hot and so ardent that she did, indeed, feel drugged.

"I want to do a whole lot more with you than just necking." Jack trailed a line of soft wet kisses from her lips to the flesh that plumped just above her low scoop neckline. "In fact," he cupped Meredith's breasts and brushed his thumbs across her nipples, watching as they beaded beneath his touch, "I don't ever want to let you go again. Just tell me that you'll give me another chance to prove myself to you, baby. I swear to you that I'll never hurt you like that again—ever."

Just then Karyn returned from the kitchen, balancing a tray laden with three glasses. "I think a little celebration is in order," Karyn said, setting the tray in the center of the coffee table. "And since you've eaten and you're not taking any medication you're free to indulge." She handed a glass to Meredith, another to Jack and then hiked her own into the air.

"What's this?" Meredith examined her glass.

Karyn shrugged. "Since there's no champagne this is what we're having to toast your return." She glanced at Jack and Meredith and laughed. "Hey, what's with those apprehensive looks? Okay, so I'm no expert when it comes to bartending, but I think this should probably be good. I just poured a little of each of the liquor bottles I found in one of the cabinets, plus some ginger ale into the glasses and added some maraschino cherry juice."

Meredith sniffed the glass and then took a sip. Her eyes went wide. Just as Karyn brought her glass to her lips, Meredith screamed, "Nooooo!" Then she bolted to her feet, vaulted over the coffee table and knocked the drink out of Karyn's hand. "Karyn, what the hell do you think you're doing?"

As the glass went sailing through the air and then smashed on the floor, Jack shot to his feet and he and Karyn whipped their heads toward Meredith, looking aghast.

"Honey...what—" Jack started

"Never, Karyn," Meredith cut him off, wagging a finger at Karyn. "Never do I *ever* want to see you drinking anything with whiskey in it, do you hear me? Never!" And then Meredith burst out crying in shoulder-shaking sobs. With the first whiff of whiskey from her glass those horrid images of Karyn draped over Meredith's grave, drunk and sobbing, came rushing back. And then Dev's sick cackle of delight when Karyn's car crashed into the tree rang in Meredith's ears. She clapped her hands over her ears. "Stop it! I don't want to see it or hear it anymore!"

Karyn and Jack stood silent for a few moments, still drop-jawed and stunned.

"Um...yeah..." Karyn said cautiously. "Maybe alcohol's not such a good idea after all with you just coming out of amnesia and all, sweetie." She went to Meredith's side and draped her arm over her shoulder. "I, uh, I wasn't really thirsty anyhow."

"Right. Me neither." Jack set his glass down, far out of Meredith's reach. He came close, taking her hand in his and rubbing it softly. "Why don't we all sit down quietly now and relax, honey? Do...do you want me to call a doctor or something?"

As he and Karyn gingerly moved Meredith toward the sofa she stiffened. "A doctor." She swiped at the tears on her cheeks and scanned their worried faces. "Oh dear Lord, you think I'm crazy, don't you?"

"No, no, not at all," Jack and Karyn blurted in unison while shaking their heads.

They were pathetically unconvincing and Meredith couldn't help laughing. Clearly, poor Jack and Karyn were scared shitless that she'd become a raving lunatic during her absence. "Don't worry. I haven't lost my mind. Honest. It's just...well, it's just that I've been through a lot...seen a lot, and I guess I'm still dealing with the repercussions."

They sat scrunched together on the sofa and Karyn nodded. "You must have seen the results of some alcohol-related accident or something, is that it?"

"Yes," Meredith said without hesitation. "Exactly. A woman who reminded me so much of you, sweetie," she clasped Karyn's hands tightly, "who died a horrible death after driving under the influence. The poor woman was an alcoholic. The," Meredith paused and cleared her throat, "the memory came flooding back when I saw you with that drink in your hand. I would die if anything like that ever happened to you, Karyn. Please promise me that you'll never start drinking that stuff."

"But, Meredith, you know that I'm not a big drinker — and God knows I'd never drink and drive. Trust me, the last thing you have to worry about is me becoming an alcoholic."

"That's true, honey," Jack chimed in, massaging the back of Meredith's scalp with his fingers. "You know Karyn better than that."

"Heck," Karyn added, "my only indulgence is when we get together and have our chocolate martinis." She licked her lips and chuckled. "If you're going to worry about anything, it should be my food addiction. I swear I must have put on another fifteen pounds with all that nervous eating since you disappeared."

"You look beautiful to me, Karyn. I never would have known about the extra weight if you hadn't mentioned it. And the occasional chocolate martinis we share are fine, but no whiskey. Promise." When Karyn failed to respond immediately, Meredith repeated, *"Promise!"* with added emphasis.

Karyn sucked in a deep breath and nodded slowly. "Sure...if it makes you feel better, honey, I promise. I hereby solemnly swear off whiskey forever." Slipping her right hand from Meredith's grip she crossed her heart.

Meredith breathed a sigh of relief. "Thank you, Karyn." She looked back and forth at Karyn and Jack and gave a quizzical smile. "It just dawned on me...since when did you two become such good friends? I mean, the last time we talked, Karyn, you —"

"She hated my guts." Jack laughed. "And she wasn't on my list of favorites either."

"Yeah," Meredith noted. "So how come..." She pointed to one and then the other. "Jack...were you upstairs celebrating Karyn's birthday with her?"

"Well, I wouldn't exactly call it celebrating. We were waiting for you to show up. Karyn was positive you would."

"Jack and I have gotten to know each other pretty well over the past few months," Karyn said. "And, uh…he's not half the monster I thought he was." She reached across Meredith and patted Jack's knee.

"Gee, thanks. I think." Jack laughed.

"He really and truly loves you, Meredith. I never would have believed it after all he did to you in the past. Lord knows he was a rotten cheating no-good bastard, a scumbag, a—" Jack cleared his throat with a loud *ahem*. "Oh…sorry, Jack. Guess I got carried away there." Karyn patted his knee again. "But the point is he adores you. Jeez, the man practically drove me crazy worrying about you all this time. If you hadn't come back I probably would have had to shoot him to put him out of his misery."

"Me?" Jack said. "What about you? You were a basket case. I never saw so much water come out of one human being before in my life. I can't even maneuver around Karyn's apartment without sloshing through soggy, tear-soaked tissues." He looked at Karyn and smiled, clasping her hand on his knee. "Now I understand why you two have been best friends for all these years. Karyn's a very special lady." He leaned over, lifting Karyn's hand to his lips and kissed it.

"Well, I'll be damned." Meredith chuckled. And then she straightened in her seat, thinking better of the nonchalant phrase. "No I won't—scratch that." Jack and Karyn just looked at each other and shrugged. "I'm glad to see the two people I care most about in this world on good terms. Amazed, but glad."

The telephone rang. "Just let it go to the answering machine, Meredith." Karyn waved a dismissive hand.

After the fourth ring a rich accented male voice said, "*Kah-rin, cara mia,* where are you? Don't make me sit here all alone when we could be doing *la cucaracha* together."

Karyn snatched the phone off the hook. "I'm on my way. Stay right where you are." She hung up and turned to

Meredith and Jack, grinning. It was about the biggest shit-eating grin that Meredith had ever seen. "That was the, uh…exterminator. I, uh, I gave him your phone number."

"Exterminator?" Meredith cocked her head. "What ex—" she stopped when she caught Karyn's dramatic eye signals. "Oh. *Oh!* Right. I forgot. The *exterminator.*"

"Uh-huh." Jack folded his arms across his chest and smirked. "Give it up, ladies. I wasn't born yesterday."

Karyn gave him her practiced wide-eyed innocent look, which didn't quite match the still present shit-eating grin. "Why, I don't know what you mean, Jack."

"I mean you'd better get your horny forty-year-old ass upstairs unless you want that young stud to get tired of waiting and seek gratification elsewhere." Jack shook his head and laughed. "And take your time because Meredith and I have lots of catching up to do." He gave Meredith a squeeze.

The grin still in place, Karyn flushed crimson. "Oh…well in that case," she skipped to the door and opened it, "happy birthday to me!" With a wink, a giggle and a blown kiss she was gone.

Chapter Fourteen

ဆ

"I can't believe we're finally alone," Jack said as soon as the door closed. "Thank God Karyn left when she did because if I had to wait any longer to get my hands on that sweet, delicious body of yours I would have thrown her out myself." He leapt from the sofa, grasped Meredith's ankles and yanked her into a reclining position, eliciting a surprised little yelp from her. And then Jack stood over her, arms akimbo, searing her with an intense, searching gaze.

Meredith's body reacted as it always had. Her heart rate picked up, her skin heated and her pussy drooled. She stared up into hazel eyes that gleamed with carnal intentions and licked her lips. She wanted Jack McKenna now more than she'd wanted anything in her life.

A soft growl erupted from Jack's throat as he scrutinized her from head to toe. "You're so goddamned beautiful that it makes my insides ache," he said, his voice raw and gruff with emotion. He shoved the coffee table out of the way with a swift kick and then dropped to the sofa, straddling Meredith with one knee on the cushions and one foot on the floor. Her head fell back as he slipped his hand under her back and drew her up, never taking his gaze from her eyes.

A tiny sound broke from Meredith's throat, part acceptance, part plea as her lips opened in anticipation. She gasped as he took fierce possession of her mouth, delving with his tongue. He tasted of unrestrained need and frustration and her heart broke for him at the same time that her nipples tightened beneath his hand.

"Oh Jack...my darling Jack." She stroked his face as their lips parted. "I'm so sorry for all the pain I've caused."

"Sweetheart," Jack said in a strained tone tinged with a chuckle, "the only pain either of us needs to be concerned about at the moment is the throbbing ache in my cock. It's so fucking hard it's about ready to burst out of my jeans."

"Well then I think we need to do something about that, don't you?" Meredith pulled herself up far enough so that she could get her hands on Jack's crotch. With a bit of fumbling as Jack supported her back, she finally managed to unfasten his jeans and sink her hand in the opening, wrapping it around his grand cock through his shorts. "Oh yes," she indulged in a throaty chuckle, "this is what I've been waiting for. The hope of feeling you inside of me again is what kept me going as I went through Hell and back."

Dropping Meredith unceremoniously to the sofa cushions, causing her to utter an *oomph*, Jack scrambled to his feet and jerked off his T-shirt. She moaned at the sight of his broad chest with its smattering of hair across his well-defined pecs. And when her gaze alighted on his ripped washboard stomach as he tossed the shirt aside, her cunt clenched. It had been so long...too long.

He shucked off his shoes, socks and jeans in mere seconds and then, in the blink of an eye, off came his shorts. Meredith felt her pussy trickle as he stood before her splendidly naked and breathing hard.

"Strip for me, Meredith." His voice was just above a whisper. "Give me an eyeful of those full luscious curves I've been dreaming about before I batter your pussy with my poor tormented cock."

Eager to get to the main attraction, Meredith quickly complied, tugging her sweater over her head first and then fiddling with the snap and zipper on her jeans until she could wrench them off.

"Come on, let's have it." Jack stretched out his hand, curling his fingers back and forth in invitation. "I want to see those gorgeous tits naked and bouncing.

Once on her knees, Meredith unclasped the front closure of her bra, liberating her breasts and immediately feeling her nipples crinkle under Jack's appreciative gaze. That's when she noticed the first trickle of juice down her thigh.

"Mmm, yeah. Definitely the stuff of my dreams." He closed the distance between them, cupping Meredith's breasts with his big hands and burying his face between them. A moment later he began to suckle and Meredith took in a sharp breath.

As he nibbled on one nipple and then the other, Jack groaned low in his throat, the vibrating sound thrilling her clear to her toes. He pushed her back against the cushioned arm of the sofa and the delectable, rigid feel of him brushed against her belly, making her writhe in anticipation. Jack's hand slid beneath the elastic of her panties and he coaxed them down over her hips. Suddenly, he tore the scrap of satin and lace from her body.

"I can't wait another minute, Meredith. I need you, baby. I need you right now more than I've needed anything in my life."

"Yes. Now, Jack. Do it to me now." She opened her thighs and he positioned himself over her. Her every cell tingled with expectation as his cock nestled in her thatch of curls, ready to part her pussy lips. And then he stopped as if frozen. Bracing herself on her elbows, Meredith popped her head up and chuckled. "What's the matter? Do you see something down there I should know about?" He was silent for so long she frowned. Shit. Maybe Dev had pulled some nasty trick and turned her pussy green or something. "Um...Jack?"

Jack gazed at her solemnly. "I went for a test shortly after you disappeared, Meredith," he said finally. "I'm clean. No disease. Nothing."

"Oh." She nodded with understanding. "Okay, that's good. Now go ahead and get back to work." Motioning to his immobile cock, Meredith smiled. She itched with an almost frantic need to feel him where he belonged—stuffed high and hard inside her. And if he didn't scratch that need soon she'd scream.

"And," Jack continued, "I need you to know that I haven't been with anyone since you left." And then his lip quirked into a sly smile. "So there won't be any need for cognac."

"Cognac?" Meredith gazed at him uncertainly and Jack simply nodded with a knowing smile. And then images of their night at the hotel—when she'd *sterilized* his cock against any *bimbo germs*—flashed across her mind and the realization hit her. "Oh!" She cringed, remembering Jack's reaction to the sting of the alcohol as she poured it over his cock. And then, as much as she didn't want to, she laughed. "Oh, Jack, I am *so* sorry about that. Really."

He pinned her hard against the sofa cushions and without warning, thrust himself into her, hard and unforgiving. After his satisfied growl blended with Meredith's shocked gasp, he said, "No you're not." And then he plunged into her again.

"Ooh," Meredith breathed, "if this is your way of punishing me then, please, discipline away." She hiked her hips and thrust against him as Jack pushed into her again. Needing to feel him even closer, harder, she locked her ankles behind his back and moaned with unbridled pleasure as his fingers sank into her ass cheeks and his stiff cock pummeled her cunt. They bucked, clawed and pumped wildly against each other. Meredith could tell that she was in for the orgasm of her life.

"Ah, Meredith, you feel so damned good—so juicy and so tight. I'm not going to be able to hold out much longer." Jack shifted their positions so that each pistoning motion of his cock abraded her clit.

"Yes... Just like that, Jack."

As Meredith trembled with the first vibrations of an imminent climax Jack said, "This is something else that taunted my dreams while you were missing. The sweet memory of watching myself slide in and out of your pretty little pussy. You have no idea how I've missed that, baby." His gaze glued on their joined flesh, he slammed into her with a fury that took her somewhere beyond all reason. It felt as if he had marked her—had boldly taken ownership of her body and she exulted in the primal sensation.

Digging her nails into his shoulders Meredith moaned. She knew at that moment that what Annie said was true—she and Jack were indeed soulmates, destined to be lovers for all eternity. She relished in the magnificent sensation of being sublimely fucked and then she screamed as her pussy clenched around him and she spiraled into a rip-roaring orgasm. Then it was Jack's turn to yell as the last of his control shattered and he went over the edge, joining her in carnal bliss.

Loud, boisterous and utterly unstinting in their passionate cries, they slumped into a boneless, exhausted heap. Replete and content.

"I feel like I've died and gone to heaven," Jack murmured against Meredith's throat. He started to lift his weight from her but Meredith clasped her arms around him, holding Jack in place.

"Not just yet. I want to feel the weight of you on top of me for a little while longer. I've missed that so much."

Jack raised himself a bit on his elbows and looked down at Meredith. "Have I told you lately that I love you? I mean really and truly love you?" He deposited a path of soft kisses from her forehead to her chin.

"I love you too, Jack. I always have and I always will." She smoothed the hair from his eye and pulled his head down to kiss him.

"I was such an ass, Meredith. I know I can't erase all the hurt and anguish you suffered because of me in the past but I can promise you that you'll never have to go through that again. Ever."

"We've both made mistakes," Meredith whispered. "Some real doozies. Why don't we try to forget what happened in the past and just start fresh from here?"

"Not before I get some things off my chest. It's important to me, Meredith." He gazed at her questioningly and she nodded. Jack raised himself to a sitting position, bringing Meredith up with him. "While you were gone I had plenty of time to think about the way I've treated you—taking you for granted and tossing you aside like you were nothing more than day-old bread. I was cocky and selfish and an immature prick. In the back of my mind I guess I always figured you'd still be there to come back to after I'd had my fill of the latest bimbo. But then when you disappeared and I realized you might be gone from my life forever, something snapped."

"Oh, my poor Jack." Resting her head on his shoulder, Meredith caressed his chest.

"I don't know how to explain it," he continued, clasping her hand. "It was almost like I went through one of those near-death experiences you hear about. My life sort of flashed before my eyes and I saw clearly that the finest, happiest, most satisfying moments always involved you. Not my work, not money, not other women...you, Meredith." He cupped her face in his hands and kissed her sweetly. "You are my life. You are my everything. Without you I have no soul...no reason for living."

Jack's words moved her so greatly that she was at a loss for words. Tears streamed down her cheeks while a radiant awareness of pure love lodged at the center of her heart. With an unhurried intake of breath, she studied Jack's features, finding something bright and untainted and wonderful there that she'd never seen before.

"You've always had a way with words, Jack, but never quite like this." She smiled warmly. "Believe me when I say that all I went through while I was away brought me to the same conclusions. I need you in my life, Jack. I want us to be together, always."

"You'll never know how happy that makes me." Jack captured her mouth in a kiss so concentrated with love and passion that Meredith felt the sensations shoot like liquid love straight to her soul. "I give you my word that there will never be anyone else. There will be no open relationships, no more infidelity. Period. Believe me?" He gave her a hopeful, expectant look.

Contemplating his proclamation as she noted the concern etched across his features, Meredith nodded. "Yes. For the first time I do believe you, Jack."

"And I want you to know," he continued, "that I love you just the way you are, all full and zaftig and curvy." He cupped her heavy breasts, giving them a firm squeeze. It felt so good having his hands on her again. "You're a strong, independent, curvaceous woman who exudes luscious femininity and I find that to be a major turn-on." Jack licked her slowly from her throat to her temple. As her eyelids fluttered closed, Meredith failed to muffle her rising moan.

"When I take my cock into my fist," Jack said against her ear, "stroking my erection to completion, it's your soft, yielding flesh that I'm thinking about. It's your womanly body that I picture rippling and jiggling as I pound into you." He laved her ear with his tongue and licked his way to her lips, seizing them in an evocative kiss.

When their lips parted, a whimper escaped her throat and Meredith struggled to keep herself from melting on the spot. "But...you told me before that a man wants the woman who's draped on his arm to be a svelte little thing," she said cautiously. "Are you honestly saying that you don't feel that way anymore?"

"Exactly. That was the old Jack talking—the idiot who cared more about what everyone else thought than what he thought and felt himself. I've always been attracted to your shapely body, Meredith, you know that. And I was a jerk for trying to make you over into a carbon copy of those impossibly thin model-type women. I want a real woman, dammit, not a skin-covered skeleton. I want you just the way you are, Meredith."

His heartfelt words made her feel beautiful...attractive...appealing...sexy. Better than thin. And she'd longed for Jack to feel this way, to tell her this, for oh so many years. It was like a dream come true. Like Heaven. "Well that's a good thing." Meredith kept her tone light so she wouldn't dissolve into hiccupping, messy, albeit happy sobs. "Because if I had to exist on a diet of little more than cigarettes, black coffee and lettuce leaves, with the occasional carrot stick for dessert, I'd be a hollow-eyed bitch on wheels." Jack joined her in laughter. "Food, like love, must never be a joyless experience," she added, stroking his jaw with her fingers.

"I love your passion for food, Meredith. Watching you enjoy the hell out of a glass of fine champagne, a forkful of lobster, a chunk of praline cheesecake or a spoonful of rich chocolate mousse reminds me of the same gusto you've always brought to our lovemaking. Speaking of which..." His gaze dropped to his groin and the impressive erection there and Meredith's eyes followed. When he raised his head again, Jack jiggled his eyebrows playfully.

"Hmm." Meredith folded her arms across her chest and smirked. "So, tell me...are you speaking about the gusto I bring to eating right now or are you referring to the gusto I bring to our lovemaking?"

Jack broke into a wide grin. "Both. Definitely."

"That's what I thought." Meredith smiled and licked her lips as she slipped off the sofa and got to her knees on the floor. "As a woman who fully appreciates gustatory delights, I've always loved sinking my teeth into things of...substance." She arched a brow and eyed Jack's cock, murmuring a husky chuckle. "And what could be more substantial than your delicious cock?" After a few teasing flicks of her tongue she slowly licked up one side of his cock and down the other before taking him in her mouth and biting softly.

"Oh yeah...I'm all for carnal gluttony," Jack groaned as he threaded his fingers through her hair.

After she'd spiraled her tongue around his notable girth her senses were suddenly assaulted with images of Alicia doing the same thing to her when she was in Ricky's body. *No, no, no, no, no.* Stunned by the unwelcome intrusion, Meredith pulled back and Jack's wet cock popped out of her mouth.

"Aw, please tell me you're not finished yet," he pleaded with a chuckle.

Meredith sat back on her heels, awestruck by the memories that flooded her brain. Memories that she *really* didn't want to be thinking about right now.

"Baby, is something wrong?"

"No...just give me a minute," Meredith said. One of the clearest memories that popped into her head was of the feeling of raw power that she had as Alicia sucked her...*Ricky's* cock. As Ricky, Meredith wanted to dominate, to control, to possess. And she wanted Alicia to swallow her cum. And Alicia did—every last drop. And Ricky loved it. Meredith frowned. She'd never done that for Jack. Sure, she'd given him plenty of blowjobs but she always let him pull out before he came in her mouth. The other memory at the forefront of her mind was the desire she, as Ricky, had to spank Alicia's ass. She'd certainly never engaged in anything like that with Jack either. Except for the last time she saw him when she'd swatted Jack's ass—hard. She rolled her eyes at the memory. Jack's ass...she wondered if the indelible ink was still there. With a shudder she hoped that it wasn't.

"Meredith, honey, are you okay? We don't have to do any more tonight if you need to rest or something. The last thing I want to do is to jeopardize your health after what you've been through."

Meredith sucked in a deep breath. "No, I'm fine. Healthy as a horse. Just suffering from a serious bout of brain overload, that's all." She laughed.

"Huh?"

She waved her hand in dismissal. "Nothing. Forget it." She took Jack's cock into her hands, mindlessly stroking it back to its former rigid state. His cock was longer and thicker than Ricky's, and Ricky's was damned impressive. She squeezed his shaft with one hand while she cupped his balls with the other, delighting in the way a groan rumbled up from somewhere deep within his chest.

"Have you ever wanted to spank me, Jack?"

Clearly taken aback, Jack laughed a little and shrugged. "Oh...several times come to mind, I guess." He grinned. "Why?"

Meredith got up and straddled Jack's lap, facing him. As Jack watched, she grasped her nipples and played with them, pinching, tugging and rolling as she moaned her pleasure. It was something she'd never done in front of a man before but Jack had often told her he'd love to see her play with herself. She'd always been shy about touching herself in front of him— but things were different now. With all the wild and unearthly adventures she'd recently experienced, Meredith decided that it was high time for some changes in her real life. As she played with her breasts, the look of drooling amazement on Jack's face told her she was definitely on the right track.

"Jack, I want you to spank my ass while I play with myself." Leaving one hand in place, tugging on a stiff nipple, she brought her other hand to her clit and flicked it with her finger.

Jack's jaw-dropping expression was priceless. "Jesus, Meredith... that is *so* hot."

She writhed in his lap. "Spank me!"

Jack reached behind her and swatted her ass while Meredith pleasured herself. The sensation was unique, adding just the right amount of pain to the pleasure.

"Again," she demanded. "Harder this time. Make me come for you, Jack. Make my pussy juices run down my thighs and onto yours."

"Holy shit." Jack complied, giving Meredith another stinging slap while he grabbed onto her other nipple, pinching hard. "I'm about this close to coming just watching you."

"No, not yet, Jack," a breathless Meredith instructed him. "You have to wait." The odd mixture of stinging pain and vibrating pleasure soon had Meredith bucking with a violent orgasm, shouting out Jack's name as she came in surging waves of ecstasy. And then she collapsed against his chest, with Jack caressing her and kissing her temple.

She took a moment to regain her senses and then, forcing her limp, sated body from the comfort of Jack's arms, Meredith lifted herself from his lap and returned to her position on her knees in front of him. With newfound enthusiasm, she took Jack's cock back into her mouth, sucking and nibbling and licking and doing her best to drive him to the brink of insanity.

Jack's hands grasped Meredith's head, pulling her away from his cock, but she stayed put.

"Ah...God...Meredith, you have to stop. I need to pull out, sweetheart. I'm going to come."

A few energetic flicks of her tongue at the tender tip of Jack's cock followed by a wicked round of suction and Jack's hips bucked involuntarily. Meredith's eyes widened as his cock thrust against the back of her throat. She relaxed the muscles in her throat, which made it easier for him to fuck her mouth. Yes...*this* is what she wanted to give him. She knew from her firsthand experience as a man how much Jack would enjoy the intense sensations of pleasure and power.

Fisting hanks of Meredith's hair, Jack gave in to a howling grunt as streams of his hot cum spurted down her throat.

She swallowed every last drop and then scoured his cock clean with her tongue. Licking remnants of the tangy cream from her lips, Meredith smiled—quite pleased with her newfangled skill and with the great big shit-eating grin on Jack's face.

Yup...Goody-Two-Shoes had left the building and in her place was the new and improved Meredith.

And the new improved Meredith swallowed.

Chapter Fifteen

තා

"I feel like I've died and gone to heaven," Jack said, slumping against the sofa cushions with a contented sigh. "That was...beyond description." He pulled Meredith up from her knees so that she was on the couch next to him and they snuggled.

She fully agreed. It felt so damned good to *canoodle* with Jack again. Meredith purred as she nipped at his neck, relishing in the knowledge that she'd successfully sent her man to the moon and back on a jet stream of passion. There was nothing quite so gratifying — except, of course, having him send her on an astral trip of her own. Ooh yeah...

"I'm starving."

Meredith popped her head up. "So much for soft and fuzzy afterglow." She gave him a playful pinch and laughed. "You haven't changed a bit, Jack."

"That's what you think." He planted a kiss on the tip of her nose before unwinding his arm from Meredith's shoulder and hopping off the sofa. "I'm betting you still have your favorite pizzeria on your speed dial," he said picking up the telephone.

"Mmm, pizza. I haven't had any in ages. Oh, Jack, you know me so well." Meredith smiled at him, realizing just how good it made her feel.

"Intimately," Jack said softly, a twinkle in his eyes as he gazed at her. "Inside and out."

"Martino's Pizza is number six on the speed dial," she said, aware that her words traveled on a dreamy sigh.

"Sausage, mushroom, peppers and onion still your favorite combo?"

"Sounds perfect." When he turned and bent to retrieve his jeans Meredith swallowed a silent sigh of relief to see that the wording she'd scrawled across his butt had, thankfully, worn off, although...upon closer squint-eyed inspection she noted there was a sort of faint purplish tinge to his ass cheeks. "Glad to see it wasn't permanent." She smacked his backside after he'd finished his call to the pizza place.

Smirking, Jack shrugged on his jeans, sans shorts, and eyed Meredith with a narrowed gaze. "Do *not* even get me started on that." He wagged a chastising finger. "Trust me, you don't want to know what it's like to have to scrub your own ass with a steel wool scouring pad. And the ink residue's still not completely gone."

"Yeah...I sort of noticed. Sorry." She gave an apologetic shrug. "At least the photos Ricky took didn't get published."

In the middle of fastening his jeans Jack stilled, staring at Meredith with a quizzical expression. "How did you know about the pictures...and Ricky?"

Damn. Her heart hurdled into her throat, thumping wildly. "Uhhh..." Now probably wasn't the best time to confess that she'd perfected her cock sucking skills by experiencing a blowjob firsthand while inhabiting Ricky's body. They stared at each other for what seemed like an eternity as Meredith hustled to come up with a feasible explanation. Finally, she tapped her head and gave a clueless shrug. "I'm not sure, Jack. Must be the amnesia. His name just popped into my mind." She watched carefully as he regarded her words and felt her heart slither back into place as Jack's features relaxed.

Scrubbing his chin, he nodded thoughtfully. "Maybe you ran into him or his accomplice after you left the hotel. Apparently he had second thoughts about selling the photos to the press but his girlfriend had different ideas." He paused for a moment, eyebrows furrowed. "You know, Ricky mentioned you by name before he died, so you two must have met at some point. He was a strange and mixed-up kid but there was something about him...something in his eyes that reminded me of..." His gaze zeroed in on Meredith's eyes while his mouth curved in frowning contemplation.

"Yes?" Meredith's breath hitched. He *had* recognized her! She knew it. What was that saying? *The eyes are the windows to the soul...*

With a self-conscious laugh, Jack broke his stare, waved his hand dismissively and shook his head. "Never mind. It just sounds silly."

There wasn't any need to press Jack about it. She knew exactly what he'd seen in Ricky's eyes. Meredith got up, scooping her panties from the floor and chuckling when she remembered that the scrap had been rendered useless when Jack tore it from her hips. Tossing them aside, she reached for Jack's T-shirt and yanked that over her head. It came just low enough to cover her crotch.

"Don't bother putting on anything else," he said as Meredith stooped to grab her jeans. "Because after the pizza, I'm having *you* for dessert." He winked and Meredith felt her pussy dribble in joyful expectation.

The pizza arrived a short time later. Jack set the box on the coffee table and headed for the kitchen, humming some unrecognizable tune. Although not particularly gifted with mellow vocal chords, Meredith remembered that he liked to sing, hum and whistle much of the time. Hearing him warble happily in her kitchen made her feel like she was really home at last. She smiled and hugged herself. Jack opened the bottle of cabernet he'd selected from her tiny wine rack as Meredith lit several lavender-scented candles. The subtle peach glow of the setting sun fused with the blush of candlelight, creating the perfect ambience.

As Meredith reached for her wineglass, Jack stilled her hand. "Uh...I just want to make sure you don't have any problems," he cleared his throat, "you know...of the glass-throwing sort...before we make a toast." He gave an apologetic shrug. "Because we can have water instead if that makes you feel better."

It took a minute for Meredith to figure out what he meant and then she remembered how she'd whacked the glass out of Karyn's hand earlier. "Oh," she laughed, "that." Jack nodded. "No, I'm perfectly okay with wine, don't worry." She winked.

"Good." Jack let out a deep breath and hoisted his wineglass. "In that case, let's toast to your safe return, to loving each other always and to never being parted again. Ever." Meredith nodded her agreement and smiled. Then they intertwined arms continental style and drank.

"And here's to being soulmates," she added as they clinked glasses and sipped again. Forget the fame and the fortune and all the trappings that went along with it. This was it—the glorious feeling warming her insides right at this moment. It's all she'd ever wanted. Her and Jack, together and loving each other forever.

"You'll have to catch me up on things," Meredith said after finishing her first slice of pizza and murmuring her appreciation of the gooey, crisp-crusted treat. "Has your TV show aired yet or is it still in the production stage?"

Jack chewed and swallowed. "*On the Right Track with Dr. Jack* is kaput."

"What?" Meredith almost choked on her wine. "They pulled the plug on your talk show? But I thought everything was all right. I thought the memory card with the photos is safely stuck in the mud somewhere at the bottom of the river." He looked at her strangely after that gaffe, but Meredith didn't care at this point. "Oh, Jack, this is terrible. What happened...why did they cancel it?" Meredith's hand flew to her mouth and she gasped. "Oh dear Lord, it's Alicia, isn't it? She got to the press somehow and told them about the sock puppet and all the rest, is that it? Damn," she muttered to herself before Jack had a chance to answer, "as much as I detest violence, I almost wish Kravitz would have shot her when she gunned me down. That way she never would have been able to hurt you."

"When she gunned you down?" Jack coughed an astonished gasp. "Okay, hold it, Meredith," his hand popped up like he was a cop stopping traffic. "You're scaring me here. Seriously. Part of what you said makes no sense at all and there's no way you could possibly know any of the rest unless you were there at the scene—which, to the best of my knowledge, you weren't. I think it's definitely time for you to do some explaining, don't you?" He nailed her with a solemn, no-nonsense gaze.

Meredith slouched against the cushions, offering a meek smile. "Eh...yes, I suppose so. Would you believe me if I told you that I was inhabiting Ricky's body when Alicia shot him and when Kravitz held Ricky's bleeding body before the ambulance arrived?"

Jack shifted his lower jaw from left to right as he crossed his arms over his chest. Meredith felt as if his eyes were boring a hole into her skull as Jack gave her one of those disbelieving what-the-hell-are-you-trying-to-pull looks.

"Yeah, well, I didn't think so," she mumbled, engaging in a timid shrug as she nervously twisted the hem of the T-shirt.

Jack covered her fidgeting hand with his and smoothed his thumb over her knuckles. "I know you've always had a habit of hiding behind your offbeat sense of humor when you're stressed, Meredith," he said, "but I've got to tell you, babe..." he looked at her for a long moment, shaking his head, "there's not a damned thing funny about any of that. How do you know about Ricky, Alicia, Kravitz, the photos or the rest? Tell me...please."

She looked up into his eyes and sighed. "I wish I could but I just can't, Jack."

"Sure you can." His voice was soft and soothing, as if he were speaking to a small frightened child. "Just tell me the truth, sweetheart. Be honest with me. Whatever it is I promise I won't be angry or upset."

"Really?"

"Really."

"Swear?"

Jack rolled his eyes and tsked. "I swear." He crossed his heart with his finger and smiled.

Meredith worried her bottom lip as she searched his eyes and then sucked in a deep breath. "Well, okay," she cleared her throat loudly and then gulped down some wine before proceeding, "but if you didn't buy the part about me being inside Ricky's body then it's probably a safe assumption that you're never going to believe the part about me falling down the elevator shaft of your hotel, going to Hell after I died and then being sent back to Earth by the devil, who's a female by the way, so that I could undo the damage I'd done." She looked at Jack and winced when she saw his horror-struck expression. "Or," she continued in a tiny, hurried voice, "the part about having Lysander, a muscular black angel, fly me up to Heaven where I met with Annie, my guardian angel, who was also my Grandma Kate's guardian angel, before Lysander brought me back here to Earth in my own body."

His mouth flattened in displeasure, Jack bolted from the sofa and began to pace. "Damn it, Meredith—"

Meredith shot to her feet and pointed at him. "You promised, Jack! You swore that you wouldn't get mad."

Muttering something unintelligible under his breath, Jack scrubbed his face with his hands and picked up his pacing. He kept scuffling around the living room for what seemed like an eternity until he finally came to a stop and faced her. "You're right. I'm sorry. It's just that I'm trying to get some serious answers here and for some reason you just seem compelled to keep making jokes. You're acting more like a five-year-old than a mature forty-year-old woman for chrissakes."

"I resent that, Jack." Meredith plopped back onto the sofa, crossing her arms over her chest and one leg over the other. "You asked me to be honest and I was. I told you the truth, it wasn't a joke. I know it sounds a little far-fetched—"

Jack huffed a humorless laugh. "A *little*? Jesus, Meredith..."

Meredith's head repeatedly bobbed in agreement. "I know, I know. But I swear to God, Jack, that it's all true. I never had any amnesia. There wasn't any car accident. No hospital stay, except for the time I was in Ricky's dying body." She purposefully ignored Jack's eye roll and kept going. "I just made all of that up to give you and Karyn some sort of rational-sounding explanation about what had happened to me. I was afraid to tell you the truth because I thought you'd have me locked up in some psycho ward or something." She got up slowly and walked over to Jack, wrapping her arms around his waist and resting her head against his bare chest. "With all of my heart I know what I put you and Karyn through, Jack. Do you honestly think I'd be crass enough to be cracking jokes about it when you asked me point blank to be straightforward?" Jack was silent and Meredith shook him a bit. "Well, do you?"

She felt his chest rise as Jack filled his lungs. "No," he offered softly. "No, you wouldn't do that."

The breath she'd been holding came out in a relieved whoosh and she tipped her head up to see his face. "Then you believe me?" She felt the beginnings of a hopeful smile tickling at her mouth.

With a tender gaze, Jack stroked his thumb along Meredith's jaw. "No, sweetheart. But I believe that *you* believe it. And that's good enough for me." He lowered his head and captured her lips in a kiss so sweet and tender that Meredith could almost feel the magnitude of his love permeating every cell of her being.

"And that's good enough for me too," she whispered. "Thank you, Jack."

They stood locked in an embrace, rocking back and forth for awhile until Meredith pulled back, taking his hand and leading Jack back to the sofa. "The pizza's getting cold," she said.

"We always liked it better that way anyway." He winked and grabbed a slice as they sat down.

"I remember." Meredith smiled, recalling all the cold leftover pizzas they'd shared together amidst good conversation and great lovemaking in times past. "So before we got off track," she folded a piece and brought it to her lips, "I was asking you why the network cancelled your TV show." She jammed the small portion into her mouth, licked her fingers and chewed as she waited for Jack to swallow the sizeable slice he'd crammed into his mouth.

"They didn't cancel it. I did," he said, mouth still partly full as he picked off bits of green bell pepper from another slice and set them aside. "I decided that I needed to prioritize things in my life in order of importance and being on television just wasn't at the top of the list anymore, that's all."

"You're kidding? Just like that?" Meredith snapped her fingers. "I thought having your own national talk show held the top spot on your list of goals, Jack. I don't get it."

"Oh it used to be a high priority, definitely. But your disappearance changed all that," he said matter-of-factly as he chomped on the de-peppered slice of pizza. When he saw the skewed expression of puzzlement on Meredith's face he laughed. "When you and I were starting out, Meredith, we dreamed of fame and fortune and living happily ever after, remember?" She nodded. "Well, I've got plenty of money now and I've got the recognition but I lost the happy ending in the process. Without you, sweetheart, fame and fortune are meaningless."

Tears springing to her eyes, Meredith sucked in a deep breath. "Wow," she said in a near whisper. "That's got to be the most beautiful, most romantic thing you've ever said to me."

Jack just shrugged. "I love you, Meredith. Period. No fancy-shmancy Dr. Jack gobbledygook, just the plain, simple, honest truth. I don't care about any of the glitzy frills unless I can share it all with you. Somehow along the way to success my priorities shifted. Being somewhat of a celebrity left me with a swelled head and an overblown ego that turned me into a sorry excuse for a man."

Meredith's head shook back and forth slowly. "I'm amazed, Jack. Not many men could admit to being a..." She searched for the right phrase, a nicer, less tactless synonym for *selfish bastard*.

"Selfish bastard?" Jack helped out and then laughed. Meredith recalled that eerie feeling she'd had when the otherworldly beings had read her thoughts and she swallowed hard. "Yeah," Jack continued, "well, it wasn't all that easy for me to come to that realization to be honest. I got a lot of help from Karyn."

"Karyn? I don't understand."

"Let's just say that after you disappeared, she and I got caught up in a lot of name calling and finger pointing before we finally found ourselves becoming friends. Karyn let me know in no uncertain terms what she thought about me." He laughed again and punched a fist against his hand. "Whew, that girl packs a helluva wallop with her words. But they eventually sank in and I finally realized how shallow and self-centered I'd become. Karyn told me about how despondent you became after I left you for Becky. Christ, it's no wonder you resorted to such drastic measures after the way I'd treated you all those years. And then the way I capped off your fortieth birthday by suggesting that we have an open marriage. Jeez, Karyn practically beat me to death when I told her about that."

"You actually told her?" Meredith was amazed.

"Yup. And here's a tip—never confess anything to Karyn while she has a large economy-size tube of liverwurst in her hand." Jack rubbed the back of his head and winced. "Who would have thought that lunchmeat could be a deadly weapon?"

Meredith covered her hand with her mouth and laughed. She could just picture Karyn on a righteous liverwurst rampage after hearing that. "Oh poor Jack."

"Nah. Poor Jack nothing." He shook his head. "After the way I treated you, sweetheart, it would have served me right if those damn photos had been published."

"Oh no. Don't say that, Jack. That would have been terrible." Meredith reached for his hand and clasped it. "When I think of the humiliation and degradation you would have gone through it kills me inside." Those horrid images of Jack and Karyn in the alternate future whizzed past her mind again and she shuddered.

Jack nodded and squeezed her hand. "I thank God every day that the pictures and story didn't get out to the media. I feel like I've won a reprieve, like I'd been given a second chance to right some of the wrongs I'd committed along the way to fame and fortune. And that's why I decided to turn my attention to Abundant Finds instead of the TV show."

By the grin on Jack's face Meredith figured the look she slanted him must have been more than a bit cockeyed. "My resale shop?"

"Uh-huh."

"What do you mean?"

Jack's mouth kicked up into a devilish, all-out smile as he poured them each another glass of wine, holding it to the light and studying it while he tilted the glass this way and that. "Good cab, isn't it? Rich, deep and earthy." He sipped from it, wickedly prolonging the suspense and obviously enjoying the fact that he'd so cleverly captured Meredith's undivided attention.

Well, two could play at that game.

"Mmm, yes it is." Raising her glass, she slowly tongued the rim as she eyed Jack. Then she dipped two fingers in the ruby liquid and brought the wet digits to her mouth, licking and sucking as she closed her eyes and emitted a sultry moan. "It's been so long since I've enjoyed a good glass of red wine. Makes me feel all warm inside. Hot. And, ooh, so damned horny I can hardly stand it." After sipping from her glass she trailed the same two fingers down her shirt and beneath it, watching Jack's gaze follow, riveted on what her fingers might be doing under the T-shirt.

"Ah, Jesus!" In a flash he'd set down his glass and, just as he was about to pounce on her, Meredith slapped a hand against his chest, eliciting a whoosh of air from his lungs as she stalled his approach.

With a low throaty laugh she said, "Uh-uh-uh. Not so fast, sweetie pie. You don't get any until *after* I get all the details." She winked.

"That's cheating," Jack said, feigning annoyance. "Just plain wicked."

Meredith picked up the remote control and shrugged. "Okay, maybe we'll just watch TV instead." It had been ages since they'd engaged in sassy, playful banter and she was relishing every minute of it.

"Sure, go ahead." Jack sat back and folded his arms across his chest as Meredith called his bluff and clicked the *on* button. "Maybe we can watch some nice old-fashioned chick flick together, you know, the ones that make you cry? It's a shame though..."

Heaving a sigh as music from some game show blared from the television, she took the bait. "What?"

"That I won't get a chance to lick you into a screaming orgasm. Or have the pleasure of keeping you gasping and quaking all night." Meredith shivered and he closed the distance between them. "Pity, because I've been dying to slide my tongue across that slick little clit of yours. Remember how I can make you tremble with just one swipe of my magic tongue, baby? And how you squirm when I close my teeth over—"

"Whoa!" Meredith fanned herself with both hands. "Okay, now *you're* cheating."

"Truce?"

"Truce," she agreed.

"I'll tell you everything you want to know," Jack offered, "and then we'll make ourselves nice and comfy on your bed and commence to screwing each other's brains out."

"Deal." Meredith nodded and clicked the *off* button on the remote. She hiked her wineglass and they clinked. "But you better talk fast because thinking about screaming orgasms tends to make it rather difficult for me to concentrate."

"Tell me about it." Jack's eyes dropped to the sizeable bulge in his jeans and Meredith's followed. Mmm, yes, they were in for a fun night of hot and heavy make-up sex all right.

"So…about your involvement with Abundant Finds?"

"Karyn was having a tough time holding everything together after you were gone. Between her constant worrying about you and having your full-timer quit—"

Meredith gasped. "Tanya quit?"

"Her husband got transferred to New Jersey unexpectedly." Jack nodded. "Karyn had to fire Tanya's replacement for stealing and had a difficult time finding someone else." Meredith cringed. "Anyway, Karyn was running herself ragged with all the extra hours she was putting in and if she didn't get help she was afraid she'd have to close the store. I know how much Abundant Finds means to both of you, so I offered to help out for awhile. It was easy to see all the love and hard work you and Karyn put into the place. The store's well laid out, inviting, offers a great selection of high-end clothing and has a strong customer base. But without the staff to man the place, it was losing business. Women just didn't want to stand in line waiting that long to purchase a few items of clothing."

"That was wonderful of you, Jack." Meredith had a difficult time picturing Jack catering to, much less relating to, the plus-size clientele, but she was surprised and delighted he'd stepped in to help. "So when are you there, on the weekends?"

"Full time."

"Full—" Her eyebrows shot up in astonishment. "How did you ever manage that with your heavy schedule?"

"That's where all that prioritizing and setting new goals came in," Jack explained, rubbing his hands together. Meredith smiled when she saw the excited twinkle in his eye. "I asked myself how you would feel if you came back and discovered that the shop you'd worked so hard to build and turn into a thriving venue was rapidly failing or that it had closed. I couldn't let that happen. So Karyn and I put our heads together and came up with a few strategies that would not only keep Abundant Finds prosperous but, hopefully, help it to flourish. And it seems to be working."

"Fascinating." Folding her arms across her chest, Meredith sat back against the sofa cushions and nodded. Truly the last thing she'd ever expected was for Jack to show a sincere interest in her shop. "So tell me about it."

"Well," Jack shrugged, "I figured that I could be of the most help by employing my strengths and talents—the very skills that you helped me to attain when you worked to put me through school."

Meredith wanted to say, *will wonders never cease?* but thought better of it. Instead, she nodded again and said, "I see." Evidently Jack wasn't kidding when he'd said that he was a changed man.

"I knew what a struggle you'd had due to weight-related concerns over the years," Jack continued. "Including low self-esteem and, worse yet, having to deal with thoughtless comments from jerks like me who couldn't understand why overweight people couldn't just push themselves away from the table and lose the weight." He rolled his eyes. "I am *so* sorry about all of that, Meredith. I didn't understand the depth of the emotional issues involved."

"Thanks, Jack. That really means a lot to me." Meredith smoothed her hand over his thigh. She was flummoxed...just as disoriented as if he'd clunked her over the head with a frying pan. All this compassion and understanding was coming from Jack? *Her* Jack?

"That's a little too close for comfort, baby." Jack eased her hand closer to his knee, patting it. "I'll never be able to focus on what I'm saying with your hand that close to my cock. If it gets any harder I won't be able to hold up my end of the deal."

"We wouldn't want that to happen," Meredith purred, gently patting the erection nestled inside his jeans with her other hand before she looped her arm through his.

"You are such a bad girl."

"Thanks. I do my best."

He huffed a laugh and tweaked her nipple, getting the little gasp of surprise his action had obviously intended. "So anyway, I listened to the customers at the shop talking about the problems they were having. All sorts of stuff from diets to exercise to motivation to finding stylish clothes that fit, etcetera. And I started asking them questions about what they were looking for in the way of help. That's when I decided to make good use of my semi-celebrity status and offer reasonably priced motivational classes for plus-sized women — given by *Dr. Jack*." He grinned just like a little boy who'd brought home a report card with straight As.

At that moment Meredith had never loved him more. "Brilliant," she said. "And very generous."

"No big deal." Jack shrugged off the praise. "But the good news is that your customers love the classes so much that I've had to add more — and they're filled to capacity with a waiting list. From among your happy customers, Karyn's hired two full-time sales clerks and two part time. And she's very pleased with them. In addition, Karyn and I co-authored a self-help book with all the proceeds to be donated to the Meredith McKenna Foundation."

She turned in her seat and gaped at him. "The what?"

"We set up a nonprofit organization to help educate the public about weight-related issues. You've always said you hated the way the media uses its power to make females feel bad about themselves if they're not a size three or less. And Karyn said you're very concerned about young girls and their obsession with weight loss so they look like all the skinny celebrities. The foundation will address those issues and strive to change the public's perception and attitude about size. I'll be one of the spokespeople and we'll also employ..." he laughed, "well, as Karyn calls them, *beefy young hunks* who'll be paired with big beautiful women for print and TV ads. We'll focus on showing plus-sized women in a positive and desirable light. We have lots of other ideas, but that's enough for now. So what do you think?"

Stunned beyond belief, Meredith couldn't speak at first. "Are you kidding?" she finally managed to say. And she felt the slow smile spread across her features until it became so wide her cheeks ached. "I think that you are the most incredible, wonderful, compassionate, giving, romantic, sexy man I have ever known." She planted a series of exuberant kisses across his face and chest.

"Wait a minute... Sexy only comes in at number six?" Jack teased.

"Listen you gorgeous, sexy stud," Meredith scribbled invisible patterns across his pecs with her finger, "I have never wanted to feel your cock inside of me as much as I do at this very moment. Ever. Does that answer your question?" Batting her eyelashes for effect, her fingers traveled down his torso, coming to rest at his crotch where she squeezed the promising bulge.

"That's it." His eyes blazing with desire, Jack grabbed Meredith's hand and yanked her off the couch. "We're done talking. Come on." He gazed down at her with an intense scrutiny so sultry that her pussy throbbed with slick, pulsing need. Oh God how she needed to feel him against her, over her, inside her. Skin to skin, ensnared in a lusty haze of hot sweaty passion.

Just a few steps before they reached the bedroom the doorbell rang, followed by a flurry of knocking.

"Goddamned sonuvabitch." Whipping his head toward the door, Jack belted out another string of obscenities before turning back to Meredith. "Do not even think about answering that," he warned, tugging her toward the bedroom. "I mean it."

"I won't," Meredith assured him. "It can't be anything important. Nobody even knows I'm back yet aside from Karyn and she'd never interrupt—"

"Hey, open up." More ringing and banging against the door.

Jack and Meredith looked at each other. "Karyn," they said, shoulders slumping simultaneously.

"I know you guys are in there," Karyn persisted. "Let me in for a minute. It's important!"

"No," Jack said to Meredith, pressing his fingers into the soft flesh of her upper arms as he pinned her with his gaze. "No way. I love Karyn like a sister but you know what a blabbermouth she is. If we open that door now we'll never get her to leave. And my cock is stretched so damned taut that I'm in danger of losing control if it doesn't get appeased almost immediately."

Meredith nodded. "I know...but she said it's important." She shrugged. "What if it's an emergency?"

"I can hear you guys whispering in there."

Grumbling something fierce, Jack tramped to the door and Meredith scrambled into her jeans, tripping several times before she managed to hike them up all the way. "This damn well better be important," Jack barked as he swung open the door, "or you are *so* dead, Karyn."

Karyn poked her head in, finger-waving at Meredith. "Hi. I hope I'm not interrupting anything." Her question being met by stony silence, Karyn cleared her throat and continued. "Silly question I guess." She chuckled. "Honest, I never would have bothered you except that I'm just on my way out and I needed to check with both of you first."

Jack slanted her a skewed, impatient look. "About what?"

Meredith stepped closer and grasped Karyn's elbow, pulling her into the apartment. "What is it, honey?"

"I know it's short notice, but I just wanted to know if you two could manage without me for a couple of days at the shop."

"Yeah. Sure. Okay. Goodbye," Jack urged, pushing Karyn back toward the door.

"Jack, stop it." Meredith tried not to laugh. "Is something wrong, Karyn? Family emergency?"

Karyn shook her head and giggled like a schoolgirl. "Nope. Everything is peachy. Perfect. Astounding," she gushed. "Cristoval won a two-night stay at a hotel on the coast and he wants me to come with him to celebrate my birthday. Isn't that fabulous?"

"Oh, honey, that's wonderful!" Meredith grabbed her friend into a hug and squeezed hard.

"I feel bad leaving right after you just got back, Meredith, but, well…"

"Are you insane?" Meredith nearly screeched. "For heaven's sake, sweetie, give yourself a fortieth birthday present you'll never forget. I promise that I'll still be here when you get back and then we can catch up on everything, okay?" Meredith winked.

"Thanks," Karyn said, squeezing Meredith's hand. "Cristoval's waiting downstairs in the lobby for me, so I have to hurry."

"Good," Jack said. "Well, don't let us keep you."

"All right already," Karyn said, throwing her hands into the air. "I get the hint. I'm gone. I'm outta here."

Meredith stilled Karyn, placing her hand on her arm. "Now see what you've done, Jack? You've hurt Karyn's feelings."

Karyn waved her hand in dismissal. "Aw, not really. Actually I'm just as anxious to get back to Cristoval as you two are to get back to..." her gaze alighted on the coffee table. "Ahem...to eating your pizza." She grinned.

Jack clearly couldn't help laughing. "A rendezvous with your boy-toy exterminator, huh?" He nodded, tongue in cheek. "You naughty girl, you." Karyn blushed and then he shot her a serious expression as he folded his arms across his chest. "But you could have just called, you know." Karyn looked stricken and Jack sighed. "Aw, come here." He pulled her into a hug. "Go on, have a good time. Stay as long as you like. You deserve it." He gave her a peck on the cheek. "Just do me one favor, okay?"

"Anything," Karyn said, nodding with enthusiasm. "Name it."

"Do not, under any circumstances call me or Meredith unless you and Cesario—"

"Cristoval," Karyn corrected.

"Whatever." Jack waved his hand. "Unless you two are rendered helpless and encased in full body casts in the hospital. Got it?"

"Oh, Jack," Meredith chastised, "that's terrible."

Karyn laughed. "Don't worry. I won't call, I promise—at least not until I get back so I can fill you in on all the juicy details." She directed the last part to Meredith with a waggle of her eyebrows.

Jack's face fell. "Come on, you guys are kidding, right? You don't really get together and go over all the particulars after...after..." he twirled his finger in some sort of explanatory gesture. "You know."

Meredith and Karyn exchanged glances. "Never," they chorused with far too innocent smiles. Jack just shook his head.

"Thanks again for setting things up with Cristoval," Karyn said, clasping Meredith's hands. "We just really hit it off, Meredith. And," her voice fell to a surreptitious whisper, "he says he loves my full, womanly curves."

"And why wouldn't he?" Jack asked. "You're a big beautiful woman, Karyn, and this young man obviously knows a good thing when he sees it."

Obviously taken aback, Karyn's eyes suddenly misted and she grabbed Jack into a firm hug. "That means a lot to me, Jack. Thank you." She planted a kiss on his jaw.

Meredith actually thought she saw Jack blush. "Yeah, yeah," he said, trying to sound like a tough guy as he scooted Karyn out the door, "now go on and get out of here so Meredith and I can get back to...our pizza." He graced Meredith with a private, sinful grin.

"Right." Karyn huffed a laugh as she looked at one and then the other. "Like I believe that. Have fun. I love you both." She blew them a kiss and then she was gone.

Before Meredith could take her next breath Jack scooped her up into his arms and marched toward the bedroom. Meredith had a sensation of buoyancy, almost as if she were as weightless as a hollow-boned size zero the way he'd effortlessly boosted her into the air.

"I don't care if the whole fucking building burns down around us, Meredith." Jack kicked the bedroom door open wide, tossing her unceremoniously onto the bed so hard that she bounced. A great shuddering breath squeezed from her lungs as she watched him stripping off his jeans, allowing his cock to spring free. Damn. He wasn't kidding about its expanding size.

"And I don't give a damn," he continued, "if the devil or your angels or Ricky's ghost or Kravitz or the entire Portland police department comes banging on your door." He leapt onto the bed, straddling her and ripping at her jeans. "You and I are going to fuck uninterrupted until I'm utterly fuck-depleted and you're a boneless orgasmic puddle of contentment, do you hear me?"

Chapter Sixteen

ഔ

"Loud and clear!" Meredith breathed, her pussy so sodden with expectation that she was soaking the bedspread.

Jack pushed the T-shirt up over her breasts, rumbling hums of approval as he grasped the mounds and dug his fingers into her pliable flesh. He plucked her nipples until they hardened into aching points then swooped close to capture one needy peak between his teeth. With each nibble, spiky flashes of ecstasy throbbed to her clit.

She whimpered as his mouth left her breast cold, wet and lonely and then purred when she felt him nipping at the soft flesh down her belly while his tongue licked a damp path in search of her pussy. An almost unbearable spike of anticipation sprinted clear through to her nerve endings as she waited to feel his mouth where she needed it most.

"Open for me, sweetheart," he coaxed. Jack certainly didn't have to tell her twice. Meredith moaned her acquiescence and immediately complied by spreading her thighs until she lay fully exposed to his slow appreciative gaze. She watched as he looked down at her cunt, licking his lips as if he were a kid in a candy store. "I want to see all that pretty pink flesh," he said, "all juicy and primed for me to fuck it with my mouth." A deep, shuddering groan escaped Meredith and Jack gave an answering growl of pleasure as he brought his face close and inhaled at her pussy deeply. "Mmm, spicy and musky and enticing. Mine. My woman. You belong to me forever, Meredith."

"Yes...all yours," she managed to hiss as Jack's hot tongue delved into her sensitive cleft and explored. "Forever..." she added, her breath hitching. A moment later his skilled mouth found her clit. He licked it and then nibbled at it with a fierceness that made her flinch. Meredith struggled to still her trembling thighs to no avail. She was completely under his spell. Without doubt, there wasn't a cell in her entire being unaffected by the magic of his mouth. She knew this was exactly where he wanted her — trapped in a state of raw sexual arousal. And Meredith wanted him to keep her there forever.

Jack's taunting fingers traveled across her breasts, pinching her stiff nipples and making her moan with delight. And then his hand inched down her belly and through her pussy fur until his fingers found their destination. With a wicked thrust, he jammed three fingers deep into her core. Stiffening as the jumble of delicious carnal sensations at her breast and pussy all but drove her insane, a hoarse cry tore from her throat.

Tunneling her fingers into Jack's hair, she held his head and writhed as he hungrily slurped at the fresh rush of juices her pussy generated. "Oh God...stop." Meredith fisted the bedspread as her legs wavered. "Too much, Jack." She wasn't sure whether she needed mercy or brutality at this point, but Jack knew from experience exactly what she needed. How much...how long...how intense...

Increasing the deliberate hypnotic rhythm as he finger-fucked her pussy and ate her tender clit, Jack brought his other hand to her tits and savagely pinched one nipple and then the other, twisting and tugging until she dissolved in a low groan. That's when Meredith felt it take hold. The distinct deluge of pleasure that started with a tickling twinge somewhere deep inside and then swelled until she became wholly engulfed in its fierce undulating waves.

Just as Jack had predicted, she screamed as she came. Raw, unabashed cries of wild, convulsing pleasure. Primal growls of deepest fulfillment...supreme satisfaction. And finally ending on a drawn-out throaty moan.

Through heavy-lidded eyes she watched Jack as he brought his fingers to his nose, breathing in her scent. And then he sucked them, taking her taste, her wetness, her essence into his mouth and groaning his enjoyment.

Her head lolled from side to side as she lifted her arm and stroked Jack's shoulder. "I don't know what to say, Jack. That was magnificent. It was—oh!" She gave a sharp intake of breath as Jack's eyes ignited with a primal, almost feral hunger.

Without giving her a chance finish what she was saying or to fully regain her senses, he dug his fingers into her ass cheeks, sliding Meredith down to meet his cock and then forcefully impaling her. The action was so swift, so urgent that it took her breath away. She never remembered a time that his cock had felt so rigid, so insistent, so powerful.

"Ah, God, Meredith..." His hips moved again and he took blatant ownership of her body, pounding into her with an impatient, almost ferocious eagerness. Sparing her little time to think or speak or do much of anything other than writhe beneath him, Jack tilted Meredith's hips and thrust hard, watching his cock sliding in and out. She gasped as he pummeled her so profoundly that she actually felt his cock connecting with previously undiscovered spots deep inside. Points she hadn't even realized had existed—or, at least, that she'd forgotten about for years. Whatever it was, the sensations were inconceivably pleasurable. So much so that it almost frightened Meredith because she had the sensation that she was on the brink of an otherworldly experience. And she'd already had quite enough of being hauled off to different dimensions, thank you very much.

"Never leave me again," Jack commanded as he slammed into her again. Meredith found her breath catching in her throat as she gazed into his eyes. There in the depths she glimpsed raw, tender emotion amidst the haze of lust and passion. Jack's features were etched with a curious mix of pain, fear, anger and something else. Meredith felt certain that it was love. The elusive, deep, soul-connecting happily-ever-after kind of love that she yearned for more than anything.

"Promise me," Jack demanded. "Promise me, Meredith!" He squeezed her arms hard, shaking her.

She clutched at his forearms, needing to comfort him, to reassure him. And then she realized she was crying when her vision blurred. "I won't, Jack. Never again. I promise." She was so caught up in the rapture, the passion, the all-encompassing awareness of hammering pain and tantalizing pleasure combining with earnest devotion that she could barely formulate words.

"I love you," they said at once.

Just as her consciousness catapulted her into a mind-blowing orgasm, Meredith heard Jack's mighty, feral grunt and then felt the heat of his cream surging into her. It was a perfect storybook caveman-type fuck like no other she'd ever experienced.

As the final waves vibrated through her body, Meredith's gaze absently fell on a sliver of the crescent moon through her bedroom window as it illuminated the inky violet sky. Its soft lavender-tinged light enveloped them, reminding Meredith of the radiant colors of Heaven. She sighed. Two bodies highly tuned to each other. *How perfect. How sublimely, utterly perfect.*

"Oh Jack..."

"I'm sorry." He collapsed at her side, one arm thrown possessively over her.

"Sorry?" Meredith said, astonished. "For what?"

"That was selfish." He took a few ragged breaths. "I didn't mean to take you so forcefully, so hard, so fast. I just couldn't help it. I looked at you with your creamy thighs spread open beneath me and the pretty pink buds on those beautiful breasts of yours poking up at me and I needed to feel myself inside of you with such a burning desire that I lost control."

Meredith snuggled against him, resting a hand on Jack's chest and feeling his racing heart begin to slow. "Oh my dear, darling Jack. You have my unqualified permission to lose control like that anytime you damn well please." She indulged in a throaty laugh. "A little rough and forceful can be nice sometimes. It brings out the animal in you."

"*You* bring out the animal in me," he growled before brushing his lips across hers and indulging in a long, hard sigh. "Speaking about turning me into a rabid animal, remember our wedding night?" Jack scooted up into a half-sitting position, propping against the pillows.

Dragging herself up beside him, Meredith chuckled. "Which one?"

"Ouch." Jack winced through a laugh. "The first one. Remember how perfect that night was, starting with the magnificent view of the city lights from our honeymoon suite to you doing that sexy wedding gown striptease — right down to your peek-a-boo undies — and, of course, all the sensational sex we had that night?"

"I remember." Meredith nodded, indulging in a tuneful sigh as the magical memories of that first night as husband and wife came flooding back. She'd been so nervous and excited. "We were young and so much in love then."

"You were my innocent semi-virgin bride," Jack said. "My sweet little goody-two-shoes." He laughed.

"Yeah, well I would have been a *full* virgin if you hadn't corrupted me before we got married." Meredith gave him a playful elbow nudge in the ribs. "But I forgive you. That was one temptation I definitely didn't mind giving in to."

"Know what I remember best about that night?"

"Oh I think so," Meredith said. "Probably the same thing that immediately pops into my mind when I think about our honeymoon."

"MAGCC. The Michigan Avenue G-Clit-Cock," they said in unison and then laughed.

"That was hot stuff," Jack said with a boastful smile. "If I do say so myself."

"Pure magic," Meredith agreed.

"It's even better now, isn't it?"

Meredith breathed in, enjoying the delicious scent of cologne and hot male flesh. "The sex?"

"Yeah. The sex, us, all of it. We were always good together but somehow it's different now. Better."

"I think you're right, Jack. I honestly never thought we'd surpass the magic of our first wedding night but when I felt you deep inside of me a little while ago it was like nothing I've ever experienced before."

"I felt it too. Maybe as my cock and your G-spot have grown and matured they've become more sensitized." He gave a toothy grin. "Well, what do you know? Older really *is* better!"

"I think it just might be." Winking, Meredith pulled Jack off the pillows and into an embrace, kissing him soundly. "Or maybe it's a combination of age, wisdom and the magical power of true love."

"That's gotta be it." Jack rolled on top of her and gazed into her eyes. "Because I love you so damn much, baby, that it almost hurts."

And his impassioned kiss left Meredith without a single doubt.

Daisy Dexter Dobbs

Chapter Seventeen

ഔ

"Sometimes it takes a lot of heartache before we finally realize what's most important to us, I guess," Meredith said, kneading the firm flesh on Jack's chest. "I know that's how it was for me."

Jack rolled onto his back, heaving a weighty sigh. "It kills me to think about all the pain and heartache I've caused you over the years, sweetheart. You're the last person in the world to deserve that."

"No, Jack, I didn't mean—"

"Every time I remember what a shallow, self-centered prick I used to be and how shabbily I treated you, my guts coil into a knot." A remorseful groan rumbled deep in his chest. "I had the perfect woman at my side—beautiful, loving, supportive, giving and caring—and all I could focus on was my own gratification. Somehow this inferior male brain of mine," he tapped his fingers against his temple, "decided that happiness was equated with how many women and how much money a guy could stockpile."

"And you certainly did a fine job of that, darling." Stifling a chuckle, Meredith patted Jack's shoulder.

"I was an ass." Jack cringed. "An egotistical jerk. It's a wonder you didn't give me a good whack in the head with a baseball bat because God knows I needed it."

"I'd be lying if I said it hadn't crossed my mind once or twice," Meredith said, humor evident in her voice. "But that head of yours is far too handsome to bash."

"You have my undying gratitude." With a twinkle in his eye, Jack feathered a kiss across Meredith's lips. "It's easy to laugh about all of that now but believe me, I wasn't laughing

228

when you disappeared from my life. The flashy women, the big money, the media attention and all the accolades were meaningless, pointless. When you vanished, Meredith, any real possibility of true happiness vanished right along with you. I'd never felt so empty and lost in all my life." Jack's voice caught and he breathed deeply. "The worst part was being left with the memory that I'm the jerk who'd driven you to desperate measures through my callous, selfish words and actions."

"Oh, Jack..." Feeling as though her heart was about to burst from the sheer enormity of love swelling within, Meredith wrapped her arms around Jack's neck and pulled him close for a kiss.

"I never want to go through the pain and anguish of losing you again, Meredith," Jack whispered once their lips parted. "I swear to God I couldn't take it. I was so damned emotional while you were gone, on the verge of tears all the time — like a fucking crybaby — and that's something I've never experienced before. Believe me, you don't know how painfully awful it is for a man to go through that."

Oh yes I do. "It's all over now, Jack." She kissed his chin, his cheek and his temple, brushing her fingers through his hair. "We're here together and nothing's going to separate us ever again. Believe me, not even death can come between us, because we're true soulmates. We'll be reunited in Heaven."

Levering himself up on one elbow, Jack pinned Meredith with a somber gaze. "Don't talk about dying. Please, Meredith." He dragged himself up, slouching against the pillows at the headboard and drew Meredith up beside him. "If one of us has to die then let it be me because I could never bear the pain of living without you." He grabbed Meredith into his arms and nearly squeezed the life out of her, hugging, rocking, patting and clutching her as if he were afraid to ever let her go again.

Overcome with emotion, Meredith searched for the right words to comfort him, assure him, but what could she say?

She couldn't promise not to die. For all she knew she could step out into traffic and end up at the Pearly Gates again tomorrow.

"Our bodies die, but our love continues forever. Trust me, Jack, I know it for a fact. When I was in Heaven I—"

"Aw, sweetheart," he groaned, "please don't start with all that heaven and hell stuff again." Jack held her closer yet, making Meredith wheeze. "Seriously, I don't think I can deal with that right now. I know that in your heart you believe it really happened, Meredith, but it didn't, honey. It was just some sort of dream, maybe some hallucination brought on by heavy medication after your accident."

Meredith jerked free. "I told you, Jack, there wasn't any accident. It was a genuine paranormal experience. I wasn't hallucinating."

Jack wrapped his arms around her, gently drawing her back into his embrace. "Shh-shh-shh. It's all right, sweetheart. Let's not talk about it anymore. We're here now. Together. That's all that matters."

"Jack," Meredith began and then she paused, stricken because she yearned to soothe him, to calm his fears—to somehow make him believe that her experience had been real—but the words just wouldn't come. In desperation she sent up a silent plea to her guardian angel. *Oh please help me, Annie. I don't know what to tell him.* In the silence that ensued, she chastised herself with a tsk. She wasn't in Heaven anymore. She didn't communicate with angels now. She was just plain flesh and bones Meredith—and she was on her own. Annie was right...the memories were beginning to fade. Images once so crystal clear were now like the shards of an incredible dream that remain upon waking.

The thought made Meredith shudder.

Dear God...what if Jack was right? What if none of it had really happened? What if she'd simply dreamed it all up? Dev and Annie and Lysander and being in Ricky's body and...

"Oh, Jack...I think I must be losing my mind. It all seems so fantastical now, so unreal. You're right. It probably never happened." Drawing in a deep shuddering gasp, Meredith's hands flew to her face, covering her eyes, and she burst into tears. "Oh dear God. None of it."

Jack stroked her hair. "Go ahead and cry if it makes you feel better, sweetheart. Just let it all out. It's okay...it's okay..."

Suddenly, the room was bathed in gentle lavender light. Her tears stopping abruptly, Meredith felt a serene sensation of peace wash over her as she looked around the room and then at Jack who, it appeared, saw the light too.

"Hush now, children," came the calming voice Meredith immediately recognized as Annie's. "There's no need to fret, no need for tears or anxiety."

"What the —" a clearly startled Jack began.

"Annie! Oh, Annie you are real!" Meredith cried. "It wasn't all a dream!"

"Adjusting is a bit difficult after a multi-realm experience like yours, my dear. Rest assured that it was, indeed, real."

Jack whipped his head around to look at Meredith. "What's going on?" he whispered cautiously.

"You mean you can actually hear her?" Meredith asked, amazed. Jack nodded almost imperceptibly and she smiled. "It's my guardian angel, Jack. It's Annie!"

"What?!" Jack shook his head. "No...no way." He grabbed a pillow, covering his naked package, and then he slapped a couple of pillows over Meredith. With lightning speed and pillow in hand he bolted from the bed, snatched his jeans from the floor and hiked them up.

"Okay, whoever you are," Jack said, brandishing the nearest object he could find, which happened to be Meredith's antique porcelain doll, "come on out where I can see you."

"My hero." Meredith slapped her hand over her mouth, struck mightily with an untimely case of the giggles as she watched her big brave man shaking her doll in the air as if to warn off the fiercest intruders. At the same time the room reverberated with Annie's tittering.

Jack cast Meredith a sharp look of annoyance. "What in the goddamn hell is so funny?" he barked.

"Ooh," Meredith warned, waving her finger at him. "I'd watch my language if I were you, Jack. And, um...if you're intent on fulfilling the role of my protector, I kind of doubt that Elizabeth is going to scare anyone off."

"Elizabeth?" Jack looked clueless.

Meredith cleared her throat and gestured to the doll Jack held aloft. "Elizabeth," she repeated, nodding.

With a sidelong glance, Jack realized what he was holding, rolled his eyes and groaned before tossing the doll back to the chair.

"Neither you nor Meredith have nothing to fear from me, Jack," Annie's disembodied voice said. "Guardian angels protect, they don't harm."

"Karyn," Jack said through gritted teeth, swinging his head left and right so fast he looked like a wind-up toy, "if this is your idea of a joke it's not funny."

Annie's transparent form shimmered before them. "I'm real, Jack. I'm here because Meredith sent up a prayer. She needed me. And you're seeing and hearing me right now because you need to believe." And then she spread her wings in all their angelic glory.

Jack stood drop-jawed. "Holy fuc—"

"I'd advise you to listen to Meredith," Annie said, wagging a chastising finger, "and watch your language, young man." She chuckled.

"Who...what...?" Jack stepped closer, hand outstretched and gingerly waving horizontally through the ghostly vision. "No...this just isn't possible," Jack said, grasping at air. And that's when Annie walked right through him.

"Shit! Shit! Shit!" Looking at his body in disbelief, Jack shivered before scrambling to the bed, jumping in beside Meredith and yanking her into his arms. "An angel," he sputtered, pointing frantically at Annie. "She's an angel!"

"Calm down, my big strong he-man." Meredith smoothed her hand over his shoulder and kissed his cheek. "I'll protect you."

"Meredith!" he warned.

"Sorry, I couldn't resist." She kissed the tip of his nose. "As for Annie," Meredith gestured toward her guardian angel, "that's what I've been trying to tell you all along, Jack. But you wouldn't believe me." She shrugged.

Jack shifted his gaze from Meredith to Annie and back again. And then he shook his head as if trying to clear it. "An angel," he mumbled several times with varying intonation. "I'm sorry, Meredith," he said, cupping her face. "I promise never to doubt you ever again."

"My time here is short, children," Annie said. "So we'd best get down to business." Jack and Meredith dutifully nodded. "This is a special one-time-only visitation. While I'll always hear your prayers, don't expect me to be popping in and out of your lives in the future." She winked. "Jack, dear, be comforted in the certainty that Meredith was correct. Love never dies. The two of you will have many long, happy years together before either of you need be concerned about dying." Annie perched her ample fanny on the edge of the bed. "Now, does that make you feel better, Jack?"

Wide-eyed, Jack nodded. "Yes, ma'am."

That got a laugh out of both Annie and Meredith.

"Good. Neither of you will fully remember that I was here but you'll both keep the knowledge of my message in your hearts after I leave and that will bring you peace when you need to draw upon it."

"So," Jack said tentatively, "after we die we'll be together again up in heaven, right? I mean, I guess since angels are real that means heaven is too…right?" He shook his head. "I can't believe I'm even having this conversation," he muttered, half chuckling to himself.

"There is a heaven, indeed. But," Annie cautioned with a raised finger, "there is also a hell. As of now neither of you is in danger of going there but don't get too complacent and overconfident. Always be on your guard to avoid the palpable temptation to do wrong. That's what Dev waits for and then," she clapped her hands together with a thunderous *whap*, "she's got you in her clutches, right where she wants you. Isn't that right, Meredith?"

With a sharp intake of breath, Meredith shuddered at the memory. "Yes. And I will never, *ever* do anything that foolish again. Trust me."

"Do what?" Jack asked, searching Meredith's eyes. "What are you talking about?"

Annie huffed, waving a dismissive hand. "She's referring to the whole unfortunate sock-puppet fiasco," she said matter-of-factly.

Jack's jaw dropped in an incredulous expression and Meredith suspected he was actually blushing. "You were sent to Hell for *that*?"

Meredith patted his knee. "It's a long story. We'll talk about it later."

Annie gazed warmly at her charge. "You've always wanted a child, my dear."

"Yes." An unexpected tear trickled down Meredith's cheek as she nodded. "We both did." She held Jack's hand, squeezing tight.

"We kept trying," Jack added, smoothing his fingers over Meredith's, "starting on that first wedding night but we weren't able to have any."

"Life grows within you as we speak, Meredith," Annie said, extending her hand palm up toward Meredith's stomach.

"You mean...?" Meredith squeaked, clapping a hand over the pillow covering her belly. "I'm pregnant?"

"A baby?" Jack said with reverence. "We're going to have a baby?"

Annie smiled and nodded. Jack and Meredith exchanged gasps of amazement before falling into each other's arms and embracing.

"Twins. One boy and one girl. Conceived with great passion and in a moment of true unselfish love," Annie said. "Just a few moments ago, in fact," she added in way of explanation.

"Twins..." Meredith grinned. "I always dreamed of having twins." She frowned then. "But, Annie, I'm forty," she noted, her face etched with concern. "Isn't that too old?"

"Bosh." Frowning, Annie waved her hand through the air. "Of course not. I had the first of six babies when I was just your age. This child will keep you young and young at heart. And you will both remain on this plane long enough to welcome each of your grandchildren into this world."

"We'll get married tomorrow," Jack announced excitedly.

"We can't, Jack. Not tomorrow."

Jack looked stricken. "Why not? You have to marry me, Meredith. Our babies need their father and mother together. Please say you'll be my wife..." now he definitely blushed, "again."

Meredith chuckled. "How can I refuse? After all, they say the third time's a charm." She winked. "But not tomorrow. I want to wait until Karyn is here so she can be my maid of honor." And then she laughed. "For the third time."

Jack expelled a sigh of relief. "Sure, sweetheart."

"You'll be standing up for her next," Annie announced.

Meredith slanted her a befuddled look. "Karyn? Karyn's getting married?" Annie nodded and Meredith squealed with delight. "Oh that's wonderful! But to who? When?"

"She's with her intended soulmate as we speak," Annie said, breaking into a wide grin.

"Cristoval?" Meredith asked with incredulity.

"The exterminator kid?" Jack followed.

"They are destined for each other." Annie nodded. "Cristoval de Medina is a good man. He'll cherish Karyn always. He will become an integral part of Abundant Finds and of your foundation as one of the model spokesmen or, to borrow Karyn's term, *beefy young hunks*." Annie paused, nodding and smiling at the looks of wonder on Jack's and Meredith's faces. "The de Medina and the McKenna children will grow up together."

Jack slapped his knee. "Well, I'll be dam—"

Annie clapped her hands together again and the room vibrated. "Uh-uh," she warned. "Be very careful what you wish for, young man. And watch that language when you're in the presence of an angel."

"Sorry," Jack said. "What I meant to say was, golly! Gee whiz that's great!" He laughed and Annie and Meredith joined in.

"I don't think I've ever been happier than I am at this very moment," Meredith breathed a sigh of perfect contentment. "I'm with the man I love. We're going to have the family we always dreamed about. My..." she looked at Jack and smiled, "*our* best friend has found her soulmate. And," she grasped both of Jack's hands and squeezed tight, "now Jack and I both know that we'll be together forever."

"I agree," Jack said. "I've never been happier. I love you with all of my heart and soul, Meredith. I couldn't possibly love you any more if I tried." He cupped Meredith's face in his hands and kissed her. It was a sweet, tender kiss full of love and promise that said more than words could ever convey.

Annie got up from the bed, gracing the pair with a genuine smile that warmed their hearts. "Good." She nodded. "Then my work here is done." She started to fade.

"Thank you, Annie," Meredith whispered.

"Yes, thank you," Jack echoed. "For everything."

"Be good to each other always, children," Annie called as she grew fainter. "You can both call on me anytime you need me and I'll answer directly to your hearts."

Before she fully disappeared, Annie waved her hand over Jack and Meredith and they both fell into a deep, restful slumber.

And then Annie and the lavender light that preceded her were gone.

* * * * *

"Look at them all snuggled together. Have you ever seen anything more pathetic? It won't last. He'll cheat on her again. You'll see."

"Nonsense, Dev," Annie said. "He'll never risk losing her again, I guarantee it."

"Baloney, Annie. Once their little twin brats are born and he's had a taste of diaper changing and middle-of-the-night bottle feedings that meat-missile of his will be itching to zero in on a fresh new target."

Annie sighed. "As usual, Dev, you're crass, crude and indubitably wrong. Not to mention being a sore loser. Jack and Meredith are under my protection so don't even think about trying to work your wicked ways with them or any of their offspring, you hear me?"

Now it was Dev's turn to sigh. "Spoil sport."

"Don't you have some coal that needs tending to? Why don't you stop annoying me and go back to your catacombs?"

Dev cackled. "You think you're such a smarty-pants, don't you? Well, I've got news for you, Annie. The next case on file won't be nearly as cut and dried as this one."

"Is that so?" Annie said with indifference.

"Yup. Because this time the soul in question is not, was not and never will be a goody-two-shoes. Mine," she said with glee. "All mine!"

"I've always enjoyed a challenge," Annie said with enthusiasm. "Bring it on."

Also by Daisy Dexter Dobbs

ဢ

eBooks:

Accidental Foursome
Absolutely Not
Caroline's Christmas Viking
Dragon by Day
Embracing the Tiger
Finding Cupid
Forever, Blue Eyes
Last Strathulian Standing
Polly's Perilous Pleasures
Samantha and Her Genie
Wednesday Nights With Jamie
Wicked Payback

Print Books:

Polly's Perilous Pleasures
Wednesday Nights with Jamie
Wanton Winter (*anthology*)

About the Author

ഔ

Daisy Dexter Dobbs has a valid reason for lying when she's asked where she gets the ideas for her books. She knows most people wouldn't believe the truth about the madcap mayhem that goes on in her daily life. Case in point: Imagine frantically trying to file your way out of a locked bathroom door with a teeny nail file, dressed in nothing but a too-small towel while you're waiting for a real estate agent and a family with three small kids to arrive for a showing of your house. Okay, now picture the contents of a box of just-delivered sex toys (purely for research purposes, you understand) strewn on the bed just outside that locked bathroom door. Mmm-hmm, it really happened.

Happily married to her soulmate, the award winning artist and writer believes in love, happily-ever-afters and the wondrous, magical escapism of reading and writing.

Daisy welcomes comments from readers. You can find her website and email address on her author bio page at www.ellorascave.com.

Tell Us What You Think

We appreciate hearing reader opinions about our books. You can email us at Comments@EllorasCave.com.

Why an electronic book?

We live in the Information Age—an exciting time in the history of human civilization, in which technology rules supreme and continues to progress in leaps and bounds every minute of every day. For a multitude of reasons, more and more avid literary fans are opting to purchase e-books instead of paper books. The question from those not yet initiated into the world of electronic reading is simply: *Why?*

1. *Price.* An electronic title at Ellora's Cave Publishing and Cerridwen Press runs anywhere from 40% to 75% less than the cover price of the exact same title in paperback format. Why? Basic mathematics and cost. It is less expensive to publish an e-book (no paper and printing, no warehousing and shipping) than it is to publish a paperback, so the savings are passed along to the consumer.

2. *Space.* Running out of room in your house for your books? That is one worry you will never have with electronic books. For a low one-time cost, you can purchase a handheld device specifically designed for e-reading. Many e-readers have large, convenient screens for viewing. Better yet, hundreds of titles can be stored within your new library—on a single microchip. There are a variety of e-readers from different manufacturers. You can also read e-books on your PC or laptop computer. (Please note that Ellora's Cave does not endorse any specific brands.

You can check our websites at www.ellorascave.com or www.cerridwenpress.com for information we make available to new consumers.)

3. *Mobility.* Because your new e-library consists of only a microchip within a small, easily transportable e-reader, your entire cache of books can be taken with you wherever you go.

4. *Personal Viewing Preferences.* Are the words you are currently reading too small? Too large? Too… ANNOYING? Paperback books cannot be modified according to personal preferences, but e-books can.

5. *Instant Gratification.* Is it the middle of the night and all the bookstores near you are closed? Are you tired of waiting days, sometimes weeks, for bookstores to ship the novels you bought? Ellora's Cave Publishing sells instantaneous downloads twenty-four hours a day, seven days a week, every day of the year. Our webstore is never closed. Our e-book delivery system is 100% automated, meaning your order is filled as soon as you pay for it.

Those are a few of the top reasons why electronic books are replacing paperbacks for many avid readers.

As always, Ellora's Cave and Cerridwen Press welcome your questions and comments. We invite you to email us at Comments@ellorascave.com or write to us directly at Ellora's Cave Publishing Inc., 1056 Home Avenue, Akron, OH 44310-3502.

Discover for yourself why readers can't get enough
of the multiple award-winning publisher
Ellora's Cave.

Whether you prefer e-books or paperbacks,

be sure to visit EC on the web at
www.ellorascave.com

for an erotic reading experience that will leave you
breathless.